"The Blue and "Jibaro Death"

TWO CLASSIC ADVENTURES OF

THE Shadow ™

by Walter B. Gibson
writing as Maxwell Grant

with a new historical essay
by Will Murray

Published by Sanctum Productions for
NOSTALGIA VENTURES, INC.
P.O. Box 231183; Encinitas, CA 92023-1183

The Shadow Volume 20 copyright © 2008 by Sanctum Productions.

"Postscript" copyright © 2008 by Will Murray.

This Nostalgia Ventures edition is an unabridged republication of the text
and illustrations of two stories from *The Shadow Magazine,* as originally
published by Street & Smith Publications, Inc., N.Y.: *The Blue Sphinx* from the
January 15, 1935 issue, and *Jibaro Death* from the September 15, 1936 issue.
Typographical errors have been tacitly corrected in this edition. These stories
are works of their time. Consequently, the text is reprinted intact in its original
historical form, including occasional out-of-date ethnic and cultural stereotyping.
Typographical errors have been tacitly corrected in this edition.

International Standard Book Numbers:

ISBN: 1-934943-04-5   13 digit: 978-1-934943-04-5

First printing: July 2008

Series editor: Anthony Tollin
P.O. Box 761474
San Antonio, TX 78245-1474
sanctumotr@earthlink.net

Consulting editor: Will Murray

Copy editor: Joseph Wrzos

Cover and photo restoration: Michael Piper

The editor acknowledges the assistance of Dwight Fuhro in the preparation
of this volume.

Nostalgia Ventures, Inc.
P.O. Box 231183; Encinitas, CA 92023-1183

Visit The Shadow at www.shadowsanctum.com & www.nostalgiatown.com.

Volume 20

CONTENTS

Two Complete Novels From The Shadow's Private Annals As told to Maxwell Grant

Thrilling Tales and Features

Cover art by George Rozen
Interior illustrations by Tom Lovell

this to those in the large envelope, sealed his packet and placed it in his pocket. Then he left his office.

TWENTY minutes later, Rutledge Mann arrived at an old office building on Twenty-third Street. He entered, passed through a dingy hall and ascended a flight of creaking, tilted stairs. He reached an obscure corridor and stopped in front of an office door. The grimy, cobwebbed panel was of glass. It bore the name:

B. JONAS

Mann dropped the big envelope in a mail slot and departed. His face was quizzical when he reached the street. It was not the thought of that obscure office that made Mann seem puzzled. That office was permanently deserted, from all appearances; yet it served as The Shadow's mailbox.

Mann had given up speculation regarding how and when The Shadow entered to receive reports.

What puzzled Mann was the same problem that had troubled Hawkeye. Like the crafty spotter, the investment broker was wondering how his chief would handle Tinker Furris, yet still have a free hand when he began an investigation in the town of Latuna.

Hawkeye had supplied word that Tinker planned crime; also, that Latuna was a spot where crime impended. Mann by reference to the Latuna *Gazette,* had produced tangible evidence that deep waters lay ahead. Latuna must be The Shadow's goal. Would he let Tinker Furris get away with crime in order to keep Konk Zitz lulled?

Mann decided not. Though The Shadow was a mystery, even to this contact agent, Mann, like all the other aides, knew that The Shadow allowed no spoils to evildoers. Somehow, The Shadow would thwart Tinker's scheme of crime, yet manage to keep from damaging his Latuna campaign.

How? Rutledge Mann was still wondering when he reached his office, and the only solution he could furnish was a head shake. Like Hawkeye, Mann had reached the conclusion that the problem was beyond all persons but The Shadow.

CHAPTER III
FROM THE SANCTUM

WHITE hands, agile and long-fingered, beneath the rays of a bluish light. The Shadow was in his sanctum, an unknown abode, secluded somewhere in Manhattan. Upon a polished table lay Mann's messages, together with the clipping from the Latuna *Enterprise.*

Writing faded. The clipping was thrust aside. Hands stretched across the table and obtained a pair of earphones. A tiny signal bulb glimmered on the wall. A quiet voice came across the wire:

"Burbank speaking."

Mann—in his office, during daytime hours; Burbank—in an obscure room, at night. These were the contact agents of The Shadow. Where Mann, slow and deliberate, served in the development of preliminary plans, Burbank was ready when action called. Active agents were always ready to receive his relayed orders from The Shadow.

"Instructions to Vincent." The Shadow's voice came in an awesome whisper. "Insert this advertisement in the late edition of the *Evening Traveler:* 'Wanted, Four Salesmen, preferably those knowing Midwest conditions convincingly.'"

Burbank's reply was a careful repetition of the words that The Shadow had given him. Then came another order from The Shadow.

"Instructions to Burke," was the whisper from the unseen lips. "Arrange to accompany Cardona on nightly inspection tour of the East Side. Special story for the New York *Classic."*

"Instructions received," replied Burbank.

"Instructions to Marsland," resumed The Shadow. "Pick up message in Shrevnitz cab one block above Cobalt Club, seven o'clock. Follow orders as given."

"Instructions received."

The earphones clicked against the wall. The bluish light went out with a click. A soft laugh quivered through blackened walls, rose to a startling crescendo, then faded into shuddering echoes.

With the last tones of that dying mockery came a hush amid the Stygian blackness. The Shadow had departed by his secret exit. The sanctum had returned to its inky emptiness. Day or night, that strange abode remained a chamber of blackness.

AFTERNOON hours waned. It was half past six when a personage attired in evening clothes entered a cab near Times Square. Tall, calm-faced and silent, this individual carried himself with remarkable composure.

Despite the fact that his keen, hawklike visage was most unusual, this stroller had a way of rendering himself inconspicuous in the crowd. He chose an opportune moment when he entered the cab and stepped aboard so quietly that even the shrewd-eyed driver failed to note his entry.

The first indication that the taximan received of a passenger was when a whispered voice came through the opened window to the front. The driver half started; then nodded. He stared straight ahead when he pulled from the curb.

The taxi driver's name was Moe Shrevnitz. Familiar with Manhattan's many thoroughfares, a capable man in a pinch, Moe had been mustered into The Shadow's service. The Shadow owned the independent cab that Moe drove. The taximan kept close to a chosen point near Times Square, to await The Shadow's call.

The voice from the cab was the whisper of The Shadow. Recognizing it, Moe knew that he was conveying his chief. As he neared his destination, he again caught a statement from The Shadow.

"Wait for Marsland," was the whisper. "Deliver this message to him."

An envelope dropped beside Moe as the driver wheeled toward the curb. Moe picked up the envelope as he stopped. He placed it in his pocket; then turned about. The cab was empty.

In that brief interval after the arrival, The Shadow had stepped to the curb. Though garbed in evening clothes, he had strangely vanished.

Moe settled back to await Cliff's appearance.

The Shadow had chosen a destination close to the exclusive Cobalt Club. He had turned in the direction of the club building after leaving Moe's cab. A few minutes later, the doorman bowed as The Shadow strolled into view.

"Good evening, Mr. Cranston," said the doorman. "Commissioner Barth is expecting you, sir."

"Very good" was the quiet reply. A slight smile showed on thin lips as The Shadow entered to find the police commissioner. In his visits to the Cobalt Club, The Shadow came in the guise of Lamont Cranston, millionaire globe-trotter. It was a most convenient personality, for the real Lamont Cranston was seldom in New York.

In his guise of Cranston, The Shadow had become a close friend of Commissioner Wainwright Barth. He found Barth awaiting him in the lobby. They shook hands and went to the grillroom for dinner.

SEATED at the table, the two formed a marked contrast. The Shadow's guise of Lamont Cranston made him appear as a quiet, lackadaisical individual, despite the keenness of his hawklike countenance.

Barth, on the contrary, was restless. Tall, he thrust his long neck forward from the collar of his evening shirt. His smooth pate gave him the appearance of a bald eagle, while his eyes gleamed through the lenses of his pince-nez spectacles.

"Prevention of crime," announced Barth, above his soup cup. "That is my watchword, Cranston. Despite the fact that the newspapers sometimes criticize my policies, I am achieving results."

"Ah, yes," responded the pretended Cranston. "Come here, waiter. Get me a final copy of the Evening Traveler."

"Yes, sir," said the waiter.

"The Traveler is a conservative newspaper," commended Barth. "You will find very little sensationalism in its pages. If you wish to see the outrageous crime reports that some journals are printing, I refer you to that yellow sheet, the Classic."

"I am not looking for crime reports," returned The Shadow, in the quiet voice of Cranston. "I am interested in the day's doings at the stock market. Pardon me for a few minutes, Commissioner, while I read the Wall Street news."

Barth looked annoyed while he was finishing his soup. Cranston's few minutes were longer than anticipated. He was still studying the stock market pages when the waiter appeared with the next course. Barth glowered indignantly. Then he turned suddenly as a club attendant approached.

"A telephone call for you, Commissioner," said the man. "You can take it right here, at the grillroom telephone."

"Very well," stated Barth.

As the commissioner went to the telephone, The Shadow lowered the newspaper slightly. With keen eyes, he noted every expression of Barth's face. From annoyance, Barth showed excitement; then came indignation. Flinging the receiver on the hook, he came stalking back to the table.

"A crank call!" he announced testily. "Some bounder hung up after he had delivered a message. I've had that experience before, Cranston."

"Perhaps the message was important."

"Maybe it was. Jove! I was so incensed by the fellow's action that I almost forgot what he told me. Let me have that newspaper, Cranston! This is a coincidence, your having the very one right here."

"The last edition of the Evening Traveler!"

"Yes. The want ad section."

"What did you learn about it?"

"The man who called up," explained Barth, as he went through the pages, "was insistent that I look for an advertisement that bears the key number J-547. He said that he had been reading the want ads, and that it appeared only in the last edition.

"Calling the Traveler office, he learned that the advertisement had later been recalled. He thinks it must be a hoax of some sort. A message, perhaps, with some unusual purpose.

"Ah, here is the advertisement in question. I see nothing odd about it."

LEANING over the table, Barth pointed out the ad to his companion. In Cranston's fashion, The Shadow read the words, which were followed by the key number.

"Rather unusual" was his comment.

"Why so?" demanded Barth.

"Cumbersome, to begin with," stated The Shadow. "Not as illuminating as it might be. To what conditions does the ad refer? And why the word 'convincingly' at the end?"

"Quite peculiar," agreed Barth. "I wonder, Cranston, could it be a code?"

"Read it to me," suggested Cranston, returning the newspaper to the commissioner, "word by word, while I write them down."

Barth complied. He began to nod wisely.

"Certain letters might mean something," he said, looking at the ad. "Let's try the first ones: W—F—S—no, that brings us nowhere. The second letters: A—O—A—that is quite as bad. The third letters—"

"One moment, Commissioner," interposed The Shadow. "Maybe you're on the right track, but going the wrong direction."

"How so?"

"You started with first letters; then seconds. Suppose we take the first letter of the first word: the second letter of the second word; and so on. Here I shall arrange the words in column form, marking those letters heavily. It's working—"

Barth seized the paper on which Cranston was writing, the moment that his companion had completed the column. Staring keenly, Barth saw the result:

WANTED
FOUR
SALESMEN
PREFERABLY
THOSE
KNOWING
MIDWEST
CONDITIONS
CONVINCINGLY

"Wolfenson!" exclaimed the commissioner. "The name shows up in the acrostic which those letters form. Do you suppose that it refers to Tobias Wolfenson, the chicle king?"

"Possibly," replied The Shadow. "He is the only Wolfenson of prominence. He has a magnificent estate on Long Island. He prefers to live a secluded life, I understand."

"This message," affirmed Barth, nodding wisely as he tapped the newspaper, "appears to be conveying information from one person to another. Probably naming a certain objective. Perhaps one criminal is notifying another where to strike. Cranston, this requires investigation. I shall communicate with Tobias Wolfenson at once."

"His telephone is probably unlisted."

"I shall go directly to his house on Long Island. Accompanied by a squad from headquarters. Can you come with me, Cranston?"

"Hardly. I am entertaining tonight at my home in New Jersey. But why the squad, Commissioner? I should think that your ace detective—what is his name—should be sufficient."

"Joe Cardona? Yes, I was thinking of him, Cranston. Cardona is at present an acting inspector. Making routine trips through the underworld. I shall have him drop that duty tonight. Pardon me, Cranston, while I call headquarters."

BARTH went to the telephone and put in a call. Returning, he applied himself to hasty eating, explaining the speed with which he was finishing his dinner.

"Cardona is joining me here," announced Barth. "I told him to bring three picked men. Inspector Egglestone will take up Cardona's usual duties tonight."

Just as Barth was finishing his dessert, an attendant arrived to inform him that Inspector Cardona had arrived outside. Rising hurriedly, the commissioner shook hands with his friend Cranston and departed.

A thin smile appeared upon the lips that looked like Cranston's. That smile remained until The Shadow arose, a few minutes later, and also strolled from the Cobalt Club. When he had reached the street, this being guised as Cranston indulged in a soft, whispered laugh.

By subtle measures, The Shadow had set a false trail for the impulsive police commissioner. Intrigued by hope of an unusual crime hunt, Barth was heading for Long Island. With him, he was taking Joe Cardona; the ace detective would be absent from the underworld tonight.

That was the end which The Shadow had sought. The temporary elimination of Joe Cardona fitted with the plan that he had made for tonight. Aided by his agents, The Shadow was ready to complete the steps that would frustrate crime and give him direct approach to the city of Latuna.

CHAPTER IV
IN THE PAWNSHOP

AT eight o'clock that same evening, Hawkeye entered the obscure doorway of Luke's Joint. Sidling through the room where thugs convened, he found another doorway and peered into a smaller room. He spied Tinker Furris seated at a table. Hawkeye entered.

"Hello, Hawkeye," growled Tinker. "Say—I thought you was bringing Tapper. What'd you do? Tell him to meet you here."

Hawkeye shook his head. He sat down at the table and spoke in a troubled tone.

"Tapper ain't comin'," he informed. "He can't take no chances, Tinker. I don't blame him."

"Why not?"

"On account of The Shadow."

"The Shadow!"

"Yeah. It looks like he's watchin' Tapper."

A change came over Tinker's pockmarked face. This mention of the underworld's great foe was disconcerting. Tinker laughed; but the tone was not genuine.

"If The Shadow is trailin' Tapper," asserted Hawkeye, leaning across the table, "he may be trailin' me next. It ain't safe for neither of us to make a move. We got to look like we was turnin' goody-goody. See?

"There ain't nothin' that The Shadow could pin on us; but if he's watchin', there's no chance of pullin' a dodge. I figure Tapper's got the right idea. He says stick in New York. No scrammin' for either of us—"

"Then the deal's off?" broke in Tinker, savagely. "You mean I got to pass up this cinch job at the hockshop until I can dig up some guy that's as good as Tapper?"

"I ain't sayin' that," returned Hawkeye. "I'm tellin' you first that Tapper wants to stay out of it an' I've got to stick by Tapper. Now that that's in your noodle, I'll give you the rest. I got a guy that'll work with you."

"As good as Tapper?"

"Better than Tapper."

Tinker looked incredulous. Hawkeye grinned; then threw a wary look toward the door. No one was in sight. Hawkeye spoke.

"DID you ever hear of a guy who was named Cliff Marsland?" he questioned. "Well"—Hawkeye grinned again as he saw Tinker nod —"I got hold of Cliff an' he's comin' here to work with you tonight."

Tinker was impressed. He had heard of Cliff's reputation in the underworld. In the badlands, Cliff was rated as one of the best lieutenants that any big shot could desire. He had a reputation as a killer. But there was one point that came as news to Tinker Furris.

"Cliff Marsland ain't no safe-buster," objected the pock-faced crook. "He's a good guy. If he wants to head for Latuna with me, Konk Zitz can use him there. But this box up at Cobleton's hockshop—"

"Listen, Tinker," broke in Hawkeye. "I'm wisin' you to somethin' that only a couple of guys know. Cliff Marsland can knock off any tin box that you show him—an' he don't need no soup for the job, neither.

"That's his real racket. That's why he's got the bulls goofy. He don't have to trail around with a crew of gorillas all the time. When things get hot, he loafs. Looks like he's takin' a vacation, see? But he ain't. He's workin' on his own, safecrackin'—"

"He's coming here tonight?" quizzed Tinker, convinced enough to interrupt.

"Sure!" nodded Hawkeye. "Maybe he's outside now. I told him to wait there. Didn't want to mention your name to him until I could find out if it was O.K."

"It's oke. Lamp those mugs in the outer room and see if he's there."

Hawkeye went to the door and peered craftily. His eyes lighted. He made a beckoning gesture. Backing into the room, Hawkeye made way for a stalwart, broad-shouldered chap. Tinker Furris caught sight of a firm, chiseled face. He recognized Cliff Marsland.

Introductions were brief. A few minutes later, Tinker and Cliff were engaged in a businesslike discussion as they considered the matter of Cobleton's safe. Tinker made his terms.

"Hawkeye wants to be out of it," he announced. "I was going to offer half the swag to him and Tapper. So I'll make the same proposition to you, Cliff. Fifty-fifty. If Hawkeye thinks he ought to come in for a cut, he gets it from you."

"Count me out," insisted Hawkeye.

"All right," resumed Tinker. "Well, Cliff, that means me and you. We take it on the lam for Latuna afterward. You'll break in with Konk Zitz. You, instead of Tapper."

Cliff nodded his agreement. Hawkeye, seeing that matters were settled, arose and made his exit in his usual wary fashion. Cliff and Tinker completed their plan of action. Then they left Luke's Joint.

COBLETON'S pawnshop was an isolated building despite its East Side location. The low roof of a garage was on one side; a deserted house on the other, with a street of alley proportions running between the hockshop and the empty house.

The lower floor had barred windows; but the second story offered opportunity for attack. The best means of entrance lay at the back of the house, where a high fence was an attraction for second-story workers.

But while Cliff and Tinker were on their way to Cobleton's, another visitor arrived there before them. Gliding past the front of the pawnshop, a phantom figure paused to study the building. Dim, almost invisible as it stood by a shrouding wall, this shape showed the outline of black-cloaked shoulders, with a slouch hat above.

The Shadow had arrived at Cobleton's. He had instructed Cliff Marsland to make contact with Hawkeye, through Slade Farrow. Cliff had done so; his introduction to Tinker Furris had been in pursuance of further instructions from The Shadow. With that settled, The Shadow was timing his own plans.

The far wall of the garage showed a blackened space that was to The Shadow's liking. The tall figure glided across the street and merged with darkness. Then came soft, squidgy sounds. With the aid of rubber suction cups, The Shadow was scaling the wall of the garage. He reached the roof; then proceeded toward the pawnshop.

A side window opened toward the garage roof. It was locked; but The Shadow pried the catch by inserting a thin piece of steel between the portions of the sash. He raised the window and entered; then found a stairway that led below.

A metal-sheathed door barred entrance to the front room of the pawnshop. The rays of a tiny flashlight showed other doors that led to storage rooms. The Shadow entered a storeroom where stacks of trunks and crates of theatrical equipment formed a medley that no burglar would attempt to remove.

Threading his way to a far corner, The Shadow discovered a locked door that apparently led to a storage closet. This was a spot that an ordinary prowler would have passed up; the very weakness of the door indicated nothing of consequence beyond.

With a skeleton key, The Shadow unlocked this door. His soft laugh told the wisdom of his move.

Beyond the opened door, the flashlight showed a tiny office. In a corner past a small desk was the front of a heavy safe that took up nearly a quarter of the room space. It was a formidable strongbox, this safe that old Cobleton had installed in an obscure room.

The Shadow approached the safe. His left hand came into the range of his flashlight. A quick gesture, and a black glove slipped from agile fingers. While a resplendent gem—the Shadow's girasol—was glimmering in changing hues, that deft left hand worked on the combination.

Minutes passed amid stillness. A click. The door of the safe swung open. Studying the interior, The Shadow noted a stack of jewel cases. He did not open them; instead, he closed the safe door.

The left hand took the flashlight. Leaning close to the safe, The Shadow produced a tiny magnifying glass and adjusted it to his right eye. Then he produced an engraving tool. His steady fingers made minute markings upon the combination knob. These gave the semblance of a slight scratch, quite similar to others that were already on the metal knob.

A soft laugh as the light went out. Then a slight *swish.* After that came silence. The Shadow was lingering in the darkness of the little office. Another step had been completed in the game.

OUTSIDE the building that housed the pawnshop, Cliff Marsland and Tinker Furris were crouching by the rear fence. A patrolman had just passed. They were ready to proceed. Tinker gave a whispered growl.

"That flatfoot's out of the picture," he informed. "Boost me up this fence. It ain't going to take long for me to jimmy a window."

Cliff complied. Atop the fence, Tinker set to work. Muffled sounds finally ended. Leaning down, Tinker aided Cliff in an upward scramble. They crawled through the window that Tinker had jimmied.

Using a flashlight with caution, Tinker led the way downstairs. He pointed out the storeroom with the trunks.

"It's through here," he growled. "That's what the ham told me when he described the joint. Said there was a door that led into an inside room. Look—there it is—"

Tinker broke off as he reached the door. He saw that the lock was simple. Producing a ring of skeleton keys, he found one that did the trick. He and Cliff entered the office. Tinker flashed his torch on the door of the safe.

"Can you crack it, Marsland?" he questioned, anxiously. "It looks like a tough baby."

"Leave it to me," returned Cliff.

Moving into the range of light, Cliff leaned in front of the safe. He drew a microscope from his pocket and held it in front of the knob while he motioned Tinker to come closer with the light.

"Say," whispered Tinker, "that's a new wrinkle! What's the idea of the glass, Cliff? It ain't going to give no tip on the combo—"

"I'm looking for fingerprints," interposed Cliff, quietly. "A gag of my own, Tinker."

"Fingerprints? What for?"

"So I can leave them if they're there. The cops will look for them, won't they? All right—let them find them. All they'll have will be old Cobleton's."

"That's neat, Cliff! Most guys would polish up after finishing. You don't, eh?"

"Not by a long shot. Yeah, there's prints here, all right, just on the edge of the center. Cobleton must have smudged it when he closed the safe. All right, I'll leave that for the bulls."

While he was speaking, Cliff was keenly noting the scratch near the center of the knob. Highly magnified, it showed a series of numbers that were barely discernible. Cliff put away his lens. He began to turn the knob.

Faking the job for Tinker's benefit, Cliff took a full five minutes before he utilized the combination that he had learned from The Shadow's markings. At last came the *click* that Tinker had desired. The door swung open. The flashlight showed the stack of jewel boxes.

"Hold it, Tinker," whispered Cliff. "I'm going back in the storeroom. To pick up one of those suitcases. We can load the swag in it."

"Oke," agreed Tinker. "I'll open up them boxes. Boy—they look like they ought to show some sparklers!"

CLIFF moved away while Tinker was speaking. Eagerly, Tinker drew boxes from the safe. He opened the top one and chuckled as he saw the glitter of a turquoise necklace, with diamonds set at intervals.

Holding the flashlight with his left hand, Tinker raised the necklace with his right and let the gems sparkle before his eyes.

Fancying that Cliff had returned, Tinker spoke as

he noted a slight sound behind him. He raised the dangling necklace that his companion might see it.

"Look at it, Cliff," he whispered. "How's that for a first grab?"

There was no response. Tinker's forehead furrowed. Puzzled by the lack of a reply, the crook wheeled and turned his flashlight upon the spot where he thought Cliff was standing. It was then that a hoarse gasp came from Tinker's bloated lips.

Cliff Marsland had not returned. Another, however, had entered. The necklace dropped from Tinker's numbed fingers. The flashlight wavered in his trembling hand as its glare revealed the form that Tinker had encountered.

Looming squarely before Tinker Furris was a figure cloaked in black. Burning eyes focused their fierce gaze upon the quivering crook. Just below those blazing optics, Tinker saw the huge-mouthed muzzle of a .45 automatic.

No gasp came from Tinker's frozen lips. But the pitiful blink of the crook's eyelids told that he had recognized the intruder who had trapped him. A laugh, barely audible, came from hidden lips. Tinker quailed as he heard that sinister taunt.

For Tinker saw death looming with that gun muzzle. A man of crime, caught in the act, he was faced by the archenemy of evil. Tinker Furris was trapped by The Shadow!

CHAPTER V
THE SWIFT SEQUENCE

TO Tinker Furris, hope was ended. Like others of his ilk, he had bragged that he did not fear The Shadow. But when the crisis had arrived, Tinker, like those same others, found his courage gone.

Through his terrified brain ran a medley of thoughts. Hawkeye's warning of "Tapper's" fears. Tinker wished now that he had heeded them. The merciless gaze of The Shadow told him of his folly.

No chance to pull a gun. No courage even to plead. Such was Tinker's state. On the floor lay the incriminating necklace. The Shadow had him with the goods. Tinker could see no out.

Then came the unexpected break. While Tinker crouched helpless, a beam of light broke suddenly from the door of the room. Meeting the glare of Tinker's shaking torch, it placed The Shadow between two paths of illumination.

Tinker saw The Shadow wheel to meet some new enemy. As the cloaked figure turned, a sharp cry came from the door. It was Cliff Marsland's voice. Cliff's light went out on the instant. Tinker, alone, saw all that followed.

The Shadow's automatic barked as Cliff dived into the room. A bullet whistled through the outer door. An instant later, Cliff, with automatic of his own, delivered a point-blank answer toward the shape that Tinker's light revealed.

The Shadow staggered. Tinker, amazed, came up to his feet and pulled his revolver. He saw The Shadow slumping to the floor; but before his gun was drawn, the automatic blazed again. Wounded, The Shadow was keeping up the fire.

A bullet zimmed past Tinker's ear. In response to a cry from Cliff, Tinker sprang toward the outer door. A second shot missed him by inches only. Tinker's light was no longer on The Shadow. Cliff, firing as he backed from the inner room, was following.

As they reached the storeroom, Cliff turned boldly and steadied his light back into the office. Tinker caught a glimpse of The Shadow rising. He saw the black form swing behind the open door of the safe. Then came a fierce, gibing laugh. An automatic boomed; its slug sizzled hot past Cliff Marsland's ear.

Quickly, Cliff extinguished his light and grabbed Tinker. He dragged the crook toward the hall. They were on the stairway before Tinker, stampeded, could object.

"The sparklers!" cried Tinker. "Say, Cliff, that swag—"

"Too late!" put in Cliff, tersely. "I clipped him; but he's not through. Listen!"

Again the chilling laugh. Defiant as a wounded tiger in his lair, The Shadow was inviting the enemy to return. Tinker groaned.

"No chance now," he admitted. "Back of that safe door, he's got a bead on us. Say, Cliff, maybe if we waited—"

"What for? The bulls?"

Tinker came to his senses. Instinctively, he started up the stairs. He realized that the fusillade must have been heard. Police were probably already on their way.

Again came The Shadow's laugh. Cliff, following Tinker up the steps, gave a pleased grunt.

"Let him hold the bag," he said. "That's the stunt, Tinker! The bulls, finding The Shadow at the opened safe. Catching him with the goods."

"Oke," agreed Tinker, with a nervous laugh. "Come on! Scram! Here's the window."

The two dropped to the fence and headed down an alleyway just as sounds of police whistles came to their ears. They were making a getaway, with sufficient time to escape the law.

BACK in Cobleton's little office, a soft laugh made an eerie whisper. With tiny flashlight glimmering, The Shadow stepped from behind the opened door of the safe. There was reason for his mirth. Aided by Cliff Marsland, The Shadow had played a deceptive game.

Cliff had come equipped with an automatic that contained blank cartridges. His point-blank shot had brought a faked stagger from The Shadow.

Tinker Furris had been fooled. The crook had given Cliff full credit for clipping The Shadow.

In return, The Shadow had utilized real slugs. He had relied upon master marksmanship, purposely missing his human targets by inches only. Unscathed by Cliff's phony shots, he was ready for the next stage of the game.

The flashlight showed the suitcase that Cliff had dropped by the door. Stooping above it, The Shadow drew the folds of his cloak over his head. Cloak and slouch hat dropped into the suitcase. Extinguishing his flashlight, The Shadow stepped to the wall and pressed a switch.

The office light came on. It revealed a remarkable transformation. Instead of a figure garbed in black, The Shadow had taken on the guise of a thug. He seemed to have lost in stature. Almost chunky, he was attired in dark trousers, jerseylike sweater, and bandanna handkerchief which served as a mask.

The black garments had gone into the suitcase. The Shadow moved swiftly to the safe; there he picked up jewel cases and placed them in the bag. Closing the suitcase, he moved toward the storeroom.

The shrills of whistles had penetrated here. A distant siren came faintly to The Shadow's ears. Men were pounding at the doors of the hockshop, front and back. The Shadow laughed.

As he advanced into the hall, The Shadow heard the rear door shatter. Harsh voices called; then two officers came pounding in from the rear. The Shadow stepped back into the darkened storeroom. The policemen swung past as they spied the lighted office.

The cops were holding revolvers. They paused when they arrived at the opened safe. Then they turned as they heard a jeering guffaw. They stared into the muzzle of a glittering revolver, held by the sweatered gorilla. The Shadow had followed them into the office.

"Heave dem rods in here!" rasped The Shadow. "No funny stuff, coppers! I'll drill youse guys—"

CAUGHT with revolvers lowered, the officers complied. They flung their weapons toward their captor.

The Shadow kicked the guns into the storeroom. He exhibited the bag.

"De swag's in here," he jeered, in crook fashion. "Tell Joe Cardona dis is where he shoulda come tonight. So long, saps. Dey'll be lettin' youse out soon."

Dropping the suitcase, The Shadow reached out and slammed the door. He locked it from the storeroom side, picked up the bag of swag and headed for the hall. Voices reached his ears. Again, The Shadow paused.

"Be ready with the squad, Townley," someone was saying. "I'll look up the officers who entered."

"Very well, Inspector," came the reply.

A grin appeared on The Shadow's disguised face. Inspector Egglestone had arrived. He had passed Detective Townley, who had evidently arrived at the back door to cover after the bluecoats had entered.

Two men went past the door of the storeroom, then paused. A hall light replaced the glimmer of torches. The Shadow saw Inspector Egglestone; close behind him was Clyde Burke, reporter for the *Classic*.

"Maybe they went in there, Inspector."

Clyde offered the suggestion. Egglestone, tall and sour-faced, wheeled toward him.

"I don't need any advice from you, Burke," he announced. "Because Cardona is fool enough to give you leeway is no reason why I should. You're lucky enough to be on this trip, without—"

Egglestone paused. Burke was staring past him, toward the door of the storeroom. Turning, the sour-faced inspector found himself confronted by the sweatered figure of The Shadow. He saw the leering lips that showed beneath the bandanna mask.

Egglestone stared at the muzzle of the revolver. Dully, he heard pounding sounds from far within the storeroom. The imprisoned officers were calling for aid.

"Hello, dere, Inspector!" came the harsh tone of The Shadow's disguised voice. "Just youse and a newshound, hey? Dat's soft! I don't need dis gat."

With a contemptuous gesture, the pretended crook thrust the revolver out of sight, beneath his sweater. He gestured with the suitcase.

"Old Cobleton will go cuckoo," sneered The Shadow. "Say, dese sparklers I took will fence for thoity grand! Listen to dem mugs poundin' away, Inspector. Funny, ain't it—"

EGGLESTONE'S hand was creeping to his coat pocket. With a sudden move, the inspector yanked a snub-nosed revolver and came springing forward upon the sweatered foe. Clyde Burke, staring, saw the mobster swing.

A clipping fist took the inspector cleanly on the jaw. Egglestone went backward; his opening fingers lost their hold on the gun. With a raucous laugh, The Shadow kicked the weapon into the storeroom.

"Out o' de way, boob!" he ordered, thrusting Clyde Burke against the wall. "Dis ain't your lookout! Give de inspector me regards when he wakes up."

With a contemptuous leer toward the sprawled form of Egglestone, The Shadow turned toward the stairs.

At that instant, Townley appeared from the rear of the hall. The detective yanked a gun; the fake crook was quicker. Out came the revolver from his sweater.

Three rapid-fire shots went *zizzing* just above Townley's head. The detective ducked to the floor.

Those shots came from above the banister as The Shadow headed toward the second floor. Wheeling at the top, he hurled back words to Clyde Burke.

"De commissioner's a dub" was the jeer, "yankin' Joe Cardona off de job! Put dat in de poipers, bozo!"

Turning, the sour-faced inspector found himself confronted by the sweatered figure of The Shadow.

Townley had reached the foot of the stairs. He was just in time to see the sweatered figure dart away from the top of the steps. Townley fired two wild shots; then drew a police whistle and blew it.

Bluecoats were already heading in from the back entrance. The front door suddenly came open. A withered-faced man—old Cobleton—entered with a flood of policemen. Inspector Egglestone was coming to his feet, half-dazed. Detective Townley took temporary command.

"Upstairs!" he bellowed. "Follow him! Outside, some of you, to cut him off!"

Cops responded. A trio dashed upstairs. They found an opened window at the rear; this was the exit that Cliff and Tinker had chosen. They shouted the news below. Arriving police formed a spreading cordon. Searchers went to work. But the procedure was too late.

The Shadow had made quick passage across the roof of the adjoining garage. He had scaled the roof of a house beyond; nearly a block away, he had dropped through a skylight to descend within an empty building.

A lone cop spied the sweatered figure as it appeared from an alleyway. The officer leveled a gun; then The Shadow, hurtling upon him, sent the weapon flying through the air. The officer sprawled as a quick wrench twisted his forearm. With this display of jujitsu, The Shadow headed away toward safety.

Two blocks away, he spied a waiting cab. Reaching his objective, The Shadow entered the vehicle. A hissed word to the driver.

Moe Shrevnitz grinned behind the wheel. He pulled away from the curb. Police whistles shrilled as officers, coming from another street, spied the moving taxi.

Another hiss from The Shadow. Inside the cab, he was removing the bandanna mask and peeling away the sweater. These garments went into the bag at his feet. His twisted smile was gone when he opened the cab window to meet the faces of officers who had brought Moe to a stop.

THE policemen saw the head and shoulders of a placid-faced man attired in evening clothes. They heard a voice that spoke in even, modulated tones as The Shadow inquired the meaning of the excitement.

"This ain't the guy," growled one.

"That's just what I was going to tell you," put in Moe, with a shrewd glance toward his passenger. "This fare's from Brooklyn. I'm taking him up to the Waldorf."

"An important reception, Officer," declared The Shadow, briskly. "I am already late."

"All right," agreed the cop. Then, to Moe: "What was the idea stopping down the block?"

"Heard a siren," returned Moe, promptly.

"Thought the patrol wagon was coming along. Drew up to the curb. That's all."

"Move ahead. Next time you're coming in from Brooklyn, stick to the avenues. You'll make, better time."

"I'll remember it, Officer."

The cab pulled away. Moe nodded at a new command from The Shadow. He swung around the block while The Shadow was busy with the suitcase.

Just beyond the fringe of the beleaguered area, Moe spied a patrolman on a beat. He pulled over to the curb. He saw The Shadow alight. Tall, in evening clothes, there was something pompous in his manner as he approached the officer.

Moe caught snatches of conversation. He saw the patrolman salute. Then The Shadow stepped to the cab, drew out the suitcase and tendered it to the bluecoat. Another salute; The Shadow stepped aboard and Moe drove away.

Bundling garments, The Shadow placed them on the seat beside him and indulged in a soft laugh. Moe nodded as he heard a new destination given.

BACK at the rifled hockshop, Inspector Egglestone was talking to old Cobleton. The owner of the place lived a block away. The excitement had brought him to the scene. In his little office, Cobleton lay slumped in a chair.

"Can you give us any clues?" Egglestone was demanding. "Have any suspicious characters come in here lately?"

"You ask me for clues?" questioned Cobleton. "When you found the man here and let him get away? Why ask me?"

Egglestone scowled. Clyde Burke grinned. The inspector noted the reporter's action. He wheeled.

"Feeling smart, eh?" he questioned, sourly. "Well, it's the last time any news hawk goes the rounds with me! Guess you'll do some panning in that lousy sheet of yours. Just because that crook got a break—"

Egglestone stopped. A policeman had entered, carrying a suitcase. Egglestone opened the bag and stared at an assortment of boxes.

Old Cobleton, springing forward with a happy cry, pawed into the suitcase. As he opened boxes, glimmering jewelry came into the light. Cobleton was elated.

"My gems!" he shouted. "My gems! All here!"

"Where did you get them?" questioned Egglestone, turning to the cop.

"From Commissioner Barth," returned the officer. "He came up in a taxi and handed me this bag. Told me to bring it here. I moved in off my beat on account of it being the commissioner's order."

"Get that, Burke?" questioned Egglestone, turning to the reporter. "There's your story. Police commissioner recovers the stolen gems. Don't forget; it was my case—"

"How about getting the commissioner's angle?"

"Good!" Egglestone nodded and picked up the telephone. "I'll call headquarters."

Three minutes later, Egglestone laid down the phone with a puzzled air. He turned to the patrolman who had brought in the suitcase.

"Are you sure that was the commissioner?" he questioned. "Did he identify himself?"

"He said he was the commissioner. He was wearing a full-dress suit."

"Do you know the commissioner by sight?"

"No. I did think it was kind of funny, him being in a taxi."

"That wasn't the commissioner," declared Egglestone, with a scowl. "The commissioner just called in from Long Island. He and Cardona went out there on a tip. Expected trouble at the home of Tobias Wolfenson. They found the house closed. Wolfenson is in Florida."

"Say, Burke"—Egglestone wheeled suddenly to the reporter—"you'd better stick to the fact that the gems were recovered. Get me? That crook knew I had him trapped. Surrendered the swag to a patrolman so he could make a getaway."

He drew Clyde over toward the safe and added a comment that the reporter alone could hear.

"My case," he said. "Remember that. You've got your facts. We have the stuff back—inside half an hour. Gems worth fifty thousand."

"About the crook," put in Clyde. "Sweater or evening dress—which was he wearing?"

"Either one. Better make it a sweater."

"Why not both?"

"Say—what're you trying to do? Stick to the facts. I'll tell you how to write this story."

"You don't need to. I've got my story."

With a grin, Clyde Burke turned on his heel and strode from the little office, leaving Inspector Egglestone fuming. Leaving the pawnshop, Clyde waved his way past bluecoats and detectives and reached a cigar store two blocks away. He put in a call to Burbank. His grin increased.

ONE hour later found Clyde at a typewriter in the city room of the New York *Classic*. He was finishing his usual police column, which covered his investigations in the underworld.

Inside stuff that would pass the desk, the moment that the night editor stepped out. He was leaving now. Clyde grinned and finished the column. He turned it over to an uncritical assistant editor, who gave a glance and sent the pages to the copy desk.

Clyde chuckled as he donned his hat and strolled from the city room. He had scooped the town. Tomorrow's column would be verbal dynamite, thanks to The Shadow.

CHAPTER VI
THE STORM BREAKS

MORNING. Acting Inspector Joe Cardona sat at his desk in headquarters, reading the New York *Classic*. A grim smile showed on Joe's face as he perused Clyde Burke's column. The account of last night's episodes ran as follows:

The East Side playboys are having their little jest at Commissioner Barth's new methods. Somehow they must have wised to his aptitude for taking up fancy clues that lead nowhere.

Last night our high official spotted a dummy ad in an evening newspaper. That was enough. He yanked Joe Cardona, acting inspector, from the underworld route. Just like a poker player discarding an ace from a royal flush.

With Joe off the beat, the jokers started. It began when they tapped the safe in Cobleton's Pawnshop and picked up a flock of likely-looking gems. Just so Barth's hired hands would know what was up, the raiders whooped a few shots like cowboys on a roundup. That brought Inspector Egglestone in the wake of two policemen.

The inspector arrived after the funmakers had locked the officers in Cobleton's office. But they had left a pal to take care of good old "Egg." Encountering a gorilla, the inspector found himself on the wrong end of a haymaker. While Egglestone slumbered, the crook made off with the swag.

It was all in fun, however. Half an hour later, a patrolman showed up with a suitcase filled with the missing jewels. A gent in evening attire had passed them to him. Said gent had introduced himself as Commissioner Barth.

Egg Egglestone was delighted until he found out it couldn't have been. Headquarters reported the commissioner on Long Island. Out in the lonely night, insisting that Cardona keep watch on a darkened house that later proved to be unoccupied.

Only one slipup marred the festivities. The suave deceiver who handed over the missing gems failed to wear a pair of pince-nez spectacles. But it didn't matter. The cop on the beat was not in the commissioner's social set. Never having been introduced to Mr. Wainwright Barth, he knew nothing of those famous specs. He just took the suitcase and toted it in to Egglestone. Egg took the credit.

Clues: A gentleman who cracks safes, fires a gat to make a noise, handles his dukes well, talks the 'oily boid' dialect, wears a sweater and uses a bandanna for a mask.

His pal travels in a Prince Albert, chooses taxis as a mode of riding and tells coppers that he's the police commissioner. Convincing enough to make them believe it, too.

What one takes, the other gives back. That's their idea of fun. Inspector Egglestone seemed to like it. Too bad the commissioner didn't take him out to Long Island, instead of snatching Joe Cardona off the job. Maybe he'll remember to do that next time.

If he does, the law will have more to show than the recovery of swag that was handed back to them. Cardona has a habit of rounding up funmakers for a joyride in the wagon. An art at which Commissioner Barth and Inspector Egglestone seem lacking.

As he finished reading, Joe Cardona looked up to see Detective Sergeant Markham enter. Joe pointed to the newspaper. Markham grinned and nodded.

"Just read it, Joe," he said. "Coming in to tell you about it. Looks like Burke's gone nuts, don't it?"

"Yeah," commented Joe. "Well"—he paused, thinking of last night's futile trip to Long Island—"you can't blame him. Somebody was due to cut loose with a razz on the commissioner. It's too bad for Burke, though."

"Why?"

"The commissioner will have his scalp. Wait and see."

"On account of the panning Burke handed Egg?"

"Sure. The commissioner rates Egglestone pretty high."

JOE CARDONA had made his comment in a tone of prediction. One hour after the prophecy, Clyde Burke entered the city room of the *Classic*. He was greeted by shaking heads.

"The old man wants to see you," remarked a reporter. "He's in his office."

Clyde entered a door marked "Managing Editor." He found the "old man" seated at his desk. The M.E. motioned for Clyde to close the door. Clyde complied.

"Burke," began the old man, "since when has your column called for editorial comment?"

Clyde grinned sheepishly. The M.E. remained severe.

"Commissioner Barth called me this morning," he declared. "He was highly indignant. He termed the *Classic* a yellow sheet. He said that it defied all the ethics of journalism."

"He's said that before, boss."

"Yes. But this time he is justified. I'm firing you, Burke."

"Just on account of—"

"Yes. On account of the way you wrote that column. It was poor business, Burke. Particularly from a reportorial standpoint. That type of tripe belongs in a small-town journal.

"I don't mind violent criticism. But I do object to having the *Classic* carry stuff that reads like the lead article in the Punkville *Weekly Bugle*. You're through, Burke. Two weeks' salary waiting downstairs."

Clyde nodded. He turned and walked slowly toward the door.

The managing editor looked up; then rose and reached the door ahead of him. He clapped his hand on Clyde's shoulder. His eyes carried a kindly twinkle as he spoke.

"I had to fire you, Burke," he remarked. "Now that the job's over, I don't mind telling you that you're a valuable man. You will find a berth somewhere; when you do, refer to me for recommendation.

"That column simply bore the marks of misplaced talent. Get it out of your system. Try a job in the sticks for six months until you're rid of this small-town complex. Then come back here. You'll find a new job waiting.

"I had to make an example of you to appease Barth. It will cool him when he learns that you were promptly removed from our staff. Either he will have forgotten all about you within six months, or—"

"There may be a new commissioner by that time," completed Clyde.

"Exactly!" chuckled the managing editor. "Good-bye, Burke. By the way, did I say you would find two weeks' salary downstairs?"

Clyde nodded.

"I meant four," corrected the M.E., returning to his desk.

HALF an hour afterward, Clyde Burke entered the office of Rutledge Mann. He found the investment broker seated at his desk, with clippings of Clyde's column in front of him. Mann looked up in solemn fashion. His face was slightly quizzical.

"Sacked," announced Clyde, pointing his thumb toward the clippings. "On account of that."

Mann smiled slightly. He picked up the clippings and tucked them in an envelope, which he passed to Clyde.

The reporter was a bit puzzled. He knew that he was due for some mission in behalf of The Shadow; what the clippings had to do with it was something he did not understand.

"Your recommendations," said Mann. "To a new job. They should serve you well."

"The old man promised me a recommendation of his own if I needed it for a newspaper job."

"Good! Call on him if necessary. But I think your own ability—as evidenced by today's article—will gain you a job with the Latuna *Enterprise.*"

"The Latuna *Enterprise?*"

"Yes. Here is a sample of the editorials that appear in that journal. Read it. I think that you and Mr. Harrison Knode have much in common."

Clyde nodded, chuckling, as he read the editorial that concerned the Blue Sphinx. When he looked up, Mann was politely tendering him a railroad ticket along with a green slip Pullman reservation.

"Pennsylvania Station, four thirty-five," announced Mann, in a businesslike tone. "Ticket and lower berth to Latuna. And added instructions"—

he picked up a sealed envelope and handed it to Clyde—"are to be read on the train."

At five o'clock that afternoon, Clyde Burke was seated in a corner of a club car, reading the message that Mann had given him. Coded words faded. Clyde crumpled the blank sheet and tossed it in a wastebasket beneath the writing desk opposite.

He had memorized brief added instructions from The Shadow.

AT that same hour, a slower through train was pulling out from the Union Station in Washington. Alone in the smoking compartment of a sleeper were two men who had come aboard at the last minute. Cliff Marsland and Tinker Furris formed the pair.

Cliff was reading a New York evening newspaper, in which he found brief mention of a foiled burglary in Cobleton's Pawnshop. He pointed it out to Tinker. A few minutes later, the pock-faced crook called Cliff's attention to a copy of the New York *Classic*.

"Say, look at this!" whispered Tinker, hoarsely. "Here's a guy has some funny dope on that job of ours. Some mug got away with the sparklers and another guy returned them!"

"The Shadow, probably," nodded Cliff, as he read the column. "Sure enough. That holds together."

"Whadda you mean?"

"Well, the bulls were coming in, weren't they?"

"Yeah."

"And The Shadow had to scram. So he slugged Egglestone and made a getaway."

"Why'd he run off with the swag?"

"Guess he didn't know who Egglestone was."

"I begin to get it. Then he handed the stuff over to some flatfoot. But it says here that there was a fellow in a sweater."

"That was probably what Egglestone thought. The Shadow must have handed him a quick haymaker."

"Yeah. And the cops must have been woozy when he cooped 'em in that office."

"They would have said the same as Egglestone."

Tinker nodded. Then his ugly countenance denoted perplexity. Cliff watched him closely. He knew what was coming.

"What gets me," confided Tinker, "is how The Shadow got out of it at all. You clipped him, Cliff."

"Probably grazed him with my first shot."

"You done better. You must have plugged him twice, anyway. He staggered that first time. I thought he was done."

"Looks like nobody can kill The Shadow."

"Maybe not. But I can't figure how he snapped out of it so quick. To do all he did afterward. Say— it's got me sort of jittery, Cliff."

"Why should it?" Cliff laughed as he saw a chance to swing the dangerous subject. "The more The Shadow did, the better for us."

"Why?"

"Because it kept him too busy to pick up our trail. We're sitting pretty, Tinker. Come on—it's time for chow. Let's see if this rattler has a diner."

Tinker said nothing more, and Cliff decided that the topic was ended. That was a good sign. For the fight with The Shadow had put Cliff in right with Tinker. As sworn pals, they were heading for Latuna to join up with Konk Zitz.

Uppermost in Cliff's mind was the fact that he must keep the true facts of that fight completely away from Tinker's mind. Any inkling that the battle had been framed would prove disastrous.

For where Cliff was going, any suspicion that he was an agent of The Shadow would ruin the coming campaign against crime. More than that, a discovery of the truth could spell prompt death for Cliff Marsland.

CHAPTER VII
IN THE MUSEUM

WHILE two trains were bringing new visitors to Latuna, that prosperous little city lay glittering beneath the darkened evening sky. Well-lighted streets were prevalent in Latuna; but they ended abruptly on the border of the business district. Beyond were blackened, vacant subdivisions that had ceased development with the sudden termination of a real-estate boom.

On a hill well out from the town stood a lonely marble building that looked like a vast mausoleum. This was the central portion of the unfinished Latuna Museum. It had been erected on the hill so that it might overlook the town.

Subdivisions as yet unbuilt; intervening trees that had not been cut down—these isolated the museum from the city. Instead of dominating a suburban district, the new building was actually in a rural area.

Viewed from the outside, the museum was a square-shaped building with broad steps leading up to four mammoth stone pillars. Modeled after the Parthenon in Athens, the structure was topped by a low, broad dome.

The marble front had large windows, guarded with heavy metal shutters; but the sides and back were windowless. Moreover, they lacked the marble surface of the front. These other walls were entirely of brick.

The reason lay in the fact that the museum was uncompleted. The final plans called for the addition of two wings and a rear extension which would be deeper than the rest of the structure; for the ground sloped downward at the back of the museum.

Entering the building, one found exhibit rooms in both front corners. Smaller rooms were situated along the side walls. From the center of the building back to the rear wall was a special exhibit room, directly beneath the broad dome. One entered this through a commodious anteroom. Heavy Florentine doors formed the first barrier; lighter doors were beyond, at the inner portion of the anteroom.

A main hall ran along the front of the building, just in back of the lobby and the corner exhibit rooms. Small corridors ran along the sides, between the blank walls of the central exhibit room and the small chambers at the sides of the building.

An incomplete arrangement. Many persons had predicted difficulties in the new extensions. On this particular evening, one man seemed deeply concerned with that problem. Joseph Rubal, curator of the museum, was seated in his office, which was reached by the last door on the right-hand corridor.

RUBAL was a tall, dry-faced man. His forehead showed deep furrows; his expression was perpetually solemn. He had a habit of running his long fingers through the sparse hair of his partly bald head. He was following this procedure as he studied a set of plans that lay upon his desk.

Eight o'clock. Rubal noted the time by his desk clock. He frowned as he looked toward the door; then his expression changed as he heard footsteps in the hall. The door opened and a uniformed attendant entered.

"Ah, Hollis," expressed Rubal, as he eyed the stocky, square-jawed arrival. "Have the other attendants left?"

"Yes, sir."

"You have locked up for the night?"

"Yes, sir. Until the watchmen arrive at nine."

"Remain here. I shall make sure."

Hollis watched Rubal leave the office. He shrugged his shoulders. As chief attendant, he never failed in his duty of closing the museum, yet the curator invariably insisted upon a personal checkup.

Five minutes later, Rubal returned to find Hollis standing stolidly in the spot where he had left him. Rubal gave an approving nod, a token that he had found the front door barred on the inside. Hollis started to leave the office.

"No inspection is necessary, Hollis," remarked Rubal, dryly. "Remain here. I wish to talk to you. Did you notice these plans for the new extensions?"

"No, sir. Are they completed?"

"Not quite. It is a problem, Hollis." The attendant nodded; then advanced as Rubal beckoned him to the desk. On view lay a floor plan of the museum as it now stood, with dotted lines to indicate the additions.

"As chief attendant, Hollis," declared the curator, "you are quite familiar with the present plan of this museum. Therefore, I think that my difficulties will interest you."

"They will, sir. Particularly because of the—"

"Well?" queried Rubal, as Hollis paused.

"On account of the criticism, sir," admitted Hollis. "In the *Enterprise,* I mean—"

"I understand. That muckraker, Harrison Knode, has objected to my delay. He thinks that I should have submitted the complete plans before this."

"He is a troublemaker, sir."

"I know it. Meanwhile I am handicapped." Rubal's voice rose as he pounded the desk. "Look, Hollis. See my problems! This building was designed wrong in the beginning!"

"Whose fault was that, sir?"

"No one's. You see, Hollis, old Barnaby Soyer promised the city his entire collection of priceless art treasures provided that a museum would be built within one year after his death. That was a large order."

Hollis nodded.

"A collection worth more than a million dollars," resumed Rubal. "It would have been lost to Latuna, but for the timely aid of Strafford Malden. He donated the ground and urged citizens to contribute preliminary funds. Construction began at once.

"IT was obvious that the Soyer collection could not be placed on exhibit until the entire building was completed. Many suggestions were made as to housing the treasures temporarily. Finally, we hit upon the best one, thanks to the rearward slope of the ground.

"A vault was created directly beneath the central room that stands under the dome. Barnaby Soyer's treasures were brought in through the back of that vault. Gems, golden vessels, statuettes of precious metals—none of these would suffer by long storage. So the back of the vault was sealed with solid brick, not to be opened until the completion of the wings."

Again, Hollis nodded. Very little of this was new to him. He wondered why the curator was going to such detailed explanation.

"Save for the front," stated Rubal, still talking loudly, "this museum is windowless. Doorways will be cut through brick walls to make the entrances to new corridors in the wings and back extension."

"The present corridors end abruptly, sir."

"Yes. Because they will be continued through. But there lies a problem. Shall we have a joining corridor in the rear extension?"

"In back of the Sphinx Room, sir?" Rubal chuckled.

"An excellent term, Hollis," he commended. "I shall remember it tomorrow, when the Blue Sphinx arrives. The Sphinx Room. Very good, Hollis."

"It just popped out, sir. It will look fine in that room, the Blue Sphinx will. The bare pedestal, with its wooden covering, is hardly artistic, sir."

"It is not meant to be," declared Rubal, unsmiling. "The wooden platform merely protects the stone pedestal."

"I understand, sir. When do you intend to remove the platform?"

"Not until the Sphinx is actually ready to go in its place. I shall superintend the work, Hollis."

"Very good, sir."

There was a pause. Before Rubal could speak, Hollis raised his hand warningly.

"Did you hear that, sir?"

"What?" inquired Rubal, nervously.

"A muffled sound, sir! Like something dropping!"

"Imagination, Hollis."

"There it is again, Mr. Rubal!"

"I hear nothing. Come, Hollis. Let me show you these plans."

"But I was sure, sir, that the noise could have come from the Sphinx Room!"

"I inspected that room, Hollis. The doors are closed. Come, come, man! You are making me nervous! Concentrate upon these plans. I want your opinion."

THE chamber which Hollis had so aptly termed the Sphinx Room lay directly beneath the large dome of the museum. Glass sections in the circular roof admitted pale moonlight. Beneath those whitened rays, a strange scene was taking place while Rubal talked with Hollis in the office.

The chief attendant's supposition had not been false. Beneath that dull light, shrouded figures were in motion. Like hunchbacked ghosts, they were creeping across the tiled floor, away from the wooden-platformed pedestal that was to form the resting place of the Blue Sphinx.

Doors lay open through the anteroom. Those had been unbarred from the outside. That explained why Hollis had heard some sound. The noise had carried through the corridors.

Creeping forms had completed some insidious mission, for they were moving together toward the outer door. One figure stopped on the fringe of the moonlight and carefully closed the doors that led from anteroom to Sphinx Room. Moonlight alone remained in the empty compartment that was to house the Blue Sphinx.

More whispers in the darkened anteroom. A flashlight glimmered as its bearer moved into the corridor. Doors from corridor to anteroom went shut. Locks turned in place. Prowlers continued toward the big front door. That barrier swung open. When it closed, the silence and gloom remained.

Five minutes. Then a bell tingled with a short, abrupt br-r-r. After that came new silence. Like a signal, that final touch had marked the passage of the unknown prowlers.

IN the office, Hollis looked up suddenly. His square face was troubled. Hollis stepped away from the desk and started to the door that led into the corridor.

"Hold on, Hollis," ordered Rubal. "What is the trouble now?"

"The bell, sir," explained the chief attendant. "I am sure that I heard it."

"At ten minutes of nine?" quizzed the curator, pointing to the clock. "Impossible! Those watchmen never arrive ahead of time. Besides, they ring incessantly."

"That is the trouble, sir. I heard just the slightest tingle."

"I warned you to curb your imagination, Hollis. Here, sit down at my desk. Try one of these Puerto Rican cigars. Imagine yourself to be the curator, if you must indulge in fanciful notions. I shall investigate."

Waving the attendant to the chair, the curator went out into the corridor and turned on a light. He continued to the big front hall, turning on more lights.

As he neared the front entrance, Rubal paused. He threw an anxious glance over his shoulder. Satisfied that Hollis was not following, he went to the door of the anteroom and found it tight.

Methodically, Rubal continued to the front door of the museum. The huge bar was raised from its place; but the curator did not seem perturbed. Carefully, he put the bar back in place. Mopping his forehead with a silk handkerchief, he went back along the corridors, extinguishing lights behind him.

Hollis was puffing a perfecto when Rubal reentered the office. The curator shook his head to signify that he had found nothing. He motioned to Hollis to keep the chair. Taking a cigar for himself, Rubal paced back and forth across the little office.

"What do you think of the plans, Hollis?" he questioned.

"I can suggest no improvement, sir," replied the attendant. "I consider them quite good."

"They do not suit me, Hollis. Perhaps I shall finish them. Perhaps not."

"What do you mean, sir?"

"I mean that I may resign as curator, in deference to public opinion."

"That would be a mistake, sir. Really—"

A long bell ring interrupted. It was repeated. Rubal waved his hand toward the door.

"The watchmen," he said, bluntly. "Admit them, Hollis. You may leave without returning here. I shall need you no more tonight."

"Very well, sir."

"But if you would only speak to Mr. Malden, sir."

"I shall not seek that opportunity, Hollis. That settles the matter. Go to your post at the front door. Be ready to answer the bell."

Hollis shifted and started to resume his insistence. Angrily, Rubal pointed to the door. Hollis stepped from view. Rubal caught a last glimpse of the attendant's troubled face. Then the curator began to study the papers on his desk.

FIRST, Rubal picked out a typewritten sheet. This was his formal resignation as curator of the Latuna Museum. Rubal signed the paper. The action seemed to relieve him. Laying the resignation aside, Rubal began to select other documents.

One was a floor plan of the museum. On this, Rubal made penciled notations. He picked out some bills and receipts. He added memos to these. On a blank sheet, he began to write in the halting fashion of a man making a confession.

There was a day calendar on Rubal's desk. It was the type in which old dates are tilted over, not torn off. In the course of his writing, Rubal paused to turn these day sheets down. He was going back to the first of the year, checking up on the written statements he was making.

When he had reached January 1st, Rubal arose from his desk. He walked across the office and stepped into a small room beyond. He turned on a light, to show a large filing cabinet in the corner. The curator opened a cabinet drawer. He began to search for papers that would give him information prior to the current year.

Rubal paused in this work as he heard the muffled ring of a distant bell. Coming from the inner room, he noticed the time on his desk clock. It was not long after eight. Time had gone slowly since Hollis had left the office.

Rubal went to the outer door of the office. He opened it and noted that the corridor lights were on. Having arranged for his visitor's entrance, the curator went back to the inner room of the office suite and hurriedly turned to the filing cabinet. He drew out a sheaf of letters.

Footsteps sounded at the office door. Rubal heard them; from his place in the inner room, he called to the arrival:

"Sit down, Mr. Knode! I shall be with you in a moment!"

With a last glance at the letters, Rubal drew several from the sheet and replaced the rest in the filing cabinet. He heard the sound of a closing door—the one to the corridor. Then came a *click*. Rubal turned.

The visitor had switched off the light in the outer office. Disturbed, Rubal stepped toward the office

itself. The only light that remained was that from the little filing room, where Rubal was standing.

In the doorway, with right hand against the door frame and left holding the letters from the cabinet, Rubal peered anxiously into the office. He saw his visitor over beyond the desk, a lurking figure in the darkness.

"Knode!" exclaimed Rubal. "What does this mean? Why have you turned out the light?"

Something glimmered. A horrified exclamation came from the curator's lips as his eyes caught the flash of a revolver barrel. Desperately, Rubal stepped back from the doorway. He was too late.

Framed against the light from the filing room, Joseph Rubal made a perfect target for the murderous marksman. Flame forked from the gun, accompanied by a fizzing sound, like that of a squibby firecracker.

Joseph Rubal staggered. He delivered a wild, sighing cry, dropped the letters and pressed his hands against his body. He staggered forward, step by step; past the desk, almost to the outer door of the office.

Then, suddenly, the curator collapsed. Sprawled upon the floor, he lay moaning between hopeless gasps. Joseph Rubal was dying, while his assassin, indifferent to the curator's plight, moved through the darkness of the office.

CHAPTER X
THE MAN WHO KNEW

BACK at the outer door of the museum, Hollis was seated at his table. The chief attendant was restless. Hollis glanced at his watch. Twenty minutes past eight.

Hollis had bolted the outer door, his usual procedure after admitting a visitor. It was his duty to remain here until the watchmen arrived, unless otherwise ordered by Rubal. There had been no summons from the curator.

Yet Hollis was sure that something was amiss. He had an impression that he had heard an odd, sighing cry from a distant spot of the museum. He knew that the door of the curator's office was not soundproof. Noise carried strangely through the long corridors of the museum. Could that cry have come from Rubal's office?

Hollis ended his indecision. He glanced toward the outer door. Anyone seeking admittance there would have to ring. The bell could be heard from Rubal's office. Hollis decided that it would be a good idea to visit the curator. He glanced at his watch, then nodded. He had found a satisfactory excuse.

Pocketing his watch, Hollis plodded past the Medieval Room and took to the long corridor that led to Rubal's office. Reaching his objective, the chief attendant stopped and listened intently. He heard someone moving within the office. That sound faded. Then Hollis fancied that he caught a moan.

"Mr. Rubal!"

Hollis knocked as he gave the call. He listened. There was no response. "Mr. Rubal!"

A dull *click,* like someone pressing a light switch. That was all that Hollis heard.

Perplexed, the chief attendant opened the door of the office. The barrier swung inward; something stopped its course. Hollis pushed harder; he heard a moan as the door swung clear past an obstruction that shifted on the floor. Then Hollis stood astounded.

The office light was out. So was the light of the little filing room. The click that Hollis had heard was the explanation of the inner light being gone. But Hollis was not concerned with that matter. He was staring toward the floor of the curator's office.

By the light of the corridor, Hollis could see the prone form of Joseph Rubal. The curator's face showed pallid and distorted. Gasping lips and pleading eyes registered themselves to the chief attendant's gaze. Hollis stooped beside the dying curator.

"Mr. Rubal!" blurted the attendant. "Tell me— what has happened—"

"Knode!" gasped the curator weakly. "Harrison Knode! He—he shot me; I'm dying—"

"Knode?" questioned Hollis. "Knode shot you? But—but where—where did he—"

HOLLIS paused abruptly. He caught a sound from straight ahead. The attendant looked up, then came slowly to his feet. He was looking toward the door of the filing room, where he could detect a slight motion.

Whirling impressions swept through the attendant's brain. Finding Joseph Rubal on the floor, Hollis had first thought the curator stricken by a heart attack. Rubal's words had astounded him; then had come this interruption.

Motionless, Hollis stared at that door. He realized that the murderer stood there; that the slayer had chosen the filing room as a lurking spot. Hollis did not picture what had happened. He did not know that Rubal, stepping from the filing room, had been a perfect target against a background of light.

Nor did he realize that he had stepped into a similar situation. With the light of the corridor behind him, Hollis was another target. His first cognizance of that fact came when he saw what Rubal had seen: the glimmer of a revolver.

Hollis uttered a hoarse cry. He started forward, hopelessly. Flame tongued through the darkened office; with it, the fierce sigh of the silencer-fitted gun. The second shot proved better than the first. Hollis doubled crazily and tottered.

Joseph Rubal delivered a last croaking gasp from the floor. Then Hollis came tumbling squarely on his body. The chief attendant gave a final writhe and rolled from the curator's dead form. Side by side, Rubal and Hollis lay dead.

THE murderer did not turn on the light. Instead, he prowled about the room with a flashlight. He picked up the letters that Rubal had dropped upon the floor. He found the resignation and added it to the letters. He gathered up Rubal's notations, including the marked plan of the museum. Then he extinguished his flash.

Stepping past the dead bodies, the killer sidled to the door. But he did not move into the corridor; wary, he wanted to avoid its revealing light, despite the fact that he had become the only living man remaining in the Latuna Museum.

An arm came into the corridor, reaching around the corner from the office door. A hand found a light switch that controlled the corridor lights. Three clicks. The pathway from office to the big front door was a mass of blackness.

Unaided even by his flashlight, the killer moved out of Rubal's office and made his way along the corridor to the front of the museum. He reached the steps by the big front door and felt his way to the barrier. Groping, he found the bar and raised it. He swung the huge door inward, stepped out into the night and closed the door behind him.

A clouded sky had brought pitch-blackness to the ground. Even the whitened front of the museum was barely visible. The building looked a dim, ghostly sepulchre in the darkness. Its deathlike appearance was appropriate; for it had become the tomb for two murdered victims.

The killer gave a low, evil laugh as he stalked away from the museum of death. Treading hard clay soil, he left no footprints behind him. He found a hard-beaten path in the darkness and descended the hill in back of the museum until he arrived at an old road near the quarry siding.

Tiny lights were flickering half a mile away. The killer watched them bob and scatter. Then he kept on moving through the dark. They were doing night blasting at the isolated quarry. A hundred yards along the road, the murderer paused while a muffled *boom* resounded and the earth gave a slight shudder.

Then, as clattering rocks came tumbling down the neighboring hillside, the unseen killer turned from the road and stepped amid a thick cluster of trees. He flicked his flashlight on the stony surface of an abandoned road. The glimmer showed an old coupé, parked in readiness. The killer extinguished his torch.

Entering the car, this man of murder turned on the dim lights and started the motor. He drove bounding along the old road, curving off through trees, away from both the museum and the quarry. He reached a highway and began a curving course in the direction of Latuna.

Double death had struck tonight. With evil aforethought, a murderer had spelled finish to the affairs of Joseph Rubal. Then, as a final touch, the killer had lurked to deliver death to the only man who might have served as witness for the law.

He had slain Hollis, the man who knew. With the chief attendant dead beside the slain curator, it would take the efforts of a master sleuth to pin crime on the fiend who had committed it.

Hollis ... started forward, hopelessly. Flame tongued through

CHAPTER XI
AT THE PHOENIX HOTEL

SHORTLY after murder had been enacted at the Latuna Museum, a stranger entered the lobby of the Wilkin Hotel, Latuna's most pretentious hostelry. There was something about the arrival's bearing that was oddly reminiscent of Lamont Cranston.

The stranger in Latuna was tall, like Cranston; his face was hawklike and immobile; yet his whole visage was squarer and heavier than that of the New York millionaire. Moreover, his complexion was darker than Cranston's.

The new guest at the Wilkin registered under the name of Henry Arnaud; his address: Cleveland, Ohio. He was given a room on the sixth floor front.

the darkened office ... the fierce sigh of the silencer-fitted gun.

Arrived there, Arnaud seemed satisfied. He dismissed the bellhop with a tip.

Moving his heavy suitcases from the luggage rack by the window, Henry Arnaud gazed out toward the town's main street. Half a block away was the Phoenix Hotel. Watching the front of that building, Arnaud spied two men entering the hotel. One was Bart Drury; the other Clyde Burke. Arnaud's eyes gleamed as he recognized the latter.

A soft laugh came from immobile lips as the new guest withdrew from the window. As Henry Arnaud, The Shadow had come unannounced to Latuna. His first purpose had been to learn how Clyde Burke was faring. Already, The Shadow had spied his agent.

Leaving his room, The Shadow descended to the lobby of the Wilkin. In the methodical fashion of Henry Arnaud, he strolled out to the street. He crossed the main thoroughfare and entered the Phoenix Hotel.

The Shadow discovered a large, glittering lobby that was cluttered with various slot machines. These devices were of a non-gambling type and had evidently passed police inspection. For tonight, two khaki-clad policemen were on duty; and they seemed mildly interested in watching the players at the game boards.

Bart Drury was seated in a corner chair, smoking a fat cigar. He had a complete view of the lobby and the small taproom that adjoined it. Near Bart was Clyde Burke, also on the watch.

Both were so concerned, however, with their more distant watching that they failed to notice the stranger who took a chair just past a potted palm tree to Drury's right. In fact, neither man saw the inconspicuous figure of Henry Arnaud.

Listening, The Shadow overheard the conversation between Drury and Burke.

"Grewling's got two cops on the job tonight," laughed Bart. "Guess the old man got results with that editorial."

"Are any of the riffraff around?" questioned Clyde.

"Sure," returned Bart. "There's a couple by the cigar stand. The rest are in the taproom."

"I don't see any cops in there."

"Two detectives." Bart paused to puff at his cigar. "Look through there to the corner table. See that guy with the funny-looking face? He's one of Grewling's dicks. Mushmug, we call him."

A pause. Bart's stogie began to curl. He chucked it in an ash-stand. As he started to fumble in his pocket for a fresh cigar, Bart suddenly poked Clyde in the shoulder.

"Here comes the big shot," he whispered. "Guy named Konk Zitz. See? From the taproom?"

CLYDE nodded as he saw a short, sallow-faced rogue come into the lobby. Konk Zitz was attired in tuxedo. He was chewing a cigar and looking about with beady, ratlike eyes. He spied Bart Drury, and a sour grin appeared upon his face.

"Hello, there!" greeted the newcomer, approaching the reporter. "Boy! What smoke! Did you chuck a pineapple in that ash-stand?"

"Just a cigar," returned Drury.

"Who gave it to you?" chuckled Konk. "The police chief? Trying to gas you?"

"I bought it," retorted Drury. "For a nickel."

"Well, here's a fifteen-center," offered Konk. "One for your pal, too." He looked at Clyde and added a question. "New reporter on your paper?"

"Yes," replied Drury. "Name's Burke."

Konk shook hands with Clyde. Then he took a chair near the two reporters and nudged his thumb toward the lobby.

"Looks like your boss woke Grewling up," observed the crook leader. "Two flatfeet here in the lobby. Couple more out back. Couple of dicks in the taproom."

"Watching your bunch?" quizzed Drury.

"Watching everybody," corrected Konk. "I've got no outfit, Drury. Get that out of your noodle."

"You've got a lot of friends."

"Sure! Pals who have the same idea I have. We all think Latuna is a good spot for a vacation."

"Two more blew in today, didn't they?"

"Yeah. Couple of friends of mine. I mailed them a folder about Latuna. You know the one. Chamber of Commerce puts it out. Well, they fell for the idea this city was a beauty spot and they dropped off."

"From a freight?"

"Came in by the Northeast Express," replied Konk Zitz, ignoring Drury's sarcasm. "Say—I don't get this stuff of calling me and my friends undesirables. Latuna is a vacation city, ain't it?"

"So they say."

"Well, we spend U. S. dough, like anybody else. What's more, we spend more of it than most people."

"All right, Konk. I'm not arguing. It's Knode's idea to razz you fellows; not mine. Say—who came in today?"

"A fellow named Tinker Furris; and a pal of his, Cliff Marsland. Both have a clean bill of health."

"Where are they?"

"In the taproom. You can't see them from here; but Grewling's gumshoes are watching them."

THE SHADOW had heard every iota of this conversation. Yet not even Konk Zitz had noticed the placid stranger beyond the potted palm. Watching across the lobby, The Shadow spied an approaching bellboy. He observed that the attendant was coming to speak to Konk Zitz.

"Telephone, Mr. Zitz."

Konk arose at the bellhop's statement. The Shadow watched the sallow-faced cigar smoker go to a telephone booth, while Bart and Clyde resumed their conversation. Though Konk was turned so that The Shadow could not eye the motions of his lips, the keen-eyed watcher knew that this telephone call was an important one.

When Konk came out of the booth, he wore a poker-faced expression. He started toward the tap-room; as an afterthought, he swung back and approached Clyde and Bart.

"Fine mess your boss made of things!" Konk told Drury. "With Grewling's gumshoes on the job, none of us can go out of here tonight. I had to bust a date with a swell blonde who just called me up."

"Too bad," observed Drury.

"I'll say it is!" growled Konk. "If I took her out in my coupé, I'd have a couple of these wise dicks traveling along in the rumble seat. When you see that boss of yours, Knode, tell him I don't like him! Get that?"

Konk turned and went into the taproom. His bluff had been effective with the reporters.

Not so with The Shadow. The listener who wore the countenance of Henry Arnaud knew well that Konk Zitz had deliberately tried to cover up a business call.

"Let's go up to the old man's house," suggested Bart. "Maybe he's been up to the museum, to see Rubal. We'll walk over to Knode's. It's only a couple of blocks."

As the two sauntered from the lobby, The Shadow arose and strolled to the taproom. Just inside, he paused; as before, his guise of Arnaud was an inconspicuous one. The Shadow saw Konk Zitz with a group at a table. Cliff Marsland was there, seated beside Tinker Furris. The Shadow recognized the latter's pockmarked face.

"All O.K.," came Konk's low growl. "Nobody needed tonight. Sit tight. It's great, with these dicks watching us. We want them to know that none of us moved out of here after seven p.m."

The Shadow strolled from the taproom. He knew the source of that information which Konk Zitz had passed to the band. It was an aftermath of the telephone call that Konk had received. As he left the Phoenix Hotel, The Shadow glanced at his watch. The time was five minutes before nine.

There was no need for The Shadow to remain here longer. Konk and his pals was staying in the Phoenix Hotel; Cliff Marsland, established with the outfit, would report any new developments.

The Shadow's thoughts reverted to Clyde Burke and Bart Drury. His fixed lips formed the semblance of a smile as he entered the lobby of his own hotel and took the elevator to the sixth.

IN his room, The Shadow consulted a telephone book and learned Knode's address. He extinguished the light in the room; then opened a suitcase. Black garments clicked. From that moment, Henry Arnaud was a name only; his personality had ended. The cloaked figure of The Shadow had replaced him.

Gliding phantomlike through the hallway, The Shadow arrived at a firetower exit and descended to a vacant lot beside the hotel. This was used as a parking space; The Shadow threaded his way among the standing cars.

His course became swift and undiscernible as he moved along silent, dimly lighted streets. The Shadow's speed showed that he had familiarized himself with a street map of Latuna. He knew the shortcuts; his pace was rapid. It brought him to the front of a small, old-fashioned house that stood on a secluded street.

The Shadow passed through a little gate; then merged with the blackness at the side of a porch as he heard footsteps coming from the corner.

Clyde Burke and Bart Drury entered the gate. This house was Harrison Knode's. The Shadow's swift course had beaten their strolling pace and roundabout choice of route. The Shadow watched from darkness as Drury rang the doorbell. An elderly housekeeper answered.

"Hello, Bridget!" greeted Bart. "Where's Mr. Knode?"

"He went out, Mr. Drury," replied the woman.

"When did he say he'd be back?" inquired the reporter.

"He didn't tell me that," answered Bridget. "He just told me he was going out before eight o'clock. That was right after dinner—"

"Who says I went out?" The irritable voice was Harrison Knode's. The editor was coming from a stairway. "I haven't been out at all!"

The Shadow saw Knode's figure at the doorway. The man was in shirtsleeves. His necktie was missing. He acted in a half-sleepy manner.

"I told you to call me, Bridget," snapped Knode, "so I could go out at eight! I went upstairs to take a nap. I overslept."

"I was sure, sir," protested the woman, "that you had gone out. When I saw you just now, I thought you'd come in by the back door."

"Enough, Bridget! You may go!" Knode shooed the housekeeper with an angry wave of his hands. Then to Clyde and Bart. "Come in, you fellows. We'll have a smoke."

The door closed after Clyde and Bart entered.

The Shadow lingered; then edged forward from the darkness beside the porch. He reached the door and found it unlatched. Softly, he entered to a hallway.

Beyond curtains, The Shadow saw lights that

indicated Knode's parlor. He peered into an old-fashioned room. He saw the editor offering cigars to the reporters.

"IT'S too late to go to the museum," stated Knode, as he lighted his cigar. "Rubal will be gone. Well, I'll see him tomorrow. If he's got anything worthwhile to say, I'll hear it in time for the edition."

He paused; then inquired sharply. "Where've you fellows been this evening?"

"Down at the Phoenix Hotel," replied Drury. "Talking with Konk Zitz. Couple of new pals blew in to join him."

"Was Grewling there?"

"No. Some of his men were, though."

"Humph! I wonder why Grewling wasn't there. I thought he'd be keeping tabs himself, tonight. Well, I guess he'll be there later."

Knode walked restlessly across the room; then sat down in a chair.

"It irks me," he asserted, "this fact that I over-slept. I should have seen Rubal tonight. Instead, I didn't get a chance to leave the house. I was caught napping, literally."

With that statement, Harrison Knode dropped the subject and settled down to a casual chat with his reporters. But Clyde Burke could not dispel a lurking suspicion that Bridget had been correct when she had stated that Knode had gone out at eight o'clock.

Whether or not Knode had told the truth was a matter that continued to perplex Clyde. It was something that he intended to put in his report to The Shadow. Clyde wondered what his chief's finding would be. The Shadow had a way of divining the false from the true; even when he worked on information from others.

Clyde Burke would have been amazed had he known that The Shadow had already studied the merits of Knode's statements. Listening from the hall, that cloaked watcher had heard all that the editor had said. Moreover, he had noted Knode's expression when the man had talked.

The Shadow had dropped Konk Zitz, knowing that Cliff Marsland could watch that fellow. Right now, he was dropping Harrison Knode, leaving further observation of the editor to Clyde Burke. A new, uncovered lead was the one that The Shadow intended to follow.

Knode's front door closed softly as The Shadow stole out into darkness. Swiftly, stealthily, the cloaked phantom headed townward.

A soft whisper drifted through the darkness. The Shadow had yet to learn of murder at the museum. Yet he had already gained important impressions concerning two persons in Latuna: namely, Konk Zitz and Harrison Knode.

CHAPTER XII
MORE MEN MOVE

TEN minutes after The Shadow had left Harrison Knode's, a figure strode from the Phoenix Hotel. It was Police Chief Grewling. The official had paid a brief visit to the hotel in order to hear reports from his men.

A coupé was parked just past the lighted front of the hotel. The car was Grewling's; in businesslike fashion, the official entered the coupé and took the wheel. He started the motor and shifted the gear.

Gleaming eyes from darkness. They had watched the police chief's exit from the hotel. The Shadow, arriving, had stopped at sight of Grewling's gold-braided uniform. The police chief's love of tinsel trappings made him easily recognizable.

As the coupé started, blackness swept forward. With long, swift stride, The Shadow gained the rear of the moving car. His shape blended with the curve of its body. Invisible above the rear light, The Shadow was accompanying the police chief to some destination.

For The Shadow had done more than recognize the police chief. He had analyzed Grewling's stride; he had divined that the official was bound on some important mission. Grewling, like Zitz and Knode, was a factor in the odd medley of counterpurposes that existed in Latuna. The Shadow saw opportunity to gain an inkling of the police chief's ways.

Grewling drove rapidly through secluded streets, totally unaware of the mysterious rider perched at the rear of his car. After half a dozen minutes, he pulled up in front of a large stone house. The door was open; a servant was standing there. Grewling called out to learn if Mayor Rush happened to be at home.

"I expect him any minute, sir," informed the menial. "He said something about an appointment here, at nine o'clock."

"It's after nine now."

Lights swung from the corner in front of the coupé. Grewling, using his prerogative as police chief, had parked on the left. The arriving car, a sedan, stopped on the right, its lights glaring into those of Grewling's coupé.

It was the mayor's car. Rush alighted and came pompously to the door of Grewling's coupé. He nodded to the police chief and beckoned to the servant, who came from the house door. The Shadow made no move from his perch at the rear of the coupé.

He could see a uniformed policeman who had alighted from the mayor's car. He knew that this must be an officer whom Grewling had detailed as Rush's chauffeur, the mayor's car being an official one. From his absolute concealment, The Shadow could hear Rush speaking. The mayor was addressing the servant who had come from the house:

"Any callers, Adams?"

"No, sir. Mr. Malden telephoned, though, a short while ago."

"I see. Let's go up to Malden's, Grewling. We can ride in your car. I told Malden I might be up to see him along about nine o'clock." Then, to the servant. "I'll leave my sedan here; if Mr. Rubal calls, Adams, tell him that my chauffeur will bring him up to Mr. Malden's."

"Very well, sir."

THE SHADOW made no motion while Rush was entering the coupé. Grewling started the machine; it shot rapidly from the curb and skirted Rush's sedan so swiftly that neither Adams nor the chauffeur spied the figure clinging to the rear of the coupé.

As the car swung the corner, The Shadow performed a difficult maneuver. He came headfirst over the fender at the right rear of the coupe. Flattened there, his shoulders were just in back of the opened window beside Mayor Rush.

As the coupé rolled through darkness, The Shadow could overhear all that passed between mayor and police chief.

"I lost track of time at the office," explained Rush. "I shall have that wall clock fixed someday. It stopped around eight. I did not know how late it was. Where were you this evening, Grewling?"

"Checking on the Phoenix Hotel. Knode ought to be satisfied. I had eight men watching the lobby. None of those crooks went out of the place."

"It is within your authority to watch the hotel, Grewling; but remember: I did not order it. I think you made a mistake."

"Why?"

"Knode will lampoon anything you do. Mark my words on that, Grewling. The best policy with Knode is to ignore him."

"But, today, his paper said—"

"I know. Just a wedge for more muckraking. I thought there might be a large crowd at the dedication exercises. That is why I ordered a large detail. The men were available; there was no reason why you could not have supplied them."

"Certainly. They were mostly traffic officers who had no duty until afternoon."

"But Knode saw a chance for empty talk. Well, Grewling, I took it up with Dunham, of the *Gazette*. His journal will run a suitable story tomorrow, with photographs of the museum and the Blue Sphinx."

The mayor cleared his throat; then added:

"Forget Knode for a while, Grewling. Watch the Phoenix Hotel for a few days longer at the most.

Remember, Grewling, if I took Knode too seriously, you would not be holding your job today."

The Shadow, peering through the edge of the coupé window, saw Grewling shift uneasily. The police chief darted a glance at the mayor, then looked toward the road and slowed the coupe in order to turn into a driveway just ahead.

"Like Rubal, you are an official from the last administration," explained Rush, as the car stopped in front of a massive stone mansion, well in from the road. "Ever since Darfield, our ex-mayor, disappeared from town, Knode has demanded that I air the faults of the last administration.

"I have refused to do so. I kept you and Rubal because I believed both of you, to be honest. I can give good government to Latuna without discharging capable men. My policy is to ignore dead scandals. I refuse to start a new one about those men at the Phoenix Hotel. They may look like crooks; yet they have not branded themselves as such. Men must be regarded as innocent until proven guilty."

THE SHADOW shifted backward as Rush opened the door. This house was Malden's. Its blackened foreground offered opportunity to The Shadow. He edged into darkness and reached the house while Rush and Grewling were ascending steps between two stone griffons.

The Shadow saw lighted windows at the side of the house; they indicated a conservatory. He glided in that direction.

At the front door, Mayor Rush banged pompously upon a brass knocker. The large door opened; a Japanese servant bowed the visitors into a lavishly furnished hallway.

"Mr. Malden is in the conservatory," announced the Jap. "He awaits you, Honorable Mayor."

Toya led the way to the conservatory. Entering, the visitors found Strafford Malden rising to greet them. The donor of the Blue Sphinx was attired in a dark dressing gown that accentuated the gray streaks in his hair.

"You are late, Quirby," he told the mayor, with a smile. "I thought that perhaps you did not have your official car tonight. I was ready to send my limousine to your house."

"The car is down there," replied Rush. "Waiting for Joseph Rubal."

"He is coming to see you?"

"Yes. I told the police chauffeur to bring him up here."

"I have Singler waiting here," remarked Malden, indicating a uniformed chauffeur who was seated in the corner. "If you wish to send your man off duty, Singler can take the limousine—"

"Not necessary, Mr. Malden."

"Very well. You may go, Singler." Malden

smiled. "You may resume your narrative at some later date."

"All right, Mr. Malden," laughed the chauffeur.

"Interesting chap," observed Malden, after Singler had departed. "He served for seven years in the French Foreign Legion. I started him talking after I had finished dinner and he held me spellbound until your arrival. One adventure after another. Interesting to have a chauffeur who is also a *raconteur.*

"Well, gentlemen"—Malden waved his guests to chairs—"I am pleased that you are here. I have been rather anxious to learn why you wanted me to see Rubal, Quirby."

"It's on account of his resignation, Malden."

"Has Rubal resigned as curator? This is unbelievable!"

"He intends to resign tonight. That is why he is coming to see me. I mentioned the matter to you after we left the museum today."

"You stated that Rubal had said that he did not intend to go on. I thought that you meant in regard to the plans for the museum extension."

Quirby Rush shook his head.

"Rubal is through," he declared. "Completely prepared to quit. I am bringing him here in hope that he will reconsider his decision."

"He must do so," agreed Malden. "He is the proper man for the post of curator."

"I'm thinking of myself as much as Rubal," admitted the mayor. "Harrison Knode has been after Rubal's scalp. If Rubal quits, it will appear that Knode has accomplished something in spite of me."

"I see," nodded Malden. "I can appreciate your concern, Quirby. However, I can register no sentiment politically. My interest lies in the welfare of art. So far as Latuna is concerned, Joseph Rubal is the proper man as curator of the museum. Perhaps his resignation is on account of trouble with the plans. We aided him previously. Perhaps—"

Toya interrupted by appearing.

"Honorable Police Chief," declared the Jap. "He is wanted to speak on the telephone."

Grewling arose and followed Toya. Malden and Rush gazed after the police chief. Their eyes, however, were not the only ones that observed Grewling's temporary departure. From outside an opened window, keen orbs were staring in from darkness.

THE conservatory was built on a slope that descended from this side of the house. Hence its windows were high above the ground. The Shadow, however, had scaled the masonry. From the outer darkness, he had listened in on every word of the passing conversation.

And with Toya's interruption, The Shadow had peered above the sill. He watched Rush and Malden as they began to resume their conversation. Then he saw Grewling returning; the police chief's face was purple with excitement.

"A call from headquarters!" exclaimed Grewling. "Report on a murder! Discovered shortly after nine o'clock."

"Murder?" queried Quirby Rush. "Where?"

"At the museum!"

"Not—not Rubal—"

"Yes. And Hollis, the chief attendant!"

The Shadow saw Mayor Rush and Strafford Malden exchange horrified stares. The police chief waved them to their feet.

"Call your chauffeur, Mr. Malden," he urged. "We're going to the museum."

Malden nodded. He called Toya, telling the Japanese to get clothes ready so that he could dress hurriedly. He also ordered Toya to call Singler and have him bring the limousine.

Ten minutes later, the big car rolled from Malden's front drive on its way to the Latuna Museum. From the heavy darkness at the front of the mansion, the eyes of The Shadow watched the departure of Grewling, Rush and Malden.

A grim laugh whispered from the gloom. The Shadow, though he had come to Latuna, had arrived too late to prevent the stroke of crime. He had planned a later visit to the museum. Such a trip would be useless tonight.

Death had already occurred. Two men were murdered; the law was investigating. The Shadow's only course would be to wait for better opportunity to view the scene of crime.

CHAPTER XIII
WORD TO THE SHADOW

WHEN Malden's limousine pulled up in front of the Latuna Museum, the building showed light from its open front doorway. Two policemen arrived with flashlights; they recognized their chief as soon as Grewling stepped from Malden's car.

"We've got the watchmen inside, Chief," informed one of the cops. "They're the fellows who found the bodies."

"Was the place lighted up like this?" inquired Grewling.

"It was when we got here," said another policeman. "But one of the watchmen said he switched on the lights."

"Let's go inside," suggested Grewling, turning abruptly to Rush and Malden.

The trio entered the museum. They followed the corridor on the right and came to the office. There they found a policeman outside the door, while, at the end of the corridor, stood two solemn-looking men. They were the watchmen.

The police chief stepped into the office. He saw the bodies lying on the floor. Joseph Rubal's upturned face was distorted from the dying agony that the curator had suffered. Hollis looked grim in death.

Strafford Malden and Quirby Rush viewed the bodies from the doorway. They stepped back as Grewling came from the room. They waited while the police chief quizzed the watchmen. The story that the two men told was simple and straightforward.

They had arrived at the accustomed hour of nine. When Hollis did not answer their prolonged ring, one of them had the inspiration of trying the door. It was found to be unlocked. The watchmen had naturally gone to the curator's office.

They had turned on lights all along the line. After discovering the dead bodies of the curator and the chief attendant, they had called police headquarters from the curator's telephone.

"There's not much mystery about the killing," announced Grewling, turning to Rush and Malden. "The museum closes up at eight. Somebody must have rung the bell; after that, Hollis let him in and he killed Rubal."

"What about the other attendants?" inquired Rush.

"They go out at eight o'clock, don't they?" retorted Grewling.

"I know that," replied Rush. "But it is possible that one of them could have been responsible for this crime."

"That's possible!" exclaimed Grewling. "Here, Toxter"—he turned to a policeman—"dig down to town and look up those other attendants. Bring them out here."

THE order given, Grewling paused to eye a stout man with a bag who was coming down the corridor. He recognized a local physician, who had arrived in response to a call from headquarters. He told the doctor to examine the bodies. While the physician was busy, the police chief resorted to his first theory.

"Somebody could have come in here," he declared. "Some special visitor, between eight o'clock and nine."

"Just whom would Hollis have admitted?" questioned Malden.

"Anyone who might know the curator," replied the police chief. "That's a good lead, Mr. Malden. If some ordinary thug had showed up here, Hollis wouldn't have let him in."

"He might have forced his way in," observed Rush.

"He'd have had Hollis to deal with first," returned Grewling. "No, the thing's plain, Mayor. Somebody got by the door and came in here. Hollis must have heard the shot and come in—to get his dose of lead."

"Odd that he walked into the trap so easily," said Malden.

"Not if he knew the man who was calling," declared Grewling. "He might have thought the shot was accidental."

New footsteps in the corridor. It was Singler, Malden's chauffeur. The man had come in to inquire if he might be needed. Malden told him to remain.

"Well, Doc?" questioned Grewling, as the physician finished his examination. "Anything unusual?"

"I'm not exactly sure," declared the physician, in a doubtful tone. "Death may not have been instantaneous in the case of Rubal; but it was with Hollis. In both cases, however, the wounds show tendency to enlargement. I am not an expert on bullet wounds; but I would say—"

"May I take a look at them?" inquired Singler, the chauffeur.

"What for?" snapped the police chief.

"I've seen some pretty mean wounds," replied Singler. "Seven years with the Foreign Legion. I've seen what ricochet shots can do. As for dumdums— well, the Arabs never minded using them. As for the Tuaregs—"

"Let him take a look, Doc," broke in Grewling.

Singler joined the physician and noted the doctor's comments. When he arose from beside the body, the chauffeur was nodding. He had apparently made a discovery.

"I'll bet ten to one on it," declared Singler.

"On what?" inquired Mayor Rush.

"That there was a silencer on the gun that got those fellows," said the chauffeur.

"Did they use silencers in the Foreign Legion?" quizzed Police Chief Grewling, in a scoffing tone.

"No," replied Singler, soberly, "but there were plenty of lowlifes—Apaches and what not—who had used them in the past. I've seen and heard about plenty of guns; and a silencer—particularly a poor one—will put a quiver to a bullet. Like this."

Singler paused to make a wiggling motion with his right hand, as an exaggerated idea of the course that a bullet might have followed.

"Turn it over to a bullet expert," suggested the chauffeur. "Get those slugs, Chief, and they'll tell their own story."

"This coincides with your theory, Grewling," observed Mayor Rush. "Hollis might have come back in here not knowing that anything had happened to the curator."

"We'll have the bullets extracted," declared the police chief, grimly. "You seem to know what you're talking about, Singler. Thanks for the information."

The chauffeur nodded, and Strafford Malden gave him an approving smile.

AT that moment, there was a stir from the front end of the corridor. Voices carried down the passageway as a group of men put in their appearance. Two policemen were arguing with the newcomers.

"Harrison Knode!" exclaimed the mayor. "With a couple of his reporters. They must have heard the news."

"Keep them out!" bellowed the police chief, to the cops.

"No, no," rebuked the mayor. "Let them come here. Don't be annoyed, Grewling. Remember what I told you tonight."

"All right, men," called the chief. "Let them by."

Knode arrived with Burke and Drury. While his reporters stood in the background, the long-faced editor nodded to mayor and police chief. He smiled sourly as they failed to return his greeting. Knode turned and shook hands with Strafford Malden.

Two policemen appeared with the museum attendants. They had found the men in town. There were two; and Grewling quizzed them briefly. Both stated that they had left as usual, at eight o'clock. Hollis had bolted the door behind them.

The frankness of the attendants was convincing. The police chief, already moving along a solid theory, accepted what they said. But he quizzed the two men definitely on one point: the possibility of some one having remained in the museum after closing time.

Both men stated that they had inspected with Hollis, after the museum was closed, and that Rubal could have had no lurker in his office.

Another newcomer arrived at the finish of the quiz. This was Howard Dunham, tall, cadaverous-looking editor of the Latuna *Gazette*. Dunham covered big stories in person; and his arrival pleased the police chief, for it gave Grewling a chance to bait Knode.

Stepping into the curator's office, Grewling invited Dunham to accompany him. While the editor stood by the desk, the police chief made a careful inspection. The room had been lighted by one of the watchmen; the same man who had peered into the little filing room. Grewling inspected both portions of the suite.

"Sit down," he said to Dunham, motioning the *Gazette* man to the chair behind the curator's desk. "I'm going to give you my theory, Mr. Dunham. That will give you a chance to run a story before the coroner holds his inquest."

Grewling shot a glance at the doorway where Knode was looking on with Rush and Malden. He was willing that Knode should listen in. The *Gazette* being a morning paper, it would beat the *Enterprise* with the news.

"JOSEPH RUBAL was murdered," declared the police chief, "by some visitor who came here after eight o'clock. That unknown party had a firearm that was equipped with a silencer. He shot and killed Joseph Rubal.

"The same murderer was forced to slay Hollis in order that the chief attendant would not reveal his identity. We shall have an examination made of the bullets. Through them we may be able to trace the gun and the killer himself."

Grewling paused and began to pace the room.

Dunham, pausing in his notetaking, chanced to notice the calendar on the desk. Idly, the editor of the *Gazette* lifted the pages until he came to the current date.

"Look at this!" he exclaimed. "Two notations! The first says: 'Eight p.m., appointment, office.' The second says 'Nine p.m., appointment. Mayor.' These refer to tonight!"

The police chief came to take a look at the date pad. Mayor Rush crowded through the doorway and also examined it. Grewling spoke to the mayor.

"You see?" said the chief. "Someone was due here at eight o'clock. Unless Rubal intended to go to your office."

"It says nine o'clock for me," objected Rush. "That was the time he expected to come to my home."

"He couldn't have been going to see *you,* Mr. Malden," said Grewling, turning toward the door. "You have no office. *I* was not expecting Rubal— so office means here. The question is who was due here at eight o'clock?"

"I suppose you'll be suggesting that I had an appointment here with Rubal," jeered Harrison Knode, thrusting his head through the doorway. "There's a theory for you, Grewling. Fancy that— my calling to see Rubal."

"Is that notation in Rubal's handwriting?" demanded Grewling, suddenly turning to the mayor.

Rush nodded.

"That's a break for you, Knode," stormed Grewling, turning to the door. "You and Rubal were anything but friends. It's lucky that Rubal marked this appointment himself. It shows you weren't the person he expected. It leaves you out."

"Very good," chuckled Knode. "That suits me. Good-bye, chief. I'll read the details in the *Gazette* tomorrow morning."

ACCOMPANIED by Burke and Drury, Knode left the museum. The trio rode to the editor's home. There they entered and Knode spoke privately with Drury for a few minutes. Then the editor shook hands with both men. They left together.

Drury took Clyde to a lunch wagon. He picked a spot at the far end of the counter.

"The old man asked me to speak to you," confided Drury, in a low tone. "You heard him fox Grewling. Pulled it clever on the chief, didn't he?"

Clyde nodded, as he lowered a cup of coffee.

"He wants us to keep mum about that appointment he had with Rubal," added Drury. "After all, Knode *didn't* keep it. So it means nothing. But if anybody knew about it, Grewling would be on Knode's neck. The old man wouldn't be able to cut loose in the sheet. Get the idea?"

Again Clyde nodded.

"So we're saying nothing," decided Drury. "Shake on it."

Clyde shook hands. Then he made a suggestion.

"I'd like to shoot this story to the *Classic*," he said. "They don't belong to the Interstate Press. If they could beat the other New York sheets, it would put me in right back there."

"Go ahead," agreed Drury. "You can beat the wired service by a couple of hours anyway. Dunham will be slow sending it over the Interstate Press. He'll stay late at the museum, getting his story."

"Where's the telegraph office?"

"I'll show you."

At the telegraph office, Clyde prepared a press-rate telegram. He let Drury read it.

"It says here," commented Drury, "that they're to use 'Jory byline.' What's the gag, Burke?"

"I used to write stuff under the name of 'Kirt Jory'," explained Clyde. "It will do instead of my own. They wouldn't use my own name, since they've fired me. The police commissioner would be sore."

"I get it," laughed Drury. "A good stunt, Burke!"

Clyde smiled. The ruse had passed. For that byline, "Kirt Jory," to indicate the author of the wired story, would do more than establish the story as Clyde Burke's.

The Shadow had provided for just such an emergency as this; the possibility that Clyde could best report to him through a story in the New York *Classic*. The Shadow, alone, would recognize the message in the words "By Kirt Jory."

That, to The Shadow, would mean more than the simple fact that murder had occurred in Latuna. It would signify that cross-purposes were at work; that the deaths of Joseph Rubal and Hollis might be but the beginning of other strange events.

To The Shadow, Clyde Burke's chosen byline would carry the single message: "Come!"

Clyde Burke smiled to himself as he walked from the telegraph office with Bart Drury. Outside, they passed a strolling stranger. Clyde did not even notice the hawklike visage and the keen eyes that stared in his direction.

Once more in the guise of Henry Arnaud, The Shadow was abroad in Latuna. He knew that his agent had dispatched a prearranged signal that was intended to bring him here. He had allowed Clyde to do so, unknowing that his chief was already in town.

For The Shadow's plans would begin tomorrow, after nightfall. Then would he survey the spot that Clyde had already seen. With reports received, The Shadow would fare forth to visit the Latuna Museum.

CHAPTER XIV
WITHIN CLOSED WALLS

TWENTY-FOUR hours had elapsed since the murders in the Latuna Museum. The Shadow, guised as Henry Arnaud, was seated at a writing desk in his room in the Wilkin Hotel. Across the street, he could see two khaki-clad policemen on duty near the Hotel Phoenix.

The Shadow extinguished the main light. His hands appeared long-fingered and white, beneath the glow of the desk lamp as they opened two sealed envelopes. The Shadow read reports from Clyde Burke and Cliff Marsland. The agents had left them in Henry Arnaud's box.

That had been in accord with an outlined plan. The two aides, however, did not know that their chief had checked in before tonight.

Meanwhile, another agent had arrived. Harry Vincent, a most competent worker, had seen Clyde's story in New York and had come to Latuna. He, too, had acted on instructions previously given by The Shadow.

Clyde's report laid emphasis upon his visit to Harrison Knode's. It described his trip to the museum and stressed Bart Drury's private interview with Knode, particularly Bart's warning that Knode's appointment with Rubal was not to be made public.

Cliff's report emphasized that all of Konk Zitz's pals had been at the Phoenix Hotel. None of them could have possibly visited the isolated Latuna Museum.

Finished with this report, The Shadow moved from the writing desk. He clicked on the main light; again he appeared as Arnaud.

Seating himself in an easy chair, The Shadow picked up the Latuna newspapers. The *Gazette* carried the big story. Dunham had printed Grewling's statement; also the testimony of attendants and watchmen. Theories showed that the law had struck close to the possible details of the crime.

The stumbling block was the clue that Dunham had himself uncovered. Someone had had an appointment with Joseph Rubal at eight o'clock the night before. Speculation was rife as to the identity of that person.

The *Enterprise* carried a resume of the story in the *Gazette*. A few added details of the coroner's inquest failed to add spice.

Harrison Knode had been forced to leave out an announcement that would have staggered Howard

Dunham. He could have made a scoop by printing the name of the man who had the eight o'clock appointment with Rubal. He had omitted that name because it was his own.

A SOFT laugh came from the lips of Henry Arnaud. The Shadow was considering the oddity of the case. Then he noted an item stating that the museum had been closed to the public, pending solution of the murders. Instead of ordinary watchmen, nine picked policemen were on duty, working in three shifts, each of three men.

Reverting to the morning newspaper, The Shadow picked out a statement by the police chief. It stood apart from the murder story. It referred to the lack of criminal activity in Latuna; and stated that the police had been watching all suspected crooks who happened to be in town. This statement, The Shadow knew, was for the benefit of Harrison Knode.

Police Chief Grewling had spiked the crusading editor's verbal cannon. Grewling's action of putting watchers at the Phoenix Hotel, stood as proof that the police were vigilant. Neither Knode—nor anyone else—could say that the murders in the museum were caused by the police ignoring the criminal element in Latuna.

Some lone wolf had performed the murders. Timing his deed to the hour when the museum offered the best chance for entry, this crafty killer had played a one-man game. His motive had been to rifle Rubal's files. He had succeeded in his game, at a time when the curator was on the verge of resigning his post.

Harrison Knode had made no editorial comment. But The Shadow could foresee the editor's future action. Once the excitement of the murder had died down, Knode would have his opportunity to link up the past with the present. Now was no time to drag the dead curator's name through the mire. That would come later.

A laugh was The Shadow's soft recognition of the policy that he could foresee. Rising, he extinguished the light.

He donned his black garb and descended to the parking space; there he entered a black coupé. The car was one that Harry Vincent had hired and left there after arriving in Latuna. Harry had later registered at the Wilkin Hotel.

THE coupé rolled from the parking space. It came to a highway that curved out of town and kept along until it neared the hill where the museum stood. The Shadow parked his car in a field and alighted.

The *boom* of a quarry blast came through the night air as The Shadow glided close to the museum. Barred doors and windows at the front; brick walls at sides and rear. These did not deter The Shadow.

From his cloak he drew forth suction cups of rubber, which he attached to hands and feet. He began a precipitous ascent up the side wall of the museum, accompanied by the soft, squidgy noise that he had never been able to eliminate from these concave disks without impairing their necessary efficiency.

Moonlight, trickling through rifted clouds, showed the spectral shape as it reached the roof. The Shadow had arrived at a flat ledge that led to the low, rounded dome above the Sphinx Room. Heavy frames containing frosted glass, formed the sections of the broad dome.

Scraping sounds came from the spot where The Shadow rested as a shapeless blotch. Then a soft laugh as the slight noise ceased. A glass section moved free in the fashion of a skylight.

The Shadow had found the weak spot of this building which others regarded as impregnable. To him, the dome had offered a mode of access. Sheer walls had been regarded as an insurmountable hazard. Conquering those walls, The Shadow had found access easy.

The Shadow's task, however, was not ended. As he lowered himself into the museum, The Shadow hung above a forty-foot space. He was poised above the floor of the central room that housed the Blue Sphinx.

Lowering his body in precarious fashion, The Shadow tilted his head and spied the wall close by. Coming in at the edge of the dome, he was close to an ornamental ledge that lined the Sphinx Room.

Clinging by one hand, The Shadow swayed his body like a pendulum. His free hand caught the ledge. He released his upper hand and swung against the wall. Both hands then gripped the ledge. The Shadow began a swinging, sidewise course along the wall.

He reached a space between two half pillars that came up from the floor. Smooth surfaced, these afforded no grip. But they served The Shadow as a mode of descent. Swinging his body between the block-shaped pillars, The Shadow wedged himself in place as he released his hold upon the ledge.

Braking his descent, he slid straight downward to the floor. Doubling himself for the final jar, he broke the force of the arrival as skillfully as a parachute jumper ending a long drop.

Rising, The Shadow found himself beside the massive shape of the Blue Sphinx.

WITH a soft laugh, the weird intruder turned and went to the doors that led into the anteroom. He found them locked. With tiny flashlight glimmering, he used a blackened pick and gained results. Opening the doors, The Shadow stepped into the anteroom.

More formidable doors lay ahead. The Shadow worked on them with greater care. He knew that patrolling watchers were beyond. He muffled the sounds of his probing pick, until the *clicks* were almost inaudible.

When the doors opened, The Shadow peered carefully into the front hallway of the museum. The place was dimly lighted. No watcher was in sight. Softly, The Shadow emerged from the anteroom and closed the doors behind him.

Footsteps were clicking from a far corridor. They were coming from the turn beyond the Antiquity Room. The Shadow moved swiftly in the opposite direction. As he neared the Medieval Room, he heard new footsteps coming along the corridor from the curator's office.

The Shadow swung swiftly into the Medieval Room, which offered a darkened, ghostly harbor. Stealthily, he moved among the huge oddities that furnished this chamber. A bulky object loomed beside him. It was the Iron Maiden.

A flashlight at the door. One policeman was coming in to make a routine inspection. The Shadow swung swiftly behind the opened door of the Maiden and stood between its hiding surface and the wall. The officer made his round and went to the door. The Shadow heard him pause to speak to a second patroller.

"What took you so long, Steve?" came a question. "I finished my side of this morgue five minutes ago."

"Yeah?" questioned the cop who had just inspected the Medieval Room. "Well, you've got a cinch compared to me. I've got to look careful through all this junk collection."

"I've got the room with all the statues. I had to look through there."

"Yeah? Well, who's going to be hiding in that joint? Nobody could duck out of sight in that gymnasium. This place is different. Say—a guy could even hide in that iron coffin over there, if he wanted to pull the door shut after him."

"Fat chance anybody would," scoffed the first cop, turning a flashlight toward the opened interior of the Iron Maiden. "How'd a guy close the door on himself, with all those spikes ready to run him through. Say, Steve—where's Jerry?"

"In the office, Bill. He'll join us in the front hall. We can chew the fat for half an hour, then make another round."

The policemen left. The Shadow emerged and glided toward the door of the room. He waited there until he heard new footsteps coming along the corridor from the curator's office. Bill passed and went along to join his companions inside the entrance of the museum.

With the way clear, The Shadow strode noiselessly along the deserted corridor and reached the curator's office. Entering, The Shadow closed the door behind him and turned on the light. He was here to study the scene of crime.

OFTEN, The Shadow, on excursions of this sort, could uncover clues that upset the finest police theories. Tonight, he observed nothing that conflicted with existing conjectures. The Shadow, between the accounts that he had read and the reports that he had received from his agents, was in conformity with the existing opinions.

As he spied the inner filing room, however, The Shadow gained a mental picture that others had failed to view. He turned on the light in that little room. He went to the curator's desk; arose and strode to the filing room; then across to the outer door. He looked at the spot where the bodies had been found.

A soft laugh. The Shadow was visualizing exactly what had occurred. The murderer had found the curator in the filing room and had shot him down from the outer door. From the filing room, the same killer had clipped Hollis.

There was no day calendar on the desk. It had been removed as evidence. Yet The Shadow knew the details of that memo; how Howard Dunham had chanced to notice it. He also knew that certain papers had been taken from this office.

Obviously, the murderer had overlooked the desk calendar. Its pages closed—as Dunham had first seen them—the killer had not noticed the memo made by the curator. But The Shadow saw a link between that calendar and the murderer's purpose here.

Joseph Rubal had been going over past dates. He had been looking up documents in the filing room. These papers must certainly have concerned the museum itself. Rubal, long silent and long stalling, had been gathering data that might have caused someone trouble.

Searching the files, The Shadow came upon various papers that referred to the museum. Studying them swiftly in the light of the filing room, he noticed certain gaps. One notation referred to a temporary delay during a period of inspection. There was no paper, however, that told of the inspection itself.

This date was prior to the completion of the museum as it now stood; before the final day when the lower vault was bricked and the museum completed in its temporary form, for visits by the public.

The Shadow also found reference to three sets of plans. Referring to another folder, he discovered only two sets that showed the details of the museum. Where was the third? Had it been taken at the time of the murder? If so, why?

The Shadow studied the list of collections that

out on top. Then he can report that he was watching us. I told the gang to mention it to Konk."

"He'll take care of it, Tinker."

"Yeah. Mushmug's just a dumb dick."

ACROSS the street, a young man had watched Cliff and Tinker come from the Phoenix Hotel. It was Harry Vincent; and this agent of The Shadow had noted Cliff's difficulties with the match.

Crossing the street, Harry strolled into the Phoenix lobby. He bought three picture postcards and went to the table where Cliff had been figuring his roulette system.

Harry wrote messages and addressed the postcards. He picked up the blotter that Cliff had used. On its surface, Harry noted the imprint of the blotted figures. They formed a coded message.

The numerical code was one that The Shadow's agents used frequently. They were trained in reading it in looking-glass fashion. Briefly, the marks on the blotter told Harry Vincent the all-important news: Konk Zitz had set tomorrow night.

Harry blotted his postcards, thus obliterating traces of Cliff's penmanship. He walked across the lobby, posted the cards and strolled from the Phoenix Hotel.

A few minutes later, he entered his own hotel and rode up to the sixth floor. In his room he inscribed a brief message to The Shadow, thrust it under the door of Room 640 and went out.

WITHIN that room, a quiet-looking personage noted the arrival of the note. As Henry Arnaud, The Shadow arose and extinguished the big light. By the writing table lamp, he opened and read the message. He laughed softly as he clicked off the lamp.

A short interval; then faint swishes announced his departure in the attire of The Shadow.

Half an hour later, a beetlelike form scaled the side wall of the Latuna Museum. The Shadow entered the dome and swung to the ledge. Here, he performed an action which proved that he had made more than one previous visit to the museum. Clinging to the ledge, he found a wire and carried it down with him during his descent.

On the moonlit floor beside the Blue Sphinx, The Shadow drew upon this wire. It was affixed to a bar in the dome; as The Shadow pulled carefully, the stout strand tightened. A box swung from the ledge, up toward the dome. It descended as The Shadow carefully paid out the wire. The box settled to the floor.

The Shadow had brought this to the museum on some previous visit. He had planted it upon the ledge. It was to serve him in some fashion tonight. This was the time for which The Shadow had been waiting. He had needed surety that crooks were ready to move.

The box was a foot square. From its interior, The Shadow removed an object that looked like a drill. He paused suddenly as the museum trembled slightly in response to a muffled blast from the neighboring quarry. Then he closed the box and set it between the huge front paws of the stone sphinx.

The pedestal on which the statue rested was made in sections, which were mortared together. Picking one of these vulnerable spots, The Shadow set to work with the drill. The strength with which he handled the implement brought immediate results. Mortar crackled and fell with slight *clicks*.

The noise was not great enough to be heard outside the Sphinx Room. The Shadow never desisted from his work. The drill penetrated further.

Ending his work, The Shadow moved along the pedestal and attacked another mortared crevice.

Gauged by the time that he had taken with the first drilling, this hidden worker would have a few hours of work ahead, if he intended to drill holes all along the pedestal. Whatever his purpose, The Shadow showed no great haste.

tonight, he had gained Cliff's definite report that crime was not slated until the morrow. Tonight belonged to The Shadow. He was using these hours to anticipate some scheme which he knew was in the making.

Time moved slowly by while The Shadow continued his steady, methodical drilling. Moonlight, filtering through the glass dome, showed that untiring figure as a blotch of swaying blackness, close beside the time-scarred surface of the great Blue Sphinx.

CHAPTER XVII
THE BAD BREAK

"SO you were talking to Mushmug, eh?"

Cliff Marsland heard Konk Zitz put the question to the gorilla called "Dopey." Cliff and Tinker had just returned from dinner, to find Konk holding court with a couple of his thugs.

"Sure, Konk," said Dopey, taking a cigarette from his pasty lips. "He started to talk to me; so I talked to him."

"What did he have to say?"

"Nothin' much. Kinda soundin' me out about the crew. I told him we was just vacationin' here. Liked the climate—that's what I said."

"What else?"

"Nothin' else. I dodged one question that he handed me."

"What was that?"

"About this guy Drury."

Konk became interested. Cliff saw a gleam in the big shot's ratlike eyes, as Konk rasped the question:

"What did he ask about Drury?"

"Wanted to know why the guy was gettin' so chummy with birds like you an' me," returned Dopey, promptly. "I told him I didn't know nothin' about Drury. Said I hadn't noticed him much aroun' here."

"What did Mushmug say to that?"

"Nothin', because I didn't give him no chanct. I walked out on him. Told him I'd be back later."

Konk arose from his chair. He turned to Tinker Furris and put a question.

"Is Mushmug the only gumshoe hanging around here?" asked the crook leader.

"All I've seen," returned Tinker.

"Same here," affirmed Cliff.

"All right," decided Konk. "I've got an idea—just to figure if the guy's a plant. We're going out tonight. You two"—he pointed to Tinker and Cliff—"and myself. We'll use the back route, by the freight elevator. I've got it fixed.

"The rest of you stick here, all except Dopey. I'll let him go down and stall Mushmug. Some phony talk about Drury. Tinker, you and Marsland go out by the back and make sure it's clear. You other fellows go downstairs a while, until I've finished talking with Dopey. When he shows up, it means I'm out and you're to come back here. Start your poker game. I won't be gone long."

The men nodded and strolled from the room. Cliff and Tinker followed, leaving Dopey alone with Konk Zitz. Tinker led the way to the freight elevator. A wise-looking operator took them aboard. Konk had fixed this hotel employee.

OUT in the darkness of an alleyway behind the Phoenix Hotel, Cliff and Tinker waited for a full fifteen minutes before Konk Zitz joined them. He beckoned them off to a parking lot. They entered a sedan. Konk took the wheel and drove without comment.

Reaching an isolated part of town, Konk told the pair to wait. They saw him stroll down a side street and stop by a coupé that was obscured beyond a hedge. When Konk returned, he was carrying a suitcase. Cliff and Tinker were in the back seat of the sedan, so Konk dropped the bag beside him in the front.

He drove a few blocks and pulled up by a deserted house. Alighting with the suitcase, he whispered to the others to follow him. They went past the empty house and came to the back door of another home where a dim light showed from an upstairs window. Konk tried a key in the back door. He found no difficulty in entering.

Using a flashlight, Konk found a room near the center of the ground floor. He brought the others in with him and ordered them to lower the blinds. This done, Konk flashed his light upon a safe in the corner.

With a chuckle, he ordered Tinker to close the door.

Konk turned on a light and revealed a desk close by the safe. He placed the suitcase there.

"Do you know whose house this is?" he questioned, in a low tone.

Headshakes from Cliff and Tinker. They had stayed close to the Phoenix Hotel since their arrival in Latuna.

"This," chuckled Konk, "is where the smart aleck editor lives. You know the mug I mean. Harrison Knode."

Cliff and Tinker were genuinely surprised.

"Knode is up at that hearing," resumed Konk. "There's a housekeeper here; but she's upstairs and won't hear us—if we're quiet. Listen, now, while I tell you the lay.

"Maybe Knode's got something on us." Cliff detected a peculiar wariness in Konk's tone. "Maybe that's why he's had Drury hanging around the Phoenix. Whatever Knode's got, will be in this safe. So I'm going to take a look in it."

"Why the suitcase, Konk?" questioned Tinker.

"Well," replied the leader. "I wanted to make sure, that's all. Maybe I won't be able to tap this box. If I fail, I'll use drills. They're in that bag. I didn't want to have them around the hotel. I had a guy plant them in a car near here."

As Konk paused, Cliff felt positive that he was holding back something. That, however, was a habit of Konk's. Of one thing, Cliff was sure. This visit to Knode's was not the blow-off. That was still set for tomorrow night.

"I brought you fellows," stated Konk, "so you could keep an eye on the doors. It may take me some time, to do this job. I don't want to use the drills if I can help it. Say, Tinker, it's too bad you didn't bring that bird Tapper along to Latuna."

"To open that box for you, Konk?"

"Sure. I could have used a guy like him."

"What about Cliff here?"

"Can he crack a safe?"

"Better than Tapper."

"Say—what've you been holding back?"

Tinker shifted uneasily as he caught Konk's beady glare. Then the pock-faced fellow gave a weak grin.

"IT was this way, Konk," he explained. "When I couldn't get Tapper, I heard about Cliff. I wanted to see if he had the goods. So he and I slid into an old hockshop I knew about and he took a hand at the box. That's right, ain't it, Cliff?"

Cliff nodded. He knew that Tinker did not want to admit planning a job of his own without Konk's knowledge. It was best to stick with Tinker, Cliff decided.

"Yeah?" quizzed Konk. "Well—how'd you make out?"

… The Shadow set to work with the drill.… Mortar crackled and fell with slight clicks.

"Cliff opened the box," explained Tinker, slowly. "But then The Shadow showed up."

"The Shadow?"

"Yeah. Nearly rubbed me out, too! Only Cliff plugged him and we made a getaway."

"Wait a minute. Marsland here plugged The Shadow?"

"I just clipped him," put in Cliff. "We had to scram without the swag."

"It wasn't worth much," added Tinker. "We was just practicing on that box."

"So you came to Latuna," growled Konk, "when you had The Shadow on your trail!"

"He wasn't on our trail," said Tinker, quickly. "Honest, Konk. He had to duck the bulls himself. He ain't been around here, The Shadow hasn't."

"No telling where that guy may be."

"Well, anyway"—Tinker sought to change the subject—"Cliff here can tap that box in no time. If you let him crack it, Konk, you'll have more time to go through the safe while Cliff and I are watching the doors."

Konk Zitz nodded. He eyed Cliff carefully, then pointed to the safe.

"Go to it, Marsland," he ordered. "Let's see you work."

"Got the microscope, Cliff?" quizzed Tinker.

Cliff shook his head as he stepped toward the safe. He heard Zitz speak to Tinker.

"A microscope?" Konk was asking. "What for?"

"To look for fingerprints," replied Tinker. "If he finds them, he leaves them, instead of polishing the knob. Great gag, ain't it, Konk?"

"Get going, Marsland," said Konk, to Cliff.

COLD sweat crept to Cliff's forehead as The Shadow's agent crouched in front of the safe. Luck alone could save him now. Cliff had some knowledge of cracksmanship; if the safe proved easy, he would appear to be living up to Tinker's claims. If not—The thought of consequences was one that Cliff tried to forget.

Under other circumstances, Cliff could have taken sudden action. He could hear Tinker buzzing a whisper to Konk Zitz, adding new details of that episode in Cobleton's hockshop. It would be a cinch, Cliff knew, to pull his automatic and cover these two rogues.

That, however, would ruin The Shadow's plans. It would mean a fight, a breakup of Konk Zitz's crew. Behind this little crook was some supercrook whom The Shadow sought. That crime dealer could be trapped only if his plans were allowed to reach their climax. Cliff's only course was to bluff Konk Zitz.

Steadily, despite his tenseness, Cliff worked on the combination. He recognized that this safe was not a difficult one for a cracksman; but it was beyond his ability to open it. Cliff had no microscopic instructions awaiting him tonight.

Minutes passed; still Cliff toiled. He could hear Konk buzzing to Tinker. The tone was ominous. Cliff decided that the time had arrived for verbal bluff.

"It ought to be a cinch, Konk," he said, in a low, steady voice. "It isn't, though. One of these tricky boxes that looks easy but gets tougher the longer you work on it."

"I know," responded Konk, in an assuring tone. "Let me take a stab at it, Marsland."

Cliff arose and turned about. He thought that his bluff was working until he faced his companions. Then Cliff became rigid, his arms half extended, his hands and fingers motionless.

The Shadow's agent was staring into the muzzles of two revolvers.

Konk Zitz had drawn his .38. He had buzzed an order to Tinker to do the same. Konk's eyes were venomous as they stared through narrow slitted lids. Tinker's pockmarked face was ugly in its evil leer.

"A SAFECRACKER, eh?" snarled Konk. "Say— a punk could open that box! I've been listening to Tinker's spiel. You pulled a fast one on him, Marsland, but it don't get by with me!

"You clipped The Shadow, eh? Put him out of the fight; but didn't cripple him enough to keep him from making a getaway. That don't wash! Well, I'm wise to your game! That stunt of yours was framed.

"Plenty of guys know that The Shadow has mugs working for him. They never figured who his stoolies were. But we've spotted one of them. You're the bird! It don't take a mind reader to figure that. The way you flopped on this safe proves it.

"You were working with The Shadow in New York. He fixed that safe in the hockshop. Put the fritz on Tinker's game and let you look like a hot-shot so that Tinker would bring you down here to crimp me."

Cliff made no response. He met Konk's vicious stare. The crook snarled a low laugh.

"Maybe you tipped The Shadow already," suggested Zitz. "Maybe he's going to show up here to stop the blow-off tomorrow night. Well—we'll fox that bimbo. We'll pull the blow-off tonight!

"You'll go along with us, Marsland. And remember, it won't do you no good to try a break. I could blot you right here; or in the car; or anywhere along the line. I'm just going to keep you for a while because it'll work that way.

"If you get funny, it means a bump for you. And you won't gain nothing, because a few shots and your dead corpse aren't going to queer the blow-off. We can pull it anyhow, even if you do try to start trouble."

Turning to Tinker, Konk gave a nod. Tinker stepped past Cliff and shoved his revolver against the prisoner's ribs. With Konk close in back of him, Tinker marched Cliff out through the back door and past the empty house.

"Climb in," growled Konk, as they reached the sedan. As he spoke, the big shot found Cliff's automatic and yanked it from Cliff's pocket.

Cliff entered the sedan. Tinker jostled in beside him and kept his gat against Cliff's ribs. Konk whispered an order to his pock-faced henchman:

"Hold him here, Tinker," said the crook leader. "I'm going back and crack that box. If Marsland makes trouble, plug him and I'll join you in a hurry. We can scram and dump him somewhere."

Konk departed. Cliff sat tight, indifferent to Tinker's sullen glare. Cliff knew that this was no time for a break. Konk's threat had been no bluff.

Death loomed in the offing. Cliff's only bet was to prolong the interval. Konk would prefer to hold the matter of his execution until after the blow-off, whatever it might be. The leader would have to make new plans. By sitting tight, Cliff could learn them.

No chance to reach The Shadow. Cliff knew that he would have to make the break for himself. But he decided definitely to hold it until the final opportunity. Then, if luck enabled him to make an escape, he would know more about Konk Zitz's game.

Yet Cliff harbored little hope for safety. This situation was one that he had long anticipated. It was the worst jam that he had ever encountered in The Shadow's service. At the same time, Cliff could not forget the miraculous ability of The Shadow. Time and again, that master fighter had intervened to save his aids from the brink of doom.

FIFTEEN minutes passed. Then Konk appeared from the darkness, carrying the suitcase which he had left at Knode's. He laughed gruffly as he climbed behind the wheel and laid the bag beside him.

"Didn't have to use the drills," he informed Tinker. "That box wasn't tough. Knode's got nothing on us. Keep your gat steady, Tinker."

Konk drove the car by a circuitous course until he neared the Phoenix Hotel. He parked the car in a space between an empty garage and a dilapidated wooden building. He alighted, and growled another order for Tinker to watch Cliff.

Konk strolled away and headed for the hotel. He was snarling to himself as he walked along; and he acted in pleased fashion. He had left the car far enough from the hotel. If Cliff tried a break, Tinker could give him the works without bringing coppers to the scene.

The crook leader entered the Phoenix Hotel by the rear entrance. He strolled into the lobby, looked about and nodded as he spied Bart Drury. The reporter had arrived for his chat. Konk strolled up to Bart.

"Have a cigar, Drury," he offered. "Been waiting long?"

Drury shook his head.

"Slide up to the room," suggested Konk. "The boys are having a poker game. They know you're coming. I'll be up."

Drury arose and went to the elevator. Konk lighted a cigar of his own. As he did, he delivered a sidelong glance toward the taproom. He saw Dopey standing with the detective, "Mushmug." They had heard the words which Konk had spoken to Drury.

Konk strolled into the taproom. He stopped in feigned surprise, as he saw his henchman talking with the dick. A frown showed on Konk's face; then he grinned.

"Thought you were upstairs, Dopey," said Konk. "That's where I'm going. The poker game ought to be running high right now. How about you?"—this was to Mushmug—"Ever play any poker?"

The dick shook his head.

"Too bad," observed Konk. "I was going to invite you up. Well, I'll see you later. You'll be dropping up later, Dopey?"

"In about half an hour, Konk."

Konk turned and went back into the lobby. His lips formed a sour leer as he neared the elevator. He had talked with Dopey before. The underling knew what to do. He was to stall Mushmug while Konk and the crew departed by the rear exit of the hotel.

After that, Dopey would shake the detective and make his own departure to join one lone, waiting crook. Thus Konk Zitz's outfit would be complete, ready for the blow-off which Konk had set twenty-four hours ahead of schedule.

CHAPTER XVIII
THE NIGHT ATTACK

"SOMEBODY on the phone for you, Mr. Burke."

Clyde arose from his typewriter. He was in the local room of the *Enterprise,* rewriting stories for the morrow. The night copy boy had brought the message.

"Hello... Burke..." It was Drury's voice that Clyde heard over the wire. "Listen. I had somebody else ask for you. Don't let the copy boy know I was calling..."

"All right," agreed Clyde.

"Something hot..." Drury's tone was strangely interrupted as it continued. "Want you with me... Slide out quietly..."

"Where to?"

"Cooper's cigar store. Parking lot just the other side of it. Green sedan with a Maryland license..."

Clyde finished the call, went back to the typewriter and pulled his half-written page from the carriage. He told the copy boy he was going out for a cup of coffee. Strolling from the office, he headed toward the parking space that Drury had mentioned.

There, Clyde found the green sedan. It was empty and it stood in an obscure corner. No attendant was on duty, for the lot closed at eight o'clock and it was now half past nine. Clyde approached the car.

Two men arose suddenly from the darkness. Guns jabbed Clyde's ribs. A third man appeared; the first two shoved Clyde into the back seat of the sedan while the third man took the wheel.

Covered by the revolvers, Clyde kept grimly silent.

He knew these captors to be pals of Konk Zitz's. Though Clyde had wondered at Drury's peculiar speech across the wire, he had never believed that a trap was awaiting him. Drury was not with this trio. Clyde wondered what had happened to the star reporter of the *Enterprise*.

The thugs offered no explanations. They kept sullen silence while the driver piloted the machine through secluded streets until he reached an open road. Then came a stretch of a broad highway. They turned into a dirt road.

A boom through the night. The muffled blast brought quivers to the air. Clyde knew that they were nearing the old quarry on the outskirts. Then, peering from the side of the car, he saw the outline of the Latuna Museum, off through some trees.

The sedan stopped.

"Come along, mug," growled a tough. "Keep your trap shut!"

Clyde noticed other cars parked among the trees. He heard growled whispers. He realized that Konk Zitz had assembled his entire bunch at this spot. At least a dozen—perhaps more.

Clyde, however, was concerned with one captor. This fellow was urging him from the car and up a slope toward the side elevation of the museum.

By the moonlight, Clyde made out stealthy figures moving toward the building. He saw four men reach the front of the museum and crouch there. Then one made a motion as if pushing the bell button.

Clyde recalled that the police shifts at the museum had been irregular. He realized that one of the officers would respond to this call, supposing it to be a relief. Remaining silent because of the gun against his ribs. Clyde saw the big door swing open.

Crouching figures arose. They made hurling motions as they sprang forward. Against the white front of the museum, Clyde saw a grotesque profile as one ruffian turned and waved his arms. The others were entering the door.

Tear gas! The fellow who had waved was wearing a gas mask. Gorillas had hurled bombs upon the unsuspecting police. By strategy, they had gained entrance to the museum without firing a single shot.

NEW figures were advancing. They paused on the threshold. Clyde's captor made a motion with the gun and ordered the reporter forward. When they neared the museum, unmasked men were entering while others stood by on guard. The tear gas had evidently spread. Masks were not necessary.

The front hallway of the museum was lighted. There, Clyde came face to face with Konk Zitz. Zitz was sending stealthy raiders into the end corridors. He laughed when he saw Clyde. His tone was ugly.

"Want to see something, Burke?" questioned the crook. "All right. Come along."

He took Clyde along the corridor toward the curator's office. All the while, the other crook followed with a gat poked in Clyde's back. They found a raider outside the door of the curator's office. At Konk's orders, the fellow nodded and opened the door, to deliver a snarl to persons within:

"Konk's here."

After a moment, the peering thug swung the door open. Konk motioned Clyde to the threshold. The reporter stared with amazement into the lighted room.

On the floor were the three policemen, bound and gagged. They were coughing in muffled fashion; their eyes were blinking with the light. Evidently they had received only a brief whiff of the gas. Enough to prevent their resistance; but not sufficient to stop quick recovery.

Two gorillas were standing by with guns in readiness. But the person who caught Clyde's amazed gaze was the one who occupied the center of the room. It was Bart Drury. Revolver in hand, the star reporter was glaring fiercely at the prone forms on the floor.

"All right, Bart," chuckled Konk. "Here's Burke. You wanted him."

Bart turned. A twisted smile showed on his usually loose lips. He eyed Clyde contemptuously; then spoke in a sarcastic tone.

"So you fell for it," sneered Drury. "I thought maybe you were going to be tough. A wise guy from New York. Never figured who was running this outfit, did you? Well, you know now. I am!"

CLYDE was too flabbergasted to offer a response.

"What'll I do with him, Bart?" questioned Konk. "Take him out by the front door and keep him there until you come?"

"Sure," responded Drury. "Remember how we arranged it, Konk? Hold him until we're ready to blow."

Drury turned to stare at the captured cops. Konk motioned Clyde back into the corridor. While the gorilla paced beside them, Konk growled in Clyde's ear.

"You've only seen part of it, Burke," he told Clyde. "I guess you know what we're after. That swag that's in the vault. Drury's going after it. He's got a truck out back.

"When he comes out of the office, he's going to take a couple of soup men and blow that brick wall for a loop! He and his crew will yank the swag and roll it away. You're coming with my part of the crew. Out by the front."

They reached the front hall. They stopped near the door of the Medieval Room, where Konk motioned Clyde against the wall. Clyde made no protest. He lounged at the spot designated while the gorilla kept him covered. Konk strolled back toward the corridor to the office.

Footsteps. Konk appeared in company with Bart Drury. They were holding a confab. Clyde saw Drury scowl. Then the reporter came in his direction.

"I'm leaving you with Konk," sneered Drury. "Maybe I'll give you a break, Burke. If you don't act smart, you'll be all right. But if you try anything, you'll know what's coming."

With that, Drury raised his revolver and leveled it squarely between Clyde's eyes. Unconsciously, Clyde flinched. Then, suddenly, as he stared into the leveled revolver, he began to blink. Drury chuckled contemptuously.

"Understand, Burke?" he snarled.

Clyde nodded, staring straight into Drury's eyes. The man lowered his gun and stepped away. Three gorillas—those from the office—were prompt to join him. They went out by the front door.

Konk Zitz watched them go. Then he spoke to the gorilla who was covering Clyde. The man nodded and went out. Konk alone remained. His ready gun was a sufficient threat to keep Clyde from making a move.

"Listen, Burke." Konk's voice was an odd whisper. "Drury's giving you no break. But I am. I'll tell you why. I don't put nobody but double-crossers on the spot. Here's the lay. Drury's pulled a boner; that's why I'm going to let you out.

"Drury don't want to bump the coppers. But like a sap, he let them get a look at him. They're going to squeal on him anyway. So it won't matter if you talk, too. That's simple enough, ain't it?"

Clyde nodded.

"But Drury's bullheaded," went on Konk. "Before the cops lamped him, he had his mind set on rubbing you out. Wants me to take you along for the ride, hand you the works and drop you somewhere. Figures that the police chief will think you were working with him. In on the game. See?"

Again, Clyde nodded.

"You and Drury were pals," added Konk. "You

didn't pull nothing phony. You can't spill anymore than the cops can. So here's the gag. I'll turn you over to a couple of gorillas. They'll ride you out in a coupé. When they give the word, you make a break. They won't stop you. I'll alibi it with Drury."

THE big shot's word had gained the ring of sincerity. Clyde knew that he intended to keep it. Neither Konk nor Drury could possibly suspect that Clyde was an agent of The Shadow.

"Thanks, Konk," said Clyde.

Two gorillas entered from the outside door. Konk spoke to them; Clyde could overhear his instructions. The gorillas nodded when they heard the orders that Konk had promised Clyde.

A muffled blast from the quarry on the hillside. While the dull reverberations were dying, two new gorillas entered, lugging a man who was bound hand and foot. Clyde Burke stared.

The prisoner was Cliff Marsland!

"A double-crosser," informed Konk, turning to Clyde. "You can remember that, Burke. Tell the bulls that this guy was one of the crew. After the bulls find him."

With that, Konk motioned Cliff's captors into the Medieval Room. Leaving Clyde with the first pair of gorillas, Konk followed those who had dragged Cliff from view. He returned two minutes later.

"Curtains for that mug," chuckled Konk. "He'll look pretty when they find him. I'm leaving—this to the gorillas who held Clyde—so it's time you bozos were heading for the coupé. Follow along. Don't worry about Dopey and Duke. They'll join me after they've finished Marsland."

Konk turned and strode toward the outer door. Clyde's captors nudged him with their gats as soon as Konk had gone. It was the signal for Clyde to march out to the coupé. Nodding, the reporter obeyed. But as he started along between the gorillas, Clyde clenched his fists in readiness for a sudden break.

Though it might mean death; despite the odds against him, Clyde Burke was preparing to put up a desperate fight in the hope of rescuing Cliff Marsland.

CHAPTER XIX
THE BREAK ARRIVES

MOONLIGHT had revealed the stealthy attack on the Latuna Museum. It had shown men of crime moving in and out. And all the while, that shimmering illumination had bathed the interior of the Sphinx Room, where a blackened form was still drilling at the base of the built-in pedestal.

Barred by two sets of doors, the Sphinx Room was totally detached from the rest of the museum. That was why The Shadow had no need to muffle the work that he was doing. It also explained why The Shadow had not heard the entrance of the invaders.

He had caught the faint sound of the bell that the crooks had rung. But The Shadow, like the watching policemen, had supposed that the tinkle indicated the arrival of another shift. Had a single shot been fired during the invasion, The Shadow might have had an inkling of trouble. But shots had proven unnecessary.

The distant blast from the quarry had been the only new sound that had reached The Shadow. But now, as the cloaked worker paused in his drilling, his keen ears caught an unexpected noise.

It sounded like an echo of The Shadow's own drilling. It came from the rear of the Sphinx Room, below the floor.

Swiftly, The Shadow arose and moved to the solid wall at the back of the room. Grotesque in the moonlight, he became a listening shape, as silent as an ebony statue.

A soft laugh. The Shadow knew what was taking place. Men outside were chiseling into the bricked barrier that backed the sealed vault underneath this very room. They were trying to carve through to the spot that housed the museum's treasures.

Cliff Marsland had reported that the blow-off would not come until tomorrow night. It was possible that this was preliminary work on the part of an advance squad. But The Shadow, thinking of the police who served as watchmen, knew instantly that the risk would be too great. Something must have happened within the museum before Konk Zitz would order work outside.

SWIFTLY, The Shadow headed for the front of the Sphinx Room. The huge Blue Sphinx looked on with placid eyes as the cloaked master inserted a pick in the lock of the doors. The barriers yielded promptly. The Shadow stepped into the anteroom.

As cautiously as on his first trip to the museum, The Shadow probed the outer lock. A muffled *click* announced success. Slowly, The Shadow drew one half of the double door inward, while his keen eyes peered into the front hall. He heard the *click* of footsteps.

Clyde Burke and the two gorillas had neared the outer door. The crooks were nudging their captive with their ready guns. They were to watch this fellow until later. Such had been Konk Zitz's order. But, as they made the turn, one fellow sidled a pace ahead.

Clyde saw his chance. Twisting suddenly, he swung away from the man beside him and launched a hard punch for the fellow's jaw. The gorilla staggered. With a mad dive, Clyde sprang for the corner that they had just passed, hoping to reach it before his other guard could respond.

The gorilla was too quick. Swinging as he heard the scuffle, he leveled his revolver at the darting form of Clyde. Finger on trigger, he snarled viciously as he prepared to press.

Clyde heard the snarl. He also heard the roaring shot that followed it. Yet he found himself dashing on, unscathed.

Behind him, the gorilla was crumpling. The crook's revolver dropped clattering to the stone floor, unfired. The would-be killer had never pressed the trigger. The shot that Clyde had heard had blazed from the entrance to the anteroom.

Firing on the draw, The Shadow had loosed the thunder of an automatic to drop the aiming gorilla.

Though wiry, Clyde lacked power behind a punch. The man whom he had slugged was still on his feet. That fellow, half turned, saw the burst of flame that came from the anteroom. He did not wait to see the second gorilla fall.

Savagely, the remaining ruffian aimed his ready gat for the blackness where the enemy lurked. He fired a quick shot that clanged through the brass facing of the door, into the woodwork beneath. As he completed aim, he was ready with another trigger squeeze. It never came.

A half second was the interval. The Shadow dealt in finer fractions. The automatic roared its echoing message from the confines of the anteroom. It stopped the gorilla's second attempt. With masterful aim, The Shadow sent his adversary sprawling.

While the crook was still on the fall, the door of the anteroom swung open. Into the lighted hall came the cloaked shape of The Shadow.

CLYDE BURKE had reached the Medieval Room. It was dimly lighted; and off in the further corner, Clyde saw a terrible scene. On the instant, he realized why Konk Zitz had come out chuckling.

Cliff Marsland, bound, was lying face downward with his head forced in the trough of the guillotine. Clamped in place, he could not move. One crook was standing in the foreground, while the other was preparing to loose the cleaverlike ax that had chopped off aristocratic heads in the era of the French Revolution.

Both men stopped short as Clyde came hurtling into the room. As he rounded the corner by the Iron Maiden, they thought that he must be one of their band, coming with some new order from Konk Zitz. Dimly lighted, the exhibit room did not supply sufficient glow for prompt recognition.

"Duke," the nearer man, suddenly realized what had happened. Yanking a gun, he aimed point-blank at Clyde, while he cried to Dopey, at the guillotine:

"It's the mug reporter—"

Clyde's swinging arm struck Duke's wrist as the fellow fired. The shot went wide. As they locked in a struggle, Duke managed a glancing stroke with his gun. Clyde's hold loosened.

"Get Marsland!" ordered Duke. "I've got this mug—"

Dopey, one hand on the release, had drawn a revolver with the other. His head turned as he heard a sound at the far door. With staring eyes, Dopey saw The Shadow. He caught the sound of a taunting laugh. Dopey aimed. He never fired.

The Shadow's automatic spoke. Sizzling through between the bars of a Chinese torture cage, the bullet found its mark! The cage occupied the center of the exhibit room. To reach the far corner, The Shadow had been forced to risk deflecting bars.

That necessity had prevented him from dealing instant death to Dopey. The vicious thug sagged and dropped his gun. But with his other hand, he tried to release the axe blade. His left fist was tight. Then came another withering blast from the automatic.

Aiming higher, The Shadow shattered the dying killer's wrist. Dopey's fingers relaxed. His body slumped to the floor beside the guillotine. Cliff Marsland's life was saved.

DUKE, rolling Clyde Burke to the floor, had heard the shots. Coming to his knees, Duke forgot the reporter and aimed straight for The Shadow. He had the bead he wanted. He pressed the trigger while The Shadow was swinging toward him.

But as Duke launched his seemingly certain shot, a quick hand caught his wrist. Clyde, half groggy, had seen the menace. His thrust was just in time. His yanking hand spoiled the aim. Duke's shot whistled inches away from The Shadow's wheeling form.

Snarling, Duke yanked clear and aimed again. As he fired a quick, wide shot, The Shadow's automatic spoke in unison. Duke slumped forward to the floor. The snarl ended in a dying cough.

Clyde Burke was coming to his feet. The Shadow, by the doorway, hissed an order. Clyde turned toward the guillotine. He could hear distant cries; he knew that The Shadow must go out to repel invaders. It was Clyde's job to release Cliff.

Reaching into an opened exhibit case, The Shadow seized a poniard and sent the weapon sizzling through the air. The knife landed squarely in a broad post of the guillotine and quivered there, flashing in the dim light.

Clyde, breaking loose the clamp that held Cliff's head, looked up as he heard the whirring blade. Dragging Cliff from beneath the guillotine's menacing ax, Clyde reached for the poniard and wrenched it from the wooden post. He used the blade as a knife to cut Cliff's bonds.

Cliff came to his feet. He grabbed Duke's revolver, and Clyde snatched up Dopey's. Together, they dashed out into the hall, where they could hear the sounds of shots. They saw The Shadow, by the front corner of the hall, firing out

through the opened doorway. Returning gorillas were dropping back from his fusillade.

Wheeling suddenly, The Shadow pointed his agents to the opened door of the anteroom. Shots came from outside as they took to the designated cover. Roars resounded from a second automatic that The Shadow had drawn. A hoarse cry of a wounded raider came from beyond the outer door.

Then, with a swift whirl, The Shadow came swinging across the floor. His automatics—he was wielding one with each hand—sent blazing flames in the direction of the attackers. No shots responded as The Shadow swung into the anteroom where Clyde and Cliff were waiting.

Both agents expected to see The Shadow keep up the fight through a partly opened doorway. Instead, The Shadow swung the door shut. As he clicked the lock, Clyde suddenly realized the reason for that action.

Something thudded against the outside of the closed doors. Balked in a revolver fusillade, Konk Zitz had brought up a different method of attack. The Shadow, scenting a faint odor in the outer hall, had expected it.

Tear gas bombs. The same weapons that had enabled the invaders to overpower the police were now being used against The Shadow and his agents. The Shadow had closed the doors of the anteroom just in time.

He could not open the door to meet those incoming gorillas. Konk's rallied forces would come equipped with gas masks. The Shadow and his rescued aides had only one avenue of retreat. That lay into the Sphinx Room.

Windowless, with walls that only The Shadow could scale, that inner chamber seemed no better than a hopeless trap, so far as Clyde and Cliff were concerned. Men were already pounding at the doors of the anteroom; trying to break through metal facing.

Then, at this moment that offered nothing but despair, a dull blast came from the back of the museum. The building gave a quiver. Pounding from the hallway was resumed.

Standing in the darkness of the anteroom, The Shadow laughed.

CHAPTER XX
THE ESCAPE

THE SHADOW'S laugh brought shuddering quivers to the darkened anteroom. The tones seemed ominous, even to Clyde Burke and Cliff Marsland. Yet those agents of The Shadow knew that the weird mirth promised some prompt development.

Swishing through darkness, The Shadow opened the doors into the Sphinx Room. Staring into the moonlit vault, his agents saw him approach the huge Blue Sphinx. Serene upon its pedestal, the stone figure seemed to stare into the blackened room where the agents waited.

The Shadow was working swiftly. He was stooping at the sides of the pedestal which supported the Blue Sphinx, making a round of it that puzzled his watching agents.

Axelike blows were crashing at the doors from the outer hall. Konk and his men would soon break through. Yet The Shadow kept on with his circuit of the Blue Sphinx.

"You heard the blast?" questioned Cliff, speaking tensely to Clyde.

"Yes" was the reply. "They blew the vault."

"Where from?"

"The back of the museum."

"The vault is under us?"

"Yes! Beneath the Blue Sphinx."

The Shadow was returning. Something uncoiled behind him, along the floor of the Sphinx Room. It looked threadlike in the moonlight. Then, while terrific shocks bade fair to demolish the outer doors of the anteroom, The Shadow rejoined his agents and closed the inner doors behind him.

A tiny flame flickered suddenly in the darkness. A hiss and a sputter ran along the floor. It was the end of a fuse that The Shadow had lighted. The sparkling trail sizzled under the inner doors. Clyde and Cliff waited tensely.

At that instant, a crashing blow cleaved a portion of the brass-faced door. Light issued in from the front hall. An axe fell through the opening. A hand, with pineapple bomb clutched in it, appeared beyond.

An automatic roared in the anteroom. A man flopped from the opening, dropped by The Shadow's shot.

A momentary silence. Then, from within the Sphinx Room came a terrific blast. The building seemed to rock. The stout inner doors of the anteroom crackled on their hinges. Then came the sound of shattering glass dropping in deluge from the dome above the Sphinx Room.

Stunning even to Cliff and Clyde, who had expected something of the sort, the explosion produced a tremendous stir beyond the front doors of the anteroom. It stopped Konk Zitz and his crew before they could begin a new attack.

Then, as shudders lulled, the sound of Konk's snarling voice came through the axe-made opening. Konk was ordering a new bomb attack.

A hiss from The Shadow. As his agents turned, the cloaked fighter opened the inner doors and ordered them into the Sphinx Room. As the two men staggered there, The Shadow followed. He shut the inner doors and locked them, just as a gas-pineapple came through the outer break.

CLYDE BURKE was staring in amazement. So was Cliff Marsland. Before them, shattered into great chunks, lay the remains of the Blue Sphinx. Scattered about amidst the broken glass were portions of the pedestal on which the Sphinx had rested.

The Shadow had blown the whole structure loose. His fused charges, inserted in the holes that he had drilled, had totally demolished the pedestal and wrecked the statue with it.

The head of the Sphinx had toppled on its side. The face was staring with its blank eyes toward the doorway. The rear of the statue had rolled from the ruined pedestal, while the center section had broken in two halves that lay well apart.

Crash! Gas-masked invaders had beaten through the brass-faced doors. Closer strokes. They were attacking the inner entrance. Those inner doors were wood alone. They were already loosened by the blast that had shattered the Blue Sphinx. But that mattered no longer.

A yawning hole lay in the center of the demolished pedestal. The charge, spreading in all directions, had produced a yawning hole in the floor itself. Through the pungent room, The Shadow beckoned his agents to this outlet.

Clyde Burke noticed something as he followed Cliff down through the hole. The jagged cavity showed traces of a regular shape, as though there had been an opening through the ruined pedestal.

Cliff had dropped into the vault; Clyde followed. Then The Shadow swished beside them. His flashlight gleamed.

Again, Clyde stared. The vault was entirely empty. How had the other crooks managed to remove the treasure so quickly? Only a dozen minutes had elapsed since the first blast that had told of the entry through the bricked rear wall.

Moonlight showed through the rear barrier. At The Shadow's command, Clyde and Cliff squeezed through. The Shadow followed, just as smashing from above announced that Konk's outfit had crashed through to the Sphinx Room.

Clyde was looking vainly for the trucks that had come for the swag. He saw no signs of them. He could not understand how they had been loaded for so quick a getaway. Then a thought occurred to him. He turned to speak to The Shadow. A hiss commanded silence.

Swiftly, The Shadow swung toward the far corner of the museum, his agents close behind him. Pausing near the front, The Shadow, weird in the moonlight, pointed off toward a clump of trees. Cliff and Clyde headed in that direction.

A shout from the front of the museum. Shots blazed toward the running men. The Shadow's agents kept on. From behind them, they heard the

Gas-masked invaders had beaten through the brass-faced doors.... They were attacking the inner entrance.

sudden burst of a strident, gibing laugh that rose like a mighty challenge through the clear night air.

CROOKS heard it, too. They wheeled to see The Shadow standing in the moonlight. Viciously, they opened fire, just as The Shadow began to weave a circling course away from the museum. He was drawing the fire from the foe.

Automatics loomed in gloved fists. Those weapons barked their sharp response to enemy guns. Crooks were shooting wild, at long range. Not so The Shadow. Using the white face of the museum, he picked out his living targets against that perfect background.

Thugs staggered, firing vainly at the figure which seemed to fade and appear again between the moonlight and the blackness of the trees. Again that mocking laugh came ringing to their ears. Men dived for the open doorway of the museum. A gas-masked figure appeared there.

The Shadow fired.

The masked crook staggered back into the building. The others followed, ready to brave the last fumes of the tear gas rather than meet The Shadow. Then new foemen came into view, rounding the corner at the rear of the museum.

Like The Shadow and his agents, this group had dropped through the hole in the floor of the Sphinx Room and made an exit through the break that crooks had blasted at the rear of the vault. But these new enemies, arriving, could find no target at which to open distant fire.

The Shadow had glided to the trees. There, he reached his hidden coupé, where his two agents were already aboard. His hiss came from the darkness, questioning in tone. It brought a quick response from Clyde, for it concerned the very matter that was on the reporter's mind.

"Drury was with them," informed Clyde. "They'd have to take the road to Larkton. The only shortcut without hitting Latuna. Drury was acting as their leader. It was Drury who brought me here, by a phone call."

A hissed order from The Shadow. Cliff Marsland, at the wheel, pressed the starter. The motor roared. Clyde, breathless, added one more comment:

"About Drury—he acted as if he wanted to kill me. But I saw his revolver when he threatened. No bullets in it—"

Shouts from near the museum. The crooks had heard the car.

A hiss of understanding from The Shadow. A reply from Cliff. The coupé shot away, clearing for the road before Konk and his outfit could intercept it.

Three minutes later, a lone gorilla, an outpost, guarding a parked sedan, was conscious of a slight *swish* beside him. Turning, with gun in hand, he faced the blazing eyes of The Shadow. Before the gorilla could fire, a gloved hand swept upward and clipped the crook just beneath his square-set chin.

The gorilla gave an odd gargle as he slumped to the ground.

A figure entered the car. The motor roared. The sedan shot out from the trees. Foemen heard it and turned from their chase of the coupé. Konk Zitz's yell ordered them to open fire. The cry came too late. The sedan was jouncing off along a rocky road.

Then, as raging desperadoes came running toward the trees, the air reverberated with the sound of a parting taunt. The laugh of The Shadow rang out with all its mockery. The Shadow, like his agents, was departing.

Konk Zitz laughed hoarsely. Though half his crew had been crippled, he had put The Shadow on the run. So thought the big shot as he ordered his scattered henchmen to the remaining cars.

But Konk's shreds of triumph were ill-founded. He was wrong when he thought The Shadow was in flight. By that swift departure, The Shadow was planning to ruin schemes that Konk thought were beyond the master fighter's reach.

CHAPTER XXI
BY THE BRIDGE

THE Latuna Museum was located just south of a main highway. Between the museum and the town, a paved road cut off from the through highway and led cross-country to the village of Larkton.

Clyde Burke was familiar with that fact. That was why he had told The Shadow that the supposed trucks must have gone by the Larkton road. Little traveled, the cross thoroughfare offered a perfect route for the crooks who had gone with Bart Drury.

By choosing that course, they avoided traffic and also escaped passing through Latuna itself. Moreover, they could gain the Larkton road by means of the dirt lane that curved around the hillside at the back of the museum. This eliminated all contact with the highway.

Three miles out, the Larkton road crossed the rocky ravine of a trickling creek. The bridge was reached by a sloping grade. It bore two warnings: one, not to exceed twelve miles an hour in crossing; the other, barring all trucks of more than five tons capacity.

A bulky, antiquated truck was standing on the slope fifty feet from the near side of the trestle. Its dim lights revealed the bridge. Its wheezing motor was idling, accompanied by the clatter of a loose fan belt. Two men were standing by the big vehicle. Their growled conversation marked them as members of Konk Zitz's gorilla crew.

"I don't get the lay, Soupy," one was saying.

"First we blow the back of that museum. Then we scram without goin' in there. Say—I t'ink Konk's gone screwy."

"Yeah?" returned "Soupy." "Wid all de dough he's been flashin'? Say, if Konk's gone bugs, crack me on the dome an' make me de same way."

"Like I socked the mug that's layin' in the truck, eh?"

"Say—you hit dat guy hard, Marty. You oughta been careful about dat. Remember what Konk said."

"The guy's comin' to already, Soupy. I'm keepin' an eye on him. That's somethin' else I can't figure. There's Nick an' Lefty up ahead pullin' the props out from under that bridge. So we can ditch this junker"—a nudge toward the truck—"an' all the stuff that's in it. What's the idea?"

"Say, Marty. You must be dumb. I got de idea as soon as Konk spilled it."

"Yeah? What is it?"

"Dis old truck is supposed to be de last of a whole bunch. See? Rollin' off wid a lot of swag from dat museum. But all it's got in it is de bum stuff from upstairs. When dis truck bumps trough de bridge, de bulls'll find it here. Dey'll t'ink de real swag went out dis way."

"But where's the real swag? We didn't go in that hole we blew."

"Dat's Konk's job. Leave dat to him. We're de blind, dat's all. Dat's de way I figure it, Marty."

"Sounds likely, Soupy."

MUFFLED pounding from beneath the bridge. A timber gave way with a splintering sound. Then came a crash, seconds later, as the falling beam reached the depths of the ravine.

"Dat job oughta have been done ahead o' time," objected Soupy. "No use stickin' around here de way we is."

"No?" retorted Marty. "Well, you're the bozo that's talkin' dumb now. They don't use this road much, but supposin' somebody had come through after the bridge was fixed. That would've queered it for us, wouldn't it?"

"Yeah. I neveh figured it dat way. Say, you gotta hand it to Konk Zitz. He knows his onions, dat guy does!"

A moan from the front seat of the wheezing truck. Marty leaned in to make an inspection by the glow from the dash light.

"Comin' to," he said. "Maybe I'd better hand him another haymaker."

"Lay off it," growled Soupy. "De mug ain't to look like he'd been pasted. He's part of de blind—"

Soupy broke off as he heard the sound of approaching voices. Two gorillas came into the light of the headlamps. Nick and Lefty had finished the job at the bridge. One of them spoke to Soupy and Marty.

"How's the mug?" was his question.

"Wakin' up, Lefty," replied Marty.

"Shove him under the wheel, then," ordered Lefty. "That's the way. Now loose that hand brake."

"Ain't you goin' to shove it in gear?"

"No. Think I want to stall it?"

"O.K., Lefty."

Meanwhile, Soupy and Nick were talking. The man from the bridge was bringing up a question that had evidently been dropped upon their arrival here.

"That blast after we left," Nick was saying. "It didn't sound like it come from the quarry. It was too close—"

"I tell you it was from de quarry," broke in Soupy. "If it wasn't—"

"They'd have quit blastin', Soupy, after hearin' that load we let off—"

"Maybe dey would. But maybe dey had de charge all set an'—"

"Look out!" came Lefty's growl from the other side of the truck.

Nick and Soupy stepped away. The wheezy truck was rolling. Slow on this easy portion of the slope, it would gain speed straight for the bridge.

"We pinched dat wagon up in Rockport," chuckled Soupy. "Say—de guy dat owns it'll be—"

He stopped. Like the others, Soupy turned, then leaped to the side of the road as he heard a car come roaring from a bend behind him. Then, like a meteor from darkness, a sedan came hurtling down the slope.

Lefty, leader of this quartet, yanked a gun as the glare bore down upon him. He shouted an order that sounded above the approaching roar.

"Let 'em have it!"

AS gorillas drew, the bark of an automatic came from the left side of the whizzing sedan. Bullets sizzed into the cluster of firing thugs. Tongues of flame accompanied the staccato bursts as the sedan whirled past the crew.

Enemies sprawled—all save Lefty. He leaped for the sedan as the driver suddenly applied the brakes. Catching an opened window, the ruffian went flying to the running board and swung to aim a shot at the driver, who was now trying to avert disaster.

Brakes screeched as the car cut down its eighty-mile-an-hour pace. Lefty lost aim as the driver swerved past the speed-gaining truck. On toward the very edge of the bridge. Then the brakes jammed.

The sedan did a sudden rightabout. In its whirl it came into the path of the truck; then out of it. Lefty, losing his hold on the tilting side, was thrown onto the bridge.

The door of the sedan shot open; out sprang a figure that showed solid black as it dodged away from the oncoming truck.

The Shadow had arrived. He had stopped on the verge of disaster. In split seconds, he had summed the situation. Forgetting Lefty, who had dropped his gun and was trying to rise from the bridge, The Shadow whirled almost against the passing truck.

There was no door by the driver's seat. But a man was behind the wheel, dangling there, groggy, shaking with the jolts that the truck made in gaining a fifteen-mile-an-hour speed.

Swinging to the running board, The Shadow seized the limp figure and went rolling to the roadway, carrying the man with him. Both figures went sprawling in the dust by the sedan.

A scream from the bridge. Lefty's hoarse cry was too late. He was unable to crawl clear. His rising form went over like a tenpin, as the big truck struck him. The front wheel jolted as it passed over the crook's body. The truck veered toward the rail.

Before the lumbering Jagannath reached the side, a crackling sound came from the bridge itself. Weakened timbers gave. The wooden planking caved. The whole structure swayed and went crashing down into the gorge, the truck hurtling beyond the falling debris.

Lefty's writhing form was on the sloping brink. A clawing, helpless sight, the last of the quartet slipped with the loosening planks. While the echoes of the crashing truck were still sounding from the depths of the ravine, Lefty disappeared into the chasm.

THE SHADOW saw it, while rising from the dust. By the sedan he found a bewildered man trying to get to his feet. The Shadow helped the rescued man into the sedan. Behind the wheel, The Shadow turned on the dome light. He laughed softly as he recognized Bart Drury's face.

Groggy, grimy-faced, his clothing torn, the star reporter lay bewildered. The Shadow drew a vial from beneath his cloak. He pressed the tiny vessel to Bart's lips. A purplish liquid trickled to the reporter's tongue.

Bart stirred. The Shadow clicked out the dome light and started the stalled motor. The car was turned up the slope. As it started forward, the headlights showed the sprawled, motionless forms of three gorillas.

Then that sight was left behind. The sedan was purring toward the level road. Bart Drury, half bewildered, was mumbling:

"Burke, Burke—is that you, Burke?"

"No," came the quiet response. The Shadow's tone was assuring. "Burke is all right."

"Glad of that," mumbled Bart. "Made me call him—Konk did. Couldn't—couldn't get out of it."

"Speak on," ordered the quiet voice.

"They grabbed me," explained Bart. "In Konk's place—at the Phoenix. Konk said I'd have—to be

the goat. Said he'd—he'd bump Burke—unless I played the game."

The vial came to Bart's lips in the darkness. A taste of the potent liquid was reviving. Bart steadied, and spoke further to the silent driver beside him.

"Burke was to see me running things," explained Bart. "Konk was to let him go. Burke would pin it on me. I knew I was slated for the spot. But I played the game—to get Burke out of it.

"Maybe Burke knows I was on the level. I—I couldn't go out without trying to tip him off. They had me doing an act with an empty gun. They'd have plugged me if I hadn't played my part. But I flashed the revolver in front of Burke's nose. He—he saw, it was empty. No bullets."

Bart subsided in the cushions. His strength had lessened. But as he rested, his mind cleared. He could hear the quiet voice speaking, stating facts that Bart Drury knew, yet which he had never pieced together. Then came orders that the reporter understood.

The car came to a stop. The door opened so softly that Bart did not hear it. The Shadow stepped through darkness to a spot where a coupe was standing. He voiced a low hiss.

Clyde Burke alighted. Cliff Marsland shifted from the driver's wheel. Entering, The Shadow took his place. A questioning hiss. Cliff spoke tensely, telling of the trip to Harrison Knode's; and how he had been trapped when he fluked the safe.

A soft laugh. Clyde Burke, by the coupé, heard whispered orders. He responded. The motor started. Taking Cliff, The Shadow drove away, leaving Clyde standing by the sedan.

IN the stopped car, Drury had heard voices; then the departure of the coupe. Turning to the driver's seat, he shot a question to the person whom he supposed still sat there.

"Say—who are you?"

No response. Bart groped for the dome light and switched it on. He stared, dumfounded. The seat behind the wheel was empty. Then came footsteps. A face was thrust into the light. Bart stared at Clyde Burke.

"Hello, Bart!" smiled The Shadow's agent, opening the door to take his place behind the wheel. "I got that gun flash when you gave it. Well, old man, you're out of it—like I am. But we're diving in again."

Bart nodded. He, like Clyde Burke, had received orders from The Shadow. Like Clyde, Bart was game.

CHAPTER XXII
THE EVIDENCE

HARRISON KNODE was seated in his parlor. Opposite him were two acquaintances. They had accompanied the crusading editor to his home after attending the hearing at Strafford Malden's.

the Sphinx Room, we removed all of the Soyer collection and brought it here. The treasures now repose in my heavily locked cellar.

"The next day, the Blue Sphinx arrived. Rubal superintended the removal of the loose planking and the placement of the Sphinx. The trapdoor was a neat one. No workmen knew of its existence. The way by which the treasure had been removed was hidden beneath a five-ton mass of stone. Resting on the solid portion of the pedestal, the Blue Sphinx covered the small opening."

Malden paused and leered craftily. The listeners knew that they were to hear the following portion of his scheme.

"I KNEW that the loss would eventually be discovered. When the extensions were built to the museum; for then the vault would be opened. There was only one answer. A fake robbery by criminals; a blind trail that would lead the hunt away from me.

"I could dispose of the treasures later. All the while I did so, the law would be trying to trace the link between the Soyer collection and the crooks. That is why I called in the services of Konk Zitz and paid him to keep his henchmen in Latuna. They were ready for the climax which Zitz termed the 'blow-off.'

"My only trouble was Rubal. He wanted to get out of it, by resigning after the Blue Sphinx was installed. He had aided in the actual robbery; I knew his resignation would produce suspicion after the false raid took place. There was only one solution.

"I went to the museum, leaving Toya and Singler here to give a fake alibi later. Hollis let me in. He was glad to see me. He wanted me to talk to Rubal. He told me that Knode was coming. I knew then that Rubal intended to confess. So I went directly to the office and shot him down with this silent revolver."

Malden chuckled as he looked at the weapon on the table. Savagely, he swung toward Harrison Knode.

"I had to wait there," he stated. "I knew you were coming. I had gathered all incriminating documents. Any that might mean a clue. I was waiting for you, Knode; but Hollis came in your place. I killed him so he could not tell the truth.

"I knew that police were watching the Phoenix Hotel. That was good. It kept Konk Zitz and his men free of blame. I knew their opportunity would come. The blasting of the empty vault did not have to be hurried. While I waited, I evolved a scheme"—Malden's lips twisted in evil fashion—"that made the whole game perfect.

"I left the death gun and a few old papers"—a hand gesture toward the table—"where Zitz could get them. He planted them in your safe, Knode. Then he framed Drury, with Burke, who appeared honest, to be a witness. You have all heard the rest."

Malden tightened his hold on his revolver. He leered savagely; his eyes were almost wild.

"Someone forced himself into the game!" cried the self-confessed crook. "Someone who shattered the Blue Sphinx in order to make an outlet of escape. What does it matter? No one will ever know the truth! Traces of the trapdoor may prove damaging. But I can divert suspicion from myself, once I have disposed of all of you.

"You are going to die!" Malden's voice was steady. "All of you, here in this conservatory! There will be a fight, presumably started by order of Harrison Knode. I and my servants alone will remain alive—"

EYES were intent upon Malden. All save those of Clyde Burke. The Shadow's agent had gazed toward the side door of the conservatory. He saw that door open, behind Singler.

Malden's servant did not hear a sound. But as Clyde stared, he saw Singler shift forward. Clyde could tell that a gun muzzle had been thrust against the back of the chauffeur's neck.

Singler's knees shook. His fingers loosened; his revolver clattered to the floor, as he staggered feebly in from the door.

Malden turned quickly at the sound. So did Toya. Both found themselves staring into the muzzles of automatics. Their hands released the revolvers that they held.

Shrouded against the blackness of the opened door, The Shadow stood like a symbol of death. His form was vague; the cloak and slouch hat looked like a portion of the outer darkness. But the eyes that blazed from beneath the hat brim were living coals. The whispered voice that spoke was chilling.

"It was I," declared The Shadow, in his sinister tone, "who divined your scheme! The riddle of the Blue Sphinx! It was I who placed the charges beneath the Sphinx, ready to blast it, the night before your henchmen moved!

"That would have laid bare the empty vault. Then would come my next strokes. Against you; against your criminals. Separately. But circumstances"—the sibilance of The Shadow's tone was shuddering—"changed my plan. Your henchmen came to me. I dealt with them.

"Your turn has come, Strafford Malden. I have allowed you to declare your guilt. Confessed a murderer, you are doomed—"

A shout from outdoors. A warning cry. Clyde Burke recognized Cliff Marsland's voice. Then came the bark of revolvers.

The Shadow wheeled in, away from the doorway. His automatics thundered as he fired into the outer darkness. Answering bullets were crashing the glass windows.

Konk Zitz and the remains of his crew had arrived!

MALDEN and his servants leaped for their guns. Upon them pounced the men whom Malden had threatened to kill. Quirby Rush and Howard Dunham overpowered Malden. Chief Grewling and Harrison Knode caught Toya. Clyde Burke and Bart Drury bore Singler to the floor.

The Shadow, turning, saw the outcome. With a swift whirl, he made for the door, firing as he went. He had stemmed the crooks' gunfire; sweeping out into the night, he was bound upon new vengeance.

Cliff Marsland and Harry Vincent, crouched behind a low wall, were exchanging shots with ruffians in the offing. They and The Shadow had shot down the ones who had made for the house. The rest were stationed in the background.

A snarl came in Konk Zitz's voice. With it, a growl from Tinker Furris. The two had seen The Shadow appear in momentary fashion. Rising, they aimed for their archenemy.

Cliff Marsland spotted Konk and fired. His bullet clipped the big shot.

Tinker was shooting toward the house. His slugs were chipping stone from the wall. His aim was wide of the elusive, unseen figure in black. Then, as Harry aimed to get Tinker, a shot burst from the darkness. The gloom showed Tinker sprawling by a tree trunk.

Sweeping across the dim lawn, The Shadow sent shots after the last fleeing members of Konk's crew. Puppet forms sprawled along the gravel drive. Cliff and Harry were in view. The Shadow hissed an order for their departure. He swung back toward the house.

Sounds of conflict indicated that Malden and his two henchmen had been captured. Such was the case; but Malden, fiendish in power, was not through. He was holding his revolver; but he could not use it. A detective, arriving to aid Rush and Dunham, snatched the weapon from the archcrook's grasp.

Toya and Singler were downed. But Malden made his sudden break. He sent Rush rolling across the table. He hurled Dunham upon Mushmug, the detective. With a wild leap Malden grabbed the silencer-fitted death gun from the table and sprang free toward the side door of the conservatory. He stopped short.

The Shadow had returned.

BLACKNESS moved inward. As he heard a mocking laugh, Malden caught the glow of burning eyes. Maddened, he fired a quick shot with the weapon that he had seized. The death gun emitted a sighing sound. Its silent bullet dug deep into the door frame that stood white beside The Shadow's shoulder.

Hard on the hiss of the silencer came a roaring burst from the door. Strafford Malden sagged. The murderous gun dropped from his grasp. The death weapon had failed the supercrook.

Men turned as they heard Malden's gargling gasp. Grewling came pouncing over to trap the prostrate fiend.

The police chief stopped. His efforts were not needed. With a hideous coughing, Strafford Malden gave his last breath. His arms sprawled. He was dead.

Grewling turned toward the door. So did others. They saw blackness only. The Shadow had departed.

Silence lay without. All tokens of the outer fight were ended. With Malden dead; with Toya and Singler prisoners, the law had won its fight.

Outside lay bodies of dead killers. But those did not concern the men in the conservatory. Below lay purloined treasure; wealth in molded gold and studded gems that they must find and restore to its proper place.

Turning to his companions, Police Chief Grewling was about to give an order. Words stopped on his lips. Like others, the police chief stood rigid as he listened. From somewhere in the outer darkness, its distance indefinable, came the tones of a strange, outlandish mockery.

Rising on the night air, the weird tone reached a startling crescendo. Eerily, it burst into a shuddering, fading taunt. Echoes rifled their ghoulish answer as the laugh reached its sudden finish.

Then the night air stilled.

Clyde Burke could see the frozen amazement upon the faces of his delivered companions. He knew the reason why they stood aghast. They had heard the triumph laugh of The Shadow!

THE END

Walter B. Gibson (1897-1985) was one of the most prolific American writers of the twentieth century. An accomplished magician and former Philadelphia newspaperman, Gibson wrote 282 *Shadow* pulp novels under the house-name Maxwell Grant, creating Lamont Cranston and the characters and mythos that would later be featured in the legendary MBS radio series. The host of ABC's *Strange* also wrote more than 500 magazine stories and articles, thousands of syndicated newspaper features and hundreds of comic book and radio scripts including *Nick Carter: Master Detective, Blackstone the Magic Detective, The Avenger* and *The Adventures of Frank Merriwell*. In addition to his *Shadow* stories, Gibson wrote more than 150 books including *Hoyle's Simplified Guide to the Popular Card Games, Fell's Guide to Knots and How to Tie Them, Houdini's Escapes, Blackstone's Secrets of Magic, The Twilight Zone, The Complete Illustrated Book of the Psychic Sciences* and *The Man from Uncle: The Coin of El Diablo Affair.*

JIBARO DEATH

A Complete Book-length Novel from the Private Annals of The Shadow, as told to

Maxwell Grant

The wiles of the head-hunting Jibaros combine with the treachery of the underworld, to spread death and terror in the streets of New York for the sake of tremendous wealth! But they did not reckon with the power of The Shadow until too late!

CHAPTER I
DEATH MARK

THE man who alighted from a cab in front of the Hotel Goliath was a foreigner. That was apparent from the olive hue of his skin; the jet blackness of his glistening hair, and the dark glint of his eyes. His exact nationality, however, would have been difficult to guess.

The man's expression showed odd contrasts. The flash of his eyes; the set of his lips; the strength of his squatty frame were indicative of a person who could combat danger. Nevertheless, his eyes showed a blink; his lips carried a twitch. There was a shudder of the broad shoulders as the foreigner stepped hastily across the stretch of sidewalk between the curb and the hotel entrance.

Once inside the glittering lobby of the Goliath, the olive-skinned man regained his composure. Lights were brilliant; the lobby was thronged. The place seemed to be a meeting spot for all Manhattan. The squatty man smiled as he looked about and saw a desk that bore the sign: "INFORMATION."

When he approached the desk, however, the man became cautious. He looked warily about; studied faces that he saw nearby. He saw a light-complexioned, blond-haired man standing near the information booth, and apparently considered him of no importance. Observing no one of darkish visage, the olive-skinned man leaned across the desk and spoke to a girl who was sorting mail.

"Tell me, please," he inquired. "Senor Alvarez Rentone—is he registered here?"

The girl went to a filing case marked "R." She consulted a card; without looking toward the questioner, she replied:

"Mr. Rentone is registered here; but he has gone out of town for a few days. He left no word when he would be back."

The squatty man looked troubled. He chewed his lips; then turned away and looked across the lobby. He saw a line of telephone booths. He walked over, consulted a telephone directory and entered a booth. After some perplexity with the dial, he managed to call the number that he wanted.

"Hello?" The squatty man's voice was questioning

as he heard an answer. "Is this Senor Dundee?... Ah, *buenos!* Allow me, senor, to introduce myself. My name is Manuel Fendoza... Ah, *si, senor.* I have come from Santander."

There was a short pause, while Fendoza listened to a voice across the wire. When Dundee had finished speaking, Fendoza became voluble with further explanation.

"Ah, senor," he exclaimed, "it is not my wish to cause you bother. I have come to New York to find Senor Alvarez Rentone... Ah, *si.* He is the grandson of Jose Rentone... But he is not where I should find him... At the Hotel Goliath... Your name? Ah, senor, I heard of it by pure accident... *Gracias, senor."*

FENDOZA finished his call and stepped from the booth. He went to the cigar stand, purchased a pack of cigarettes and looked about while he was opening them. He failed to glance back toward the telephone booths. Hence he did not notice that a man was hunched in the booth next to the one that he had just left. The man in the booth was the light-haired individual who had watched Fendoza at the information desk.

A hard grin showed on the man's lips as his finger dialed a number. The call went through; the light-haired man recognized the voice that responded. Low-toned and harsh, the caller gave information.

"Hello, Zenjora." he announced. "This is Cardell, watching at the Goliath... Yeah. A fellow just came in and asked for Alvarez Rentone...

"His name? Sure. I got it. Manuel Fendoza. He just put in a call to a guy named Dundee. I caught it from the next booth... What's that? Howard Dundee? I can't say for sure. All that Fendoza called him was Dundee...

"No. Dundee didn't know anything about Alvarez Rentone. From the way it sounded, he didn't want to be bothered... Wait a minute, Zenjora! I see Fendoza going back to the information desk!... Yeah. I think he's going to fall... Sure. I'll be ready with the tip-off..."

Completing his call, Cardell stepped from the booth. He watched Fendoza approach the information desk; but Cardell made no effort to draw closer. Instead, he edged toward a side door of the lobby. From that vantage point, he could see what happened at the desk.

There, Fendoza made another polite inquiry regarding Alvarez Rentone.

"Ah, senorita!" he said to the girl at the desk. "I must ask you again regarding Senor Rentone. He is a friend of mine. Is it not possible that he has left some message here?"

The girl made another reference to file "R." She looked along the line of mailboxes; found number 1282, There she discovered a sealed envelope, a memo slip with it. She passed the envelope to Fendoza and tossed the slip in the wastebasket.

"This was left for anyone who inquired," stated the girl. "No name mentioned with it. It must be for you, sir."

Fendoza took the envelope. Clutching it, he looked about, saw the side exit from the lobby. Cardell had stepped away; Fendoza suspected nothing as he hurried through the doorway. Outside, he spied a taxi. He entered it.

"Where to?" queried the driver.

Fendoza hesitated; then replied:

"Take me to a station of the subway." Then, noting a subway station just across the street, he corrected himself: "No, no! I mean a station of the elevated railway. The one that is nearest."

Fendoza's only desire was to open the envelope in privacy. He started the task as soon as the cab pulled away. Hence he did not observe a sedan that started from the curb and followed close behind the cab. The driver of the sedan had caught a signal from Cardell, at the lobby door.

THE lights of Seventh Avenue were just what Fendoza wanted. Eagerly, he ripped the envelope open, pulled out a stiff correspondence card that was within. The card was sharp-edged; it cut Fendoza's finger, and brought an exclamation from his lips. Then, placing his finger to his mouth, Fendoza forgot about the slight cut while he studied the card. His eyes blinked in puzzled fashion.

The correspondence card was blank.

Turning it over and over, Fendoza wondered. He looked inside the crumpled envelope; found nothing there. The cab swung eastward on a gloomy side street, where no more light was available. Fendoza shoved the card and the envelope in his pocket. Drawing his finger from his lips, he muttered to himself in Spanish. Fendoza could not understand the barren message.

"Here you are, sir."

The cab driver made the announcement as he pulled up beneath a station on the Sixth Avenue elevated. Fendoza alighted and produced the fare.

As the cab drove away, Fendoza looked about and became nervous. Sixth Avenue was less brilliant than Seventh. Many of its lights were obstructed by the elevated. Glancing along a side street, Fendoza saw the brighter district that he had just left. He decided to go back to it. He hurried westward along the side street.

Halfway to Seventh Avenue, Fendoza stumbled as he passed the open front of a garage. His face showed a wild expression beneath the glare of a street lamp. Another stumble; Fendoza gave an inarticulate cry. He lost his footing and rolled to the sidewalk. The spot where he sprawled was dark.

A sedan swung up from the opposite direction. It was the one that had trailed Fendoza from the Hotel

Goliath. It had rounded the block while Fendoza was walking from Sixth Avenue to Seventh. The door of the sedan swung open; a hunched, apish figure scrambled to the curb. The sedan blocked the glow from the nearest street lamp. The apish man was scarcely discernible, as he crouched above Fendoza's body.

With quick hands, this hunched ghoul went through Fendoza's pockets. There was a momentary glimmer: an arm jabbed as though delivering a knife thrust. A low call from the sedan; the apish man bounded back into the car. The sedan shot away as its door slammed. At that instant, an attendant arrived from the open front of the garage.

"Hey, you!!" he shouted after the car. "What's going on here?"

The sedan did not stop. The garage man could not catch its license number; nor did he gain a good glimpse of the car as it wheeled around the corner. He looked toward the sidewalk, near where the car had stopped. He saw Fendoza's body.

The garage man raised a shout. Another attendant joined him. As the two shouted together, a patrol-man came on the run, from some distance down the street. Reaching Fendoza's body, the officer heard the first garage man's statement.

"There was a sedan stopped here," the fellow informed the officer. "Maybe they dumped the guy. Or maybe somebody hopped out and slugged him while he was walking past."

The policeman stopped and gripped Fendoza's shoulders. The body had tilted forward; the officer rolled it on its back. One garage man gulped. From the dead man's breast he saw the handle of a knife. Fendoza had been stabbed through the heart.

THE policeman grunted. This did not perturb him. He had seen dirked victims before. He had viewed corpses with their faces shot away. He was used to all forms of death. With one hand, the officer tilted Fendoza's face into the light, so that he could observe it better.

An instant later, the bluecoat came upward, rigid. His nonchalance was gone. His eyes were staring; his hands shook. Yet he could not turn his gaze away from the horror that lay upon the sidewalk.

The face of Manuel Fendoza looked human no longer. No person on earth could have identified that countenance as one that had been seen at the Hotel Goliath only fifteen minutes before. Death had changed it to the visage of a fiend.

Livid eyes bulged from sunken sockets; eyes that were glaring brown orbs, surrounded by a rim of bloodshot white. Olive skin seemed drawn tight across the dead man's cheekbones, pulled downward by a sagged lower jaw.

Fendoza's lips were twisted into a terrible, downward smile that contorted his entire face. Half askew, those lips looked as if they had tried vainly to deliver a shriek in response to something that the bulging eyes had witnessed.

That was not all. Upon Fendoza's face stood proof that his terror had been real. A knife thrust was not the only token that had been left upon the corpse. Upon Fendoza's forehead gleamed a mark that stood for death.

That mark was formed by three crimson lines, like narrow welts. The symbol was in the center of Fendoza's forehead; two lines horizontal, the third crossing them at the diagonal. They were like slashes, carved upon the dead man's flesh; though scratches only, they had brought blood to the surface.

Yet, terrible though Fendoza's expression had become, his face was but the countenance of a victim. The devilish glare that showed upon the dead man's visage stood as a reflection of an evil that still existed.

That was the evil of some master murderer who had ordered the doom of Manuel Fendoza.

CHAPTER II
FACES FROM THE PAST

FENDOZA'S death produced big headlines in the next day's newspapers. Though killings were not unusual in New York, this one presented sensational angles. It was seldom that a man was stabbed to death within half a block of the Times Square area.

To the police, Manuel Fendoza was an unidentified victim. There was no clue to his exact nationality; and the contorted condition of his face made it still more difficult to trace the race to which he belonged. The weapon, however, was not an ordinary knife. It was a stiletto; and that fact apparently placed an Italian angle to the murder.

One fact was mentioned by all the newspapers. The victim had died in fear and anguish. Those who had seen his face were unanimous on that point. All agreed that they had viewed a sight that they would like to forget.

The morning newspapers handled the case in rather conservative fashion. The evening journals made it more sensational. Behind Fendoza's murder, so they claimed, might lie a huge vendetta that would lead to more deaths. The newspapers announced that the police commissioner had taken personal charge of the case; and it was predicted that a roundup of criminals might be due.

Until midafternoon, reporters beleaguered the office of Commissioner Ralph Weston. Then their efforts ceased. Weston ducked out and made for the Cobalt Club, where he was a member. No one had ever crashed the gate of the exclusive Cobalt Club. The reporters gave up their efforts to gain an interview, on the assumption that Weston would issue a statement later.

Four o'clock found Commissioner Weston finishing a steak in the grillroom of the Cobalt Club. Weston was a man of brisk, military appearance; when he became ruffled, he was a hard man with whom to deal. He had foregone his lunch hour in order to avoid reporters; and he had been annoyed on that account. A meal in the quiet grillroom of the Cobalt Club had calmed him; in fact, Weston looked up with a half-pleased smile when a visitor approached his table.

WESTON recognized the newcomer as Lamont Cranston, a millionaire member of the Cobalt Club. He invited his friend to sit down at the table. Cranston complied. Weston looked across to eye a calm, hawklike countenance, with keen eyes and thin, straight lips.

As Weston recalled it, he had never seen Cranston indulge in any but the slightest of smiles. There was something masklike about the millionaire's face; his manner, too, was unusual. Cranston was always deliberate and leisurely. Weston supposed that he had cultivated that manner through his long experience as a globe-trotter. Cranston had experienced adventures in many parts of the world.

Though Weston thought he knew a great deal about Cranston, there was one fact that the commissioner had never grasped. He would have been astonished had he been told that there were two Lamont Cranstons; that the real one was seldom in New York. The Cranston whom Weston faced at present was actually another person. He was that mysterious being known as The Shadow.

Master sleuth who hunted down men of crime, The Shadow used the role of Cranston to hide his own identity. Moreover, he found it useful when he sought certain items of information. Today, The Shadow was in quest of facts; he had learned enough about last night's murder to want more. Anticipating that Commissioner Weston would be at the Cobalt Club, The Shadow had come here as Cranston.

In quiet, leisurely fashion, The Shadow expressed surprise at finding Weston at the lunch table, so late in the afternoon. The remark produced the very result that The Shadow expected. It started Weston on a tirade that led to the subject of Fendoza's murder.

"There is no rest for a police commissioner," snapped Weston. "When crime is rampant, I am criticized by the newspapers and besieged by hordes of outraged reformers. Do they give me rest when I have curbed crime? No! Then they magnify small crimes into large ones!"

"I suppose," inserted The Shadow, "that you are referring to last night's murder."

"I am," acknowledged Weston. "To read the newspaper reports you would think that a feud had begun. Bah! It is such talk that stirs up trouble!"

"The newspapers state that you have taken personal charge of the case."

"I have. What else could I do? I had to satisfy them in some fashion. However, I am handling it through Inspector Cardona. He is the best man to get to the bottom of it."

The Shadow indulged in one of his slight smiles. He knew that if Joe Cardona was on the case, Weston's part would be a small one. Cardona was the most able sleuth on the New York force. He had long served as Weston's right-hand man.

"CARDONA isn't even sure that the dead man is an Italian," confided Weston, leaning across the table. "All he knows is that the man was stabbed to death with a stiletto; and that his forehead was marked with a peculiar symbol that might be the sign of some secret society.

"But Cardona hasn't found out who the dead man is; and he hasn't located a single suspect. He's down in Little Italy today, quizzing people there. Being a native of the district himself, Cardona ought to learn something."

The waiter brought Weston his dessert. The Shadow lighted a cigar; leaned back in his chair and put a casual query to the commissioner.

"The newspapers mentioned the mark on the dead man's forehead," he remarked. "They also stated that the victim's face was distorted. Was that true, Commissioner?"

For reply, Weston reached to a briefcase beside his chair. Gingerly, he produced a photograph, turned its picture side down and passed it across the table.

"Take a look at it, Cranston," he suggested. "But don't spoil my meal by turning it in this direction. You'll see the face and the mark on the forehead."

The Shadow studied the photograph. It showed the face of Manuel Fendoza as the patrolman had viewed it the night before. The picture was a large one; it was almost as horrible as the face itself. The photograph, however, produced a gleam of interest in The Shadow's keen eyes. He made a careful study of the mark upon the forehead.

"Tell me, Commissioner," said The Shadow. "Has the dead man's face altered since this photograph was taken?"

A nod from Weston. The commissioner brought another picture from the briefcase.

"There is a shot that was taken this morning."

The Shadow eyed the second photograph. Two features intrigued him. One was the fact that Fendoza's face, though still distorted, had dulled. It no longer showed the lifelike glare that would have befitted a demon. The other point was the mark upon the forehead. It was more conspicuous than before. The reason for both changes seemed to be explained by a shrinkage that had come to the dead man's flesh.

"You seem to relish those photographs, Cranston," laughed Weston. "Have you ever seen any like them?"

"I have," responded The Shadow, quietly. "In fact, I have seen actual faces that were contorted like this one."

"Where was that?"

"In Ecuador. Commissioner, this dead man resembles those who have been victims of the Jibaro headhunters. He appears to have died from the virulent poison which the Jibaros use."

"You mean those chaps who shrink the heads of their victims and keep them as miniature souvenirs?"

"Precisely! The Jibaros apply the same substance to the heads, after death."

Weston thwacked the table with his fist. He delivered a long laugh.

"That would be a story for the newspapers," chuckled the commissioner. "Jibaro headhunters, stalking the streets of New York! Only one trouble, though, Cranston." Weston sobered, and spoke with mock seriousness. "They wouldn't swallow it, even if I told them that I believed it."

"By which I infer," remarked The Shadow, "that you reject my theory."

"You have inferred correctly," smiled Weston. "That man was stabbed to death, Cranston. We have the stiletto that was thrust through his heart."

The Shadow returned the photographs without comment. Weston packed them away in his briefcase. He glanced at his watch; decided that he would chance a return trip to his office. A few minutes later, he was on his way.

AN hour later, The Shadow left the Cobalt Club. He entered a waiting limousine; gave the chauffeur an order. The big car drove slowly through Manhattan streets. The day was gloomy; dusk had settled when the limousine reached an almost deserted street.

The figure that alighted silently bore no resemblance to Lamont Cranston. During the ride, The Shadow had donned garments of black. Cloaked, with slouch hat on his head, he was like a phantasm amid the dying daylight. Even the chauffeur did not detect his exit.

For a moment, The Shadow was visible as he crossed the sidewalk; then he was gone, beneath the gloom of a dingy building. A silent alleyway marked his route; but from the point, his course was untraceable.

Soon a click sounded amid darkness. A bluish light glowed within the corner of a black-walled room. White hands came beneath the glow. The Shadow was in his sanctum, the lone abode that formed his hidden headquarters in Manhattan.

Hands moved away from the light. When they returned, they carried half a dozen photographs and spread them on the table. Faces glared upward toward the hidden eyes of The Shadow. Those photographs looked like a gallery of demons.

Every picture displayed a countenance as contorted as that of Manuel Fendoza. Each had been touched by the same grim death that had struck the man from Santander. These were the photographs of dead men whom The Shadow had seen; the ones whom he had mentioned to the police commissioner. They were the hapless victims of Jibaro headhunters.

Not only were those victims rendered alike in death, so much so that their own identities seemed gone; in addition, each carried an unmistakable mark upon his forehead. It was the three-line symbol: two cross bars with the slashed diagonal.

Another set of pictures came into the light. They were pictures of the same victims, taken later. As with Fendoza, each had undergone a relaxation. Skin was shrunken; the symbols on the foreheads were more conspicuous.

Commissioner Weston would have expressed surprise had he seen those photographs. Perhaps some of his ridicule would have faded. But those pictures were to remain within The Shadow's files. Weston had passed up his chance.

The Shadow removed the photograph. He returned with a large-scale map that showed the northern section of South America; also stacks of clippings that he placed to one side. Studying the map, he placed a long finger upon the newly formed republic of Santander, which was close to Ecuador.

From the clippings, The Shadow produced a batch that referred to Santander. During the past few years, that country had been governed by a dictator, old José Rentone. A famous champion of liberty, José Rentone had been the idol of his people; but since his death, one month ago, revolution had been rife in Santander.

With the clippings that gave the life story of José Rentone, The Shadow found a small one that had appeared recently in a New York newspaper. It mentioned that Alvarez Rentone, grandson of the dead dictator, had arrived in New York and was stopping at a Manhattan hotel. Written on the clipping was the notation: "Hotel Goliath."

With the cooperation of his agents, The Shadow kept extensive files concerning all news that might have any bearing upon crime. South American revolutions frequently extended their ripples to the United States. Therefore, The Shadow had not neglected them.

Today, one lead had brought another. Newspaper reports of a mysterious stabbing had mentioned the distorted face of a victim. The Shadow had seen photographs of the dead man, had recognized that he could be a South American instead of an Italian.

Shrunken skin, the tri-marked forehead, had pointed to the Jibaro headhunters. A check on Ecuador had brought The Shadow to a consideration of Santander; he had further checked the fact that Alvarez Rentone, grandson of the dead Santander dictator, was registered at the Hotel Goliath.

Only a few blocks lay between the Hotel Goliath and the spot where the body of Manuel Fendoza had been found. The chain had become a circle. The Shadow could see a connection between the dead man and Alvarez Rentone. In fact, The Shadow was positive that Fendoza had encountered death either while on his way to the Hotel Goliath or shortly after leaving it.

THE bluish light clicked off. Unfathomable darkness gripped the sanctum. From the darkened depths came the whispered tone of a sinister laugh, that faded to leave absolute silence. The Shadow had departed.

Since Commissioner Weston had rejected The Shadow's theory, The Shadow knew that he could expect no immediate cooperation from the law. Any effort to push the police to a trail that Weston regarded as absurd would be worse than futile.

This case demanded lone effort, of the sort that The Shadow could provide. Slender threads must be tightened; small clues built into great ones. By the time such was achieved, the police would be through with their own futile search for an Italian assassin. They would be ready to follow new and stronger leads when they received them.

Tonight, working upon pure speculation, The Shadow had only one course; yet its very simplicity promised results. The Shadow knew Manuel Fendoza only as a man who had undoubtedly tried to contact Alvarez Rentone and had received death for his effort.

That meant that death might threaten others who attempted the same contact. To deliver death, murderers would be forced to show their hand. The Shadow intended to follow the course that Fendoza had chosen. He was ready to dare a horrible death to learn the source from which it came.

CHAPTER III
THE MESSAGE OF DOOM

DARKNESS had settled when The Shadow alighted from his limousine, in the vicinity of Times Square. During his return ride in the big car, he had divested himself of his blackened garments. That equipment was safely stowed beneath the rear seat of the limousine. The Shadow had again assumed the character of Lamont Cranston.

Strolling to a side street, The Shadow approached a parked cab. The driver was absent; that fact discouraged would-be passengers from boarding that particular taxi. Nevertheless, The Shadow entered the deserted cab. He pulled the door shut; let it swing half open; then gave a final tug that closed it.

A shrewd-faced cabby arrived immediately from a side-arm restaurant. He had spied the motion of the cab door; he knew it as a signal. This cab was The Shadow's own. Its driver was employed in his service. As soon as the driver was behind the wheel, he heard quiet-toned orders from the passenger.

The cab headed for the Hotel Goliath.

Since his departure from the sanctum, The Shadow had formulated complete plans. He had contacted agents to work with him, because his own part demanded that he bluff any watchers who might be at the Hotel Goliath. The Shadow was sure that surveillance would commence as soon as he inquired for Alvarez Rentone.

The cab reached its destination. The Shadow stepped beneath the marquee of the Hotel Goliath; waited until the cab had pulled away. He entered the lobby; saw the information desk and strolled toward it. As he approached, he spied a clean-cut young man seated in a chair near the desk. This chap looked like a guest at the hotel. He was reading a newspaper, apparently oblivious to persons who went past his lobby chair.

The young man was Harry Vincent, one of The

Shadow's agents. Harry's interest in the newspaper was genuine. His duty here would not begin until he received a signal. That was due to come.

Stopping at the desk, The Shadow made inquiry. His tone, though modulated, had a peculiar carrying quality. It reached the ears of Harry Vincent.

"Is Mr. Alvarez Rentone stopping here?"

The girl behind the desk made prompt answer to The Shadow's query. She was the same girl who had been on duty the night before. Ordinarily, she might not have remembered facts concerning one particular guest at the huge hotel; but the name of Alvarez Rentone had impressed her because it was unusual.

"Sorry, sir," responded the girl. "Mr. Rentone is out of town. We do not know when he will return."

"He left no message?"

"He left a message; but a gentleman called for it last night. I am sorry, sir, but—"

The girl paused suddenly. She had remembered Alvarez Rentone's room number. Glancing methodically toward the pigeonhole mailboxes, she saw an envelope projecting from 1282. It was identical with the envelope that Manuel Fendoza had taken.

Puzzled, the girl brought the envelope from the mailbox. With it was a penciled memo, which she tossed into the wastebasket. She handed the envelope to The Shadow with the remark:

"This was left with the day clerk. The memo says that it is to be given to anyone who inquires for Mr. Rentone."

Nodding in Cranston's leisurely fashion, The Shadow held the envelope between his hands. He turned slightly, so that the action could be viewed from the lobby. The Shadow noted people from the corner of his eye; but none was watching him.

Carrying the envelope, he strolled to the side exit; there he paused to eye the envelope once more. In indifferent fashion, he placed it in his inside pocket and walked out to the street.

HARRY VINCENT, meanwhile, was glancing over the top of his newspaper, on sharp lookout for any observers. At the moment when The Shadow pocketed the envelope, Harry caught a glimpse of a tall, blond-haired man who had just stepped from the door of the taproom, some distance from the information desk. He saw the fellow become tense; glance quickly toward the mailboxes behind the desk. It was Cardell, the same watcher who had spied Fendoza.

Cardell had been caught off watch. The Shadow, noting no lookout, had suspected that a watcher might be away from his post. The Shadow had deliberately delayed departure, as far as possible, without overdoing the ruse. His method had worked. Cardell was quick to snap up The Shadow's trail.

Harry saw the light-haired man scowl viciously; then hurry to the street. Since Cardell's attention was concentrated on The Shadow, Harry had an opportunity of his own. Rising from his chair, he tucked his newspaper under his arm. Pausing for a few moments, he waited while two chance passers went toward the side exit. Harry followed behind them.

Though scarcely more than a minute had passed, events had swung too swiftly for Harry. He thought that he would be in time to observe the actions of the light-haired watcher. Harry was wrong in that surmise.

As he reached the street, Harry saw a cab swing the corner. It was The Shadow's taxi; it had rounded the block and parked to await his reappearance. A sedan was pulling from the curb, headed for the same corner. Simultaneously, a cab was starting from beside the hotel.

Cardell had reached the street in time to see The Shadow step aboard his cab. Flashing a signal to men in the waiting sedan, Cardell had immediately taken a cab himself. Harry saw the pursuing sedan swing left after The Shadow's cab. He watched Cardell's taxi turn right. A hunch gave Harry the answer to this procedure.

Murderers had taken up The Shadow's trail. The watcher who had handed them the tip-off was on his way elsewhere. He would not return to the Hotel Goliath until assured that death had been delivered and that all clues had been eliminated.

Walking back into the lobby, Harry came to the conclusion that his presence here would be of no further avail. For Harry Vincent was confident that assassins would not deal with The Shadow as they had with Manuel Fendoza.

RIDING southward in his cab, The Shadow had quickly noted that a car was on his trail. His lips phrased a whispered laugh as he reached for a bag upon the floor. Murderers had taken the bait that The Shadow had given them. Emergency might soon arrive; The Shadow was preparing for it.

From the bag, he produced black attire; donned it and slid a brace of huge automatics into holsters beneath his cloak. Edging to a side of the rear seat, he looked back to see the sedan only a quarter block behind. The Shadow whispered an order to the driver. The cab swung right at the next street. It was heading for an avenue where traffic would be less.

The Shadow had drawn black gloves over his hands. From beneath his cloak, he brought the envelope that he had received at the Hotel Goliath. Carefully, he opened it, glimmered a tiny flashlight upon the contents. The envelope was identical with the one that Fendoza had received. It contained a stiff, sharp-edged card.

The Shadow did not make Fendoza's mistake.

He was careful as he drew the card from the envelope. Despite that fact, he could not avoid contact with the sharp edge. The paper had been tapered to almost knife-edge keenness. The Shadow, however, was equipped against the cutting edge. His hands were gloved.

Though the card edge actually jabbed through the cloth, The Shadow's glove was sufficient to protect his finger. He sensed the razor keenness; carefully shifted his hand. He let the flashlight glow along the edge of the card. There, The Shadow detected a faint brownish stain.

The card had been painted with the juice of poisonous herbs known to the Jibaro headhunters. Fendoza's sudden death was explained. The dead man had received a card like this one at the Hotel Goliath, last night. The remark made by the girl at the information desk was sufficient to prove that fact.

As The Shadow carefully replaced the blank card in its envelope, he calculated an important time element. He decided that last night's victim must have died within fifteen minutes after he had opened the envelope. Therefore, the trailers in the sedan would expect similar results tonight.

That meant that if The Shadow's cab did not stop soon, the pursuers would overhaul it. They might attempt an attack at some secluded spot, hoping for the opportunity to jab a stiletto into a dead body. False clues were important to their game.

An encounter with the murderers would be a setup for The Shadow. The killers would find a live antagonist, instead of a dead one. They would meet a battler who expected them; who could deal with greater odds than any they might produce. But The Shadow saw disadvantages as a sequel to such a fray.

The Shadow was sure that the men who followed him were mere tools in the employ of a master murderer. To eliminate them would be a double mistake. The master crook would know that his plans had failed. Chance for a trail to the superkiller would be lost.

The Shadow had a better plan; there was still time to employ it. This was no ordinary cab in which The Shadow rode; nor was the driver simply an average cabby. Moe Shrevnitz, the man at the wheel, had been chosen by The Shadow because he was one of the most capable cab drivers in New York; the cab, itself, was geared for high speed and specially equipped for camouflage.

LEANING to the front window, The Shadow gave an order that brought a pleased grin from Moe. The driver gave the accelerator a jolt. The cab increased its speed. Looking back, The Shadow saw the lights of the sedan drop away; then hurry along to keep pace with the taxi.

The increase in speed did not arouse the suspicion of the followers. It merely signified that the passenger in the cab was probably anxious to reach some destination. That was actually the case. The Shadow had spurred the cab ahead in order to gain the twisted streets of the old Greenwich Village section of New York before his fifteen-minute interval was finished.

Those thoroughfares were the very sort that The Shadow needed for his coming strategy. Moe knew them like a book.

A few minutes later, the cab swung from the avenue. It struck a short street that formed an angle; made a sharp turn a block farther on. Another half block, the cab doubled on its course; staged a quick right turn and came to a stop.

The door opened; The Shadow stepped to the sidewalk of a narrow Greenwich Village street. He spoke an order; the cab rolled away.

Soon after the taxi had turned a corner, the sedan appeared and came to a halt. The Shadow had stepped to a low, obscure doorway. Half behind a flight of descending steps, he watched the sedan's behavior. It waited a few moments; then pulled slowly ahead. It turned the next corner, but took the wrong direction.

The Shadow stepped up from the doorway. He moved back along the street, found a new lurking spot and remained there.

Five minutes passed; the sedan came hesitatingly around the corner. It had evidently circled a few blocks, stopping frequently. As the sedan rolled by, The Shadow could tell that its occupants intended to scour this district further.

Taking advantage of the sedan's new departure, The Shadow moved swiftly along the next street. He neared the front of a large apartment house and waited across the way. Soon, a cab pulled up near the apartment building. It was Moe's cab; but only The Shadow could have recognized it.

The top was down, making it an open cab instead of a closed one. One of the two rear lights had been removed. Conspicuous lettering, of washable paint, had been wiped from the cab's side; also a row of checkered ornamentation had been obliterated. As a final and most important touch, the license plates had been changed to show a new number.

Gliding across a darkened sector of the street, The Shadow stepped aboard the cab. Deep in the rear seat, he watched. He saw the sedan come from a corner at increased speed. The Shadow gave Moe the order to follow.

The sedan had ended its hunt. Threading through the streets, the driver had found a route out from the twisted thoroughfares of the Village. The sedan reached an avenue; turned northward. Half a minute later, Moe's cab nosed forth to take up the trail.

Followers had lost The Shadow. The sedan's chase was ended. The driver of the car was heading somewhere to report that he had lost all traces of a cab that was carrying a new victim. Yet, while he sped to that mission, the driver who had trailed The Shadow was providing a trail of his own.

In the very same cab in which he had given the sedan the slip, The Shadow was pursuing the quarry that he wanted. The message of doom had failed to deliver death. By avoiding its poisoned edge, The Shadow had picked up a route that could lead back to the master murderer who dealt in demonish death.

CHAPTER IV
BETWEEN THE KILLERS

FIVE minutes pursuit of the northward-bound sedan was proof that the driver of the car did not know that he was being trailed. That was not surprising; crooks seldom guessed that Moe's cab was tailing them.

Thanks to the pick-up of the special taxi, its ability to wheel corners at high speed, Moe was able to fall back without losing the trail. He could always make up for lost ground through spurts of speedy driving; furthermore, he had tricky ways of keeping behind intervening cars, whenever he closed in upon his quarry.

Reclining deep in the rear seat, The Shadow kept tabs upon Moe's methods. At last, he gave a warning signal, and the taxi driver slackened speed. The Shadow had noted that the sedan was nearing the end of its trip; for it had hesitated momentarily while passing a street corner. This was the time for the cab to lie back.

The sedan's driver found the street he wanted. He swung left. When the cab reached the corner, The Shadow sighted the sedan pulling into a garage halfway down the block. The taxi halted in front of a darkened house. The Shadow silently alighted. He approached the door of the garage.

No attendants were in sight. The sedan was in the center of the floor; one man was cautiously alighting from it. By dim illumination, The Shadow could spy a darkish face; eyes that showed a scowl as they looked about. The man straightened when he reached the garage floor; he was stocky and of more than medium height.

The Shadow expected him to beckon to some other occupant of the sedan. Instead, the man came alone toward the door of the garage, a proof that he had no companion with him.

The Shadow was back in darkness when the stocky man reached the street. The fellow paced rapidly along the sidewalk; The Shadow gave him sufficient leeway, then followed.

The trail was a short one; it ended before the next avenue. The stocky man came to an old house with high stone steps. Turning in, he went beneath the steps and entered a basement door.

The Shadow followed, to find the door unlocked. Entering a dim, gaslit passage, he heard the creak of footsteps on stairs. He followed upward; reached a dim, ground-floor hall, where doors were closed. He heard footsteps going to the second floor. As they faded, The Shadow again followed.

He reached the top of the stairs just in time to hear a door close. Picking the direction of the sound, The Shadow noted a door at the rear of the hall. It was closed; but light glimmered from beneath.

Approaching the door, The Shadow heard subdued voices from within. He knew that this must be a rooming house; hence any occupants engaged in crime would be cautious in their conversation. The Shadow had not heard the turn of a key in the lock; hence he saw opportunity to listen and observe the speakers as well.

With one gloved hand, he tried the doorknob. Soon, the door yielded imperceptibly to his touch. It opened inward, the scant fraction of an inch. The Shadow peered into the room.

THERE, he saw two men. One was the light-haired lookout whom Harry Vincent had spied at the Hotel Goliath. The other was the darkish sedan driver whom The Shadow had followed from the garage. Their conversation promptly disclosed their identities.

"You should not have lost him, Marinez," growled the light-haired man. "I gave you the tip-off quick enough. Why didn't you close in on the cab sooner?"

"Ah, Senor Cardell," returned Marinez, his teeth gleaming as he spoke, "the man is not yet lost. He must have reached the place where he intended to go. Quinqual will find him."

"Maybe, if the guy dropped dead on the street. But suppose he lives in the Village? What if he went into some apartment there? Quinqual won't be able to locate him, if that's the case."

Marinez shrugged his shoulders. Cardell changed his tone.

"If he's dead, that's the main thing," decided Cardell. "But it would have been great stuff to keep the police guessing. That's the way Zenjora wanted it."

"Emilio Zenjora is one man who has great brain," reminded Marinez. "What are police to him? They are nothing. Bah! You should know that, Senor Cardell. Like myself, Senor, you have seen Zenjora make the great fool of generals and soldiers."

"In Santander, yes," agreed Cardell. "But this is New York, Marinez. I'd handle a half dozen of those uniformed monkeys they call soldiers in Santander. But I wouldn't tackle a pair of New York cops at one crack."

DURING the pause that followed, The Shadow

summarized the facts that he had heard. The name of Emilio Zenjora was one that he had immediately recognized. It told him the identity of the super-crook with whom he had to deal; also the unusual sort of foeman who had begun a reign of crime.

Emilio Zenjora had been mentioned in news reports from Santander. He was an outlaw who had been banished from the capital city after an attempt to overthrow the government of José Rentone. Instead of accepting his banishment with good grace, Zenjora had established headquarters in the jungle near the border of Ecuador. From that base, he had made raids upon various cities; and had twice started new revolutions that had been curbed.

Since the death of José Rentone, Emilio Zenjora had not been heard from. This had caused various rumors. One had it that Zenjora was dead; another, that he was waiting until different political factions had so weakened each other that Zenjora could come from his jungle stronghold and seize the reins of government.

A third—and more definite report—was that the Lepres faction, at present the strongest in Santander, had negotiated with Zenjora. The outlaw had presumably been bribed to remain away from the capital; perhaps to wait, in reserve, until Pedro Lepres, new president of Santander, needed him.

None of these reports had carried any inkling of the remarkable truth that had just reached The Shadow, namely, that Emilio Zenjora was in the United States. Zenjora's purpose in New York unquestionably concerned Alvarez Rentone, grandson of the late dictator. Therefore, it could have a political significance, linked with recent developments in Santander.

As for Zenjora's ways of crime, the death of Manuel Fendoza had already demonstrated the supercrook's ability. The fact that Zenjora was in a strange land did not make him less dangerous. In fact, The Shadow was prepared to regard Zenjora as a more powerful foe for that very reason.

As a sample of Zenjora's cunning, The Shadow held a specimen of the little-known Jibaro poison that Zenjora used for murder. Commissioner Weston, head of the law forces that were supposed to combat such men as Zenjora, was inclined to regard the Jibaro poison as a myth.

WATCHING Marinez and Cardell, The Shadow counted upon some new clue from their conversation. All that he needed was a lead to Zenjora's present whereabouts. None came; but as the lieutenants resumed their talk, they unwittingly furnished further facts.

"Zenjora expected Fendoza in New York," remarked Cardell. "Well, Fendoza came here. You and Quinqual handled him like clockwork, Marinez."

"Gracias," returned Marinez with a grin. "It is good to hear you commend me, Senor."

"I'll take back that bouquet," growled Cardell. "On account of tonight. You should have bagged this second man, Marinez."

"Perhaps so. But you have also slipped, Senor."

"How do you figure that?"

"You did not learn the name of the man whom you saw tonight."

Cardell eyed Marinez suspiciously. The Shadow knew why. Cardell had not been close on the job tonight. Perhaps Marinez had guessed the fact. Cardell decided to change the subject.

"You'd better go over and see Zenjora," he told Marinez. "I'll stay away from the Goliath until after you've seen him. Then I'll give him a call. Maybe Zenjora won't want me to go back to the hotel."

"Why not, Senor?"

"Because if Quinqual don't find the guy that took the note tonight, the police may. Perhaps they'll get a lead that he was at the Goliath. That poison message might make trouble, if they find it and make inquiries at the hotel."

Cardell was rising. The Shadow edged back from the door. Just as he was about to close it, he heard Marinez make a last remark:

"Very well, Senor Cardell. I shall wait here a little while, in case that Quinqual returns. Then I shall go to see Zenjora."

The knob was turned; The Shadow had stepped to a darkened passage past the door; when Cardell made his exit. The blond-haired man looked back and forth along the hall; but his inspection was a brief one. He was more interested in eying closed doors than in viewing darkened corners. Cardell caught no sight of The Shadow.

Nor did The Shadow make an effort to trail this lieutenant of Zenjora. There was more to learn through watching Marinez. The darkish lieutenant had stated that he intended to contact Zenjora. That was the trail that The Shadow wanted.

THERE was a stir within the room. Listening at the closed door, The Shadow decided that Marinez was packing his few belongings, probably supposing that Zenjora would order him to move to another hideout. There was a slight, thuddish click that indicated the placing of a revolver on a table. The pacing; the crackle of a flame.

Marinez was probably burning some papers that he did not care to carry on his person. The Shadow listened closely, ready to move away the moment that he heard Marinez approach the door.

Perhaps it was that intentness that prevented The Shadow from hearing a creak upon the stairs. Possibly it was because the creak itself was barely audible. Whichever the case, The Shadow did not

**Upon the topmost step was a crouched figure.... The Shadow's eyes...
glinted as they saw the menace...**

ence in New York; it also indicated strife among Zenjora's own followers. The real reason for Marinez's death did not occur to Alvarez. He would have been amazed to know that a mysterious avenger called The Shadow had stepped into the game.

EVENTS were brewing that were to render Alvarez Rentone completely helpless, particularly since he had no knowledge of them. Others than The Shadow were at work that day. Late afternoon produced their culmination, in a sumptuous apartment high above Manhattan.

There, by a window, a tall, broad-shouldered man gazed toward the city lights that twinkled early beneath a clouded sky. The glow was palled by a lowering fog that stirred in slowly from the harbor. Night's approach was sinister; it boded an evening suited to crime. That pleased the watcher from the window.

The man's bulky build was accentuated by the fullness of his face. He was heavily bearded; his lower face formed a thick black brush of hair. The beard was well kept, cut to a perfect spade shape.

Darkish skin seemed light against the matted black of the beard. A high-bridged nose gave its owner the appearance of a vulture; sharp, glistening eyes increased the likeness to a bird of prey. Above a high forehead was thick hair, as well groomed as the beard.

The evil smile of large red lips, plain despite the beard, gave the man a satanic expression. Scores of unfortunate persons could have testified to the cruelty of that smile. None remained, however, of those who had fallen into this monster's toils. Death had been the ultimate lot of all who had ever been captured by Emilio Zenjora.

In this high apartment, Zenjora was as much at home as in the mountain strongholds of Santander. His eyes glinted with cunning; his lips leered contempt of the city that lay spread below. Zenjora liked New York; thrusts were easy in the confines of this great city. Retreat was a simple matter, when the thrusts were done. The metropolis formed a perfect setting for Zenjora's methods of evil.

Hearing the shuffle of footsteps, Zenjora wheeled suddenly from the window. He waited; smiled as he recognized the footfalls. Cardell arrived from another room. Zenjora waved his lieutenant to a chair.

"Bad news, chief," growled Cardell. "I've just come from Oakbrook's apartment house. He hasn't returned there."

"It is not late," purred Zenjora, his lips pursing as he spoke. "Perhaps he has been detained at his office."

"I faked a business call there. They say Oakbrook left for a vacation. He's wise to

something. I'll bet that Alvarez has seen him. We ought to have kept tabs on Alvarez, chief."

Zenjora's smile hardened. The supercrook did not relish suggestions from subordinates. Cardell became apologetic. Zenjora's smile relaxed.

"You have failed to understand my strategy," purred the bearded man, his eyes sharp as they studied Cardell. "We knew that Alvarez Rentone left the Hotel Goliath, fearing that he would be watched. He chose the Clearview Hotel, knowing that he could observe strangers. Therefore, I decided not to watch him; I wanted to lull him into the belief that he was safe. We watched the Goliath, however, and thereby eliminated Manuel Fendoza. We should have done the same with another visitor who came to the Goliath."

Cardell winced. Zenjora saw the strained expression of his lieutenant's face.

"You fear The Shadow," scoffed Zenjora. "I do not fear him! My ways are his! I stalk my prey as does The Shadow!"

"Quinqual didn't get The Shadow, though," objected Cardell. "And we've lost Marinez."

"Quinqual did not expect The Shadow. He will be prepared in the future. So will Incos and my other headhunters. I have four Jibaros, Cardell. As for Marinez, he was a poor lieutenant. Bandrillo is better. Tonight, we shall eliminate Alvarez Rentone. We can deal with Oakbrook when he returns to New York."

ZENJORA turned to stare from the window. Increased dusk brought a new leer to his lips. Still looking outward, Zenjora purred new statements.

"We have ceased to cover the Hotel Goliath," he declared, "because of The Shadow. Therefore, should another visitor come there, we could not molest him. Such a visitor might learn where Alvarez is. The Shadow, too, may learn. So I shall reverse my policy. Since Alvarez suspects danger, we shall watch him. I shall order Quinqual and Incos to that task."

Cardell grinned. He was willing to wager that Alvarez Rentone would never gain an inkling that watchers were close by. The Jibaro headhunters had methods of keeping undercover that were as effective in New York as in the South American jungle.

"We have arranged for Alvarez Rentone and James Oakbrook," declared Zenjora, methodically. "We shall consider others on our list. There is one who must be eliminated early. That man is Howard Dundee. If Fendoza's body is identified, Dundee may report to the police that Fendoza called him by telephone and referred to Alvarez Rentone."

Turning from the window, Zenjora hardened his tone with the order: "Call Quinqual and Incos. I shall assign them to their new duty."

NICK BROGGOLETTA, assassin, and ALVAREZ RENTONE, grandson of the former dictator of Santander, opposed one against the other in this weird battle.

THERE was reason for Zenjora to watch Alvarez Rentone. He, himself, had learned of Alvarez's new lodging. What the master crook had discovered, The Shadow might find. Proof of this very fact lay elsewhere in Manhattan, where a wiry young man was seated at a rear table in a small Spanish restaurant, talking confidentially to the mustached proprietor.

"It's a big story, Francisco," the young man was saying. "An interview with Alvarez Rentone, grandson of the late Santander dictator. It's the kind of stuff the *Classic* likes."

"Ah, Senor Burke," shrugged Francisco. "You are an *amigo,* a friend that I have known long. But I have told you too much. You ask me when Alvarez Rentone has come here to eat, last time; where he has gone since then. I ask you: *'Quien sabe?* Who can tell?' But you say you have wait all afternoon to speak of it with me.

"So I tell you I have taken a special Spanish dish, of which I am very proud, to the Clearview Hotel. That was two days ago. *Si. Dos dios,* I remember. I gave it to the man you call the clerk; I hear him say to the bellboy that it was for Meestaire Rentone."

"Thanks, Francisco." The wiry young man gripped the Spaniard's hand. "There'll be no comeback. When I see Alvarez, I won't mention that I learned where he was through you. He'll never think that the tip-off came from a restaurant where he ordered dinner by telephone."

Outside the restaurant, the wiry young man walked quickly to a telephone. He had learned important news. Clyde Burke was more than a newspaper reporter, on the staff of the New York *Classic.* He was also an agent of The Shadow.

By telephone, Clyde passed the facts along to Burbank, The Shadow's contact man. Clyde knew that the word would soon reach The Shadow.

SOON afterward, the desk clerk at the Clearview received a telephone call asking for Alvarez Rentone. He gave Alvarez's room number as 308, but added that the guest was out.

That was the second call the clerk had received; each had been in a different voice. What worried him was the fact that no one was supposed to know that Alvarez was at the Clearview. But the clerk had no instructions in case persons called up and asked. Thinking that they must be confidential friends of Alvarez's, he had given the information.

The Clearview Hotel fronted on a quiet street. Odd-shaped, the hotel had a broad front; but the extension that went through to the rear street was only half width. The rest of the space formed a courtyard. Access was easy, for there was a broad alley between the front of the hotel and an old, deserted theater next door.

Twenty minutes after the clerk had received the second call, a taxi passed the Clearview Hotel. Keen eyes peered from the rear window; a passenger whispered an important order. The cab circled the block, paused at the deserted theater. From the door glided a blackish figure that sought the shelter of darkness beneath a battered marquee.

The cab pulled away, but the shape glided onward. It neared the alleyway and entered. The Shadow had found the element he wanted; completely obscured in darkness, he was planning a visit to the hotel room occupied by Alvarez Rentone.

From the rear courtyard, The Shadow saw the outline of a fire escape against the dull glow that filtered through the increasing fog. He saw window lights in the hotel that indicated crosswise corridors. They showed that the fire escape could be reached by short passages from those main halls. Finding the hinged extension of the fire escape, The Shadow drew it down without noise.

Ascending to the third floor, The Shadow avoided entry by the passage. Instead, he went across the rail and moved along a stone cornice. Gripping the wall with clutching fingers, he passed two windows. One was lighted, with shade drawn; the next was dark. The Shadow moved slowly as he passed a third room, also dark. He stopped at a fourth window.

If The Shadow's calculations were correct, this room would be 308. Raising an unlocked sash, The Shadow entered. He used a flashlight on a telephone; saw the number 308. Calmly The Shadow awaited the return of Alvarez Rentone.

FIFTEEN minutes passed. Then a slight sound occurred. It was the click of a key in the door of the room. Close beside the wall, The Shadow waited. The door did not open; the key sounded again. This time, it rattled.

Instantly, The Shadow knew that the arrival was not Alvarez. He could tell that a skeleton key was in the lock. Someone was trying to effect an entry before Alvarez returned. Whether the entrant would be friend or foe to Alvarez was something that The Shadow intended to determine.

As the key turned, The Shadow drew an automatic. Whoever entered would be due for questioning; and kept here until Alvarez arrived. The Shadow's purpose was definite. He expected no difficulty.

Strange events were in the making beyond that opening door. Once more, The Shadow was due for a struggle that would tax him to the utmost.

Though the mere entrance of an unknown person did not betray the fact, the hand of Emilio Zenjora lay hidden in the background.

CHAPTER VII
THRUSTS THROUGH THE DARK

THE door of the room moved slowly inward. It paused, as though hesitating of its own accord. Against the framed light of the corridor, The Shadow saw a squatty form. He could not distinguish the entrant's face; for the light was behind the man.

A hand reached inward to the wall, probing for a light switch. That delay gave The Shadow an opportunity that he wanted. He had waited to view the man from the hall, to see if the fellow made a sudden move or acted as if he thought someone was within. Since the intruder was unaware of The Shadow's presence, The Shadow had chance for an excellent move.

Gliding along the darkness of the side wall, he reached the front wall of the room. There, he placed himself on a line with the man at the doorway. The door, half opened, lay as a barrier between.

Cautiously, the squatty man began to shut the door behind him. He left it open a few inches, keeping one hand upon the knob. His free hand found the light switch.

A *click* sounded. Side brackets illuminated the room. With the door no longer blocking, The Shadow saw the face of the man who had entered. It was an ugly, broad-nosed countenance that boasted puffy lips and squinty eyes.

The man's dark hair was an unkempt mass. His clothes were rough and baggy. He looked like a marauder who had sneaked in through the tawdry lobby of this old hotel. As the man's face turned, The Shadow saw a reddish scar that ran halfway across his face, on a line with his upper lip.

That mark told the man's identity. The Shadow recognized him as Nick Broggoletta, a notorious assassin.

Broggoletta was the sort who killed for hire. As such, he had served various big-shots, by disposing of henchmen who had double-crossed them. His murders had saved the police considerable trouble; nevertheless, the law had tried to pin the deaths on Broggoletta. The law had failed to do so. Nick had always been clever enough to cover up his trail.

Lately, Nick had lain low. His hideout was known; but he had presumably ended his ways of crime. Yesterday, Inspector Cardona had quizzed him regarding the death of Manuel Fendoza. For once, Nick Broggoletta had shown a clean slate. Tonight, however, the killer had bobbed into the game. Nick's entry was puzzling, even to The Shadow.

The Shadow intended to gain the answer shortly. He was waiting only until Nick closed the door completely. Then The Shadow intended to greet the assassin with the muzzle of a .45. Like most hired assassins, Nick was the sort who would turn yellow when trapped. The Shadow had dealt with his ilk before. Hired killers were usually paid in advance. They had little to lose by squealing on the man who had employed them.

A FEW seconds more, Nick would have found himself staring into the mouth of The Shadow's leveled automatic. Something occurred, however, to change the course of events.

Nick heard a peculiar sound from the corridor. He pulled the door inward; the space of six inches. He turned to peer out into the hall. As he did, he saw The Shadow, past the inner edge of the door.

Through sheer instinct, the killer performed an unexpected action. His hand was on the end of the door; wildly, Nick swung it inward. Speeding on its hinges, the door rammed straight toward The Shadow, who was starting forward in response to Nick's move. The Shadow sidestepped. The edge of the door thwacked his shoulder. The Shadow was jolted halfway to the floor.

Broggoletta whipped a long stiletto from beneath his jacket. He sprang forward, driving the weapon in a long, underhand thrust.

Resting on one hand, The Shadow swung the other up from the floor. His fist held its heavy gun; the .45 cracked Broggoletta's forearm. The assassin's stroke went wide.

Spinning, Nick made a wild dive through the doorway. The Shadow swung to aim. Before he could fire, there was a wild cry from the corridor. The Shadow saw Broggoletta stop short. With the killer's halt, there came a whizzing *swish* from the end of the corridor.

A pointed weapon drove deep into Broggoletta's shoulder. The killer staggered backward; before he could rally, another sound came from the opposite direction. A second shaft struck the back of Broggoletta's neck; it quivered there, displaying its feathered stub.

The Shadow had seen such weapons before. They were bamboo darts like the one that Quinqual had hurled last night.

Though death had been slow with Fendoza, it was swift with Broggoletta. The drives from those stubby javelins delivered more than trivial cuts. Points of bamboo, dyed with their poison, had penetrated deep. Dropping his stiletto, Broggoletta plucked the first shaft from his shoulder; then vainly tried to tug the second from his neck.

Nick's fingers failed, as they clawed the feathered barb. The killer reeled; then sagged. His face turned toward the doorway. The Shadow saw eyes that bulged from their sockets; lips that writhed, then froze into an agonized leer.

Nick Broggoletta's countenance had become the counterpart of Manuel Fendoza's. The horror of a poison death was fully registered upon the killer's face.

Nick sprawled forward; as he struck, his body gave a sidewise roll. That jolt accomplished the deed that Nick had found futile. The flounder of the dead man's head threw weight upon the feathered end of the death shaft. The Jibaro weapon twisted free from Broggoletta's neck.

PADDED footsteps thudded in the corridor. An apish form appeared beside the corpse. The Shadow saw a vicious, large-toothed face. The arrival was a Jibaro—almost the twin of Quinqual. Only The Shadow could have detected the slight difference in the slope of this Jibaro's forehead.

This headhunter was Incos, whom Zenjora had ordered to act as Quinqual's teammate. If Incos had heard the sounds of Broggoletta's scuffle with The Shadow, he must have considered them unimportant; for the Jibaro did not look into the lighted room. Instead, Incos pulled a stiletto from beneath his ill-fitting coat. He rolled Broggoletta's body on its back, then jabbed the stiletto deep into the dead man's heart.

Grinning with his gritted teeth, Incos snatched up the feathered dart that had fallen from the neck of the corpse. He used it to make quick scratches on the dead man's forehead. The Shadow saw the Jibaro's arm slash twice across; then downward at an angle.

Steadily, The Shadow was shifting to the edge of the doorway, intending to be out of sight when Incos turned. Before he could reach that vantage point, oddly chattered words sounded in the corridor. Quinqual was giving advice to Incos. Instantly, Incos whipped about and stared into the lighted room.

The Jibaro saw The Shadow.

The action that followed was instantaneous. Incos performed in a style that differed from Quinqual's. With a twist, Incos came up from the floor; but instead of driving toward The Shadow, he gave a huge, sideward bound away from Broggoletta's body.

Incos wanted to retain the safety of the corridor. He also sought to gain an angled line along which to hurl his bamboo shaft. His arm swung back, then jabbed forward, while he was still in midair. His hand loosed the poisoned weapon with incredible speed.

Simultaneously, The Shadow acted with a swiftness that equalled the Jibaro's. He faded to the wall within the doorway, making a long dive that carried his body well beyond. To stop his swing, The Shadow shot his left hand forward; he hooked the door frame with his automatic. As the metal clicked the woodwork, The Shadow pulled the trigger.

The bamboo shaft whistled above The Shadow's fist; sped through emptiness where The Shadow's shoulder had been. Incos had launched a futile thrust. But the Jibaro's high, sidewise bound had served him well. The Shadow's levered aim was too much of a makeshift. His bullet zimmed an inch wide of the Jibaro's body.

Raising his right hand quickly, The Shadow extinguished the light switch. He whisked away into the darkness, none too soon. Quinqual had arrived from the corridor, scooping up his own shaft as he came.

Half into the doorway, Quinqual sped a sidearm throw, that even a bullet could not have stopped. With uncanny skill, the Jibaro picked the exact spot where The Shadow had been against the wall.

THE second dart found blankness. From the center of the blackened room, The Shadow answered with a quick gun stab. Had Quinqual paused, counting upon his accuracy with the shaft, he would have received a bullet as reward. But the Jibaro had left nothing to chance. He somersaulted as he made his throw; his rubbery body bounded clear beyond the doorway. Quinqual was following Incos. Like his teammate, Quinqual had hurled himself to safety a scant space ahead of The Shadow's gun blast.

The Shadow sprang to the doorway of the room, reached the corridor just in time to see Quinqual dive into the passage that led to the fire escape; a route that Incos had already taken. The Shadow pursued; when he reached the passage, Quinqual had already gained the fire escape.

The Shadow arrived at the metal rail, aimed his gun straight downward and blasted bullets through the open metal work. Even as he fired, he heard a thud in the darkness of the courtyard; then another.

Incos and Quinqual had both leaped from the metal steps, ahead of The Shadow's barrage. The jump was a dozen feet for Incos; twice that for Quinqual. Yet both Jibaros must have landed with equal ease, and made instant dives to cover. Although The Shadow fired in the direction of the sounds; produced a fresh automatic and boomed additional shots, his bullets found no targets. The Shadow could hear his slugs ricochet from the cement of the courtyard.

There were nooks and spaces below by which the Jibaros could reach the street undercover. Once again, The Shadow saw that pursuit was useless. His only course was to try and find Alvarez Rentone, in accordance with the original mission that he had chosen for this night.

The Shadow hurried back through the corridor; passed Broggoletta's body and entered Alvarez's room. Flicking his flashlight, he found the bamboo shafts. The Shadow gathered them as trophies, removing his gloves to twist them about the sharp points. Thus sheathed, the poisoned weapons went beneath The Shadow's cloak.

There was the clatter of an elevator door; shouts from the corridor; a *clang* as the door closed. The Shadow's gunfire had been heard below. Investigators, up from the lobby, had spied Broggoletta's body. Fearing danger, they were descending to summon the police.

The Shadow waited no longer. He made for the fire escape. His descent was swift.

When he reached the courtyard, The Shadow heard the whine of a patrol car. He still had opportunity to gain the front street. He used it. He reached the darkened space beneath the marquee of the theater just as a police car stopped in front of the hotel.

Another patrol car arrived. Police were entering the hotel; additional bluecoats were coming on foot. Ten seconds later, a taxi sped into view; it slackened speed with suddenness and rolled lazily to a stop in front of the deserted theater.

It was Moe's cab. The Shadow gained it with a quick glide.

FROM darkness within the cab, The Shadow watched the police spread. Three officers had entered the hotel; one was on guard in front. The others were making for the rear, through the alley by which The Shadow had come. None suspected that Moe's cab had an occupant. They thought that the driver had merely halted at sight of the commotion in front of the hotel.

People from the Clearview were gesticulating, as they explained matters to the patrolman who was on guard. None—not even the bluecoat—was concerned with events in the street. It was The Shadow alone who saw a cab come past and stop in front of the hotel.

The Shadow watched the door come halfway open; he saw the face of a young man that peered toward the group on the sidewalk. The young man's face was dark-complexioned. It bobbed back into the cab. A moment later, the taxi rolled away.

The Shadow knew that the arrival must be Alvarez Rentone. The young man from Santander had returned to his hotel, to discover confusion there. Alvarez had sensed that it might mean danger to himself. He was off to a new destination.

The Shadow spoke an order to Moe. The cab started; went slowly past the hotel, then gradually quickened speed as it neared the corner. Rounding into an avenue, Moe saw Alvarez's cab a block ahead. In his usual skillful fashion, Moe took up the pursuit.

Shrouded in darkness, The Shadow kept keen watch. He had found the trail he wanted. Sooner or later, it would end in a meeting with Alvarez Rentone. That meeting gained, The Shadow could learn the vital facts that he needed to combat Emilio Zenjora.

CHAPTER VIII
NEWS FROM SANTANDER

IT was after midnight. Heavy fog had set in, hours ago. Watching from the darkened window of a small apartment, Alvarez Rentone could not see the street below. That fact pleased him. Alvarez felt that he had found a new refuge.

A key clicked in the apartment door. Alvarez calmly lighted a floor lamp. He dropped into a comfortable armchair. He was gazing toward the door when it opened to admit a young man attired in a tuxedo.

The arrival was of husky build; his countenance was friendly and jocular. When he saw Alvarez, the young man stopped in surprise.

"Close the door, Lynn," suggested Alvarez, in a hoarse whisper. "What's that you have there? A morning newspaper?"

Lynn nodded, as he handed the newspaper to Alvarez.

"Just bought it at Times Square," said Lynn. "Boy! Is the fog thick down there! No use taking a cab. I had to come by subway. Say, Alvarez— what's up? Why did you come to my apartment?"

Alvarez pointed to the front page headlines. Lynn saw news of a new stiletto stabbing.

"I started to read it," he remarked. "Thought it might hook up with the one you spoke about. Only this fellow was a real Italian. Nick Broggoletta."

"Yes," agreed Alvarez, "but he was murdered at the Clearview. The newspaper doesn't happen to mention the hotel by name."

"They were after you, then?"

"I think so," declared Alvarez. "I figure it this way, Lynn. Fendoza was killed two nights ago. He was a loyal chap; but his connections in New York may have been bad ones—persons like this

Broggoletta. When Fendoza failed to reach me, Broggoletta made the attempt."

"Maybe not," disagreed Lynn. "Perhaps Broggoletta thought that you were responsible for Fendoza's death and came after you for vengeance."

"That's possible," admitted Alvarez, "but the main point is that Brogoletta was murdered by Zenjora's assassins. They must have learned that I was at the Clearview."

As Alvarez stared with troubled expression, Lynn suddenly remembered an important matter. From his tuxedo pocket he produced a letter that bore a Colombian postage stamp: It was addressed to Lynn Jefford; but Alvarez's friend had not opened it. Alvarez recognized the handwriting; gave an elated cry.

"The letter was at the club," smiled Lynn. "I expected to hear from you while I was at the banquet. Is it from Estaban?"

Alvarez nodded; he tore open the letter and scanned the contents. He imparted brief information to Lynn.

"Estaban received my message," stated Alvarez. "He is safe at San Luis. He sent this letter across the mountain, to be mailed from Bogotá, in Colombia."

Reading the letter once again, Alvarez nodded to himself. He struck a match, applied it to the letter and dropped the flaming paper into a metal wastebasket.

"You have been a true friend, Lynn," declared Alvarez. "An old school chum on whom I could rely. That is why I sent your name and the address of your club to Estaban, telling him to mail any letters to you.

"I have told you about my grandfather's fortune; that Estaban was to tell me where it was. I said also that I would have to communicate with a man in New York. Today, I saw that man and warned him of danger. He has left New York."

Alvarez did not mention James Oakbrook by name. He had deemed it best to keep Oakbrook's identity a secret, even from Lynn Jefford.

"Estaban's letter," resumed Alvarez, "has given me the location of the treasure, Lynn. I want you to help me gain it. This very night!"

THE news brought a prompt reaction from Lynn. "I'm game," he declared. "Only you'll be letting me in on the secret that—"

"I trust you, Lynn. The treasure is in New Jersey, near the town of Roselawn. There, we shall find an old estate, once owned by a man named Kincaid. Near the empty house is a mausoleum, that was never used. There is a secret opening in the stone floor; it leads to a vault below. The vault is sealed with an emblem that bears my grandfather's coat of arms."

Alvarez drew his watch from his pocket; displayed a heavy fob and pried it open. Inside, Lynn saw a gold seal the size of a half dollar.

"When do we start?"

Lynn put the query.

Alvarez smiled. "Right away," he replied. "That is, as soon as you have changed your clothes."

"I'll wear these duds," returned Lynn. "I'll phone the garage and tell them to send over the coupé."

"No, no!" exclaimed Alvarez. "I am afraid that I was followed here, Lynn, although I had a taxi driver take me all over town and drop me a block from this apartment house. Watchers may be hereabouts; they would observe any car that appeared at this hour. Let us go to the garage, instead of having the coupé come here."

Five minutes later, Lynn and Alvarez were stealing along a side street. Even their footsteps seemed muffled by the fog. They passed a lighted corner; took to another misty stretch. They reached Lynn's garage, three blocks away.

Riding forth in the car, they headed westward. Lynn, at the wheel, found driving difficult. The coupé barely crept along; fog swallowed it completely.

That fact pleased Alvarez. He was sure that they could never be observed. Alvarez would not have believed it, had he been told that there was a being—The Shadow—to whom fog and darkness served as a welcome cloak; whose keen eyes could pierce both elements.

ONE hour out of Manhattan, the coupé reached a secluded New Jersey highway. High ground had thinned the fog; thick clouds, however, blackened the landscape. Alvarez watched ahead to identify the route that he had learned from Estaban's letter. At times, he gazed through the rear window to make sure that no car was trailing them.

Coming down a slight grade, Lynn cut off the motor. The coupé creaked as he coasted it at snail's pace. Ahead, Alvarez saw the gates of the Kincaid estate. Listening, he thought he heard the sound of a motor back along the road. He looked back, wondering if a car was following, its own lights darkened, depending on Lynn's headlamps to show the road. Alvarez decided that he had imagined the sound behind.

Lynn cut off the headlights, turned on the cowls. The coupé entered the gates; followed a curving drive. Lynn guided by the border of a lawn where the grass had grown high. Massive darkness bulked ahead. It was the abandoned Kincaid mansion. Lynn picked a space past the house; extinguished the car lights.

Using flashlights, the two young men studied the graveled driveway. Satisfied that all was well, they picked a course past the back of the old mansion. Trying to do without flashlights, they blundered against a wooden wall a few hundred yards in back of the house.

Lynn risked a flashlight, to see an old work shack, built of half-rotted pine. Through a door half off its hinges, the searchers saw stacks of old boards and bags that had once contained cement. There were a few tools: rusted wrenches and a heavy sledge-hammer. In one corner, they noted a pile of large lead pipe that varied in length from two feet to six.

"It looks as though they intended to build a garage," remarked Alvarez. "Probably at the time when the old mansion was abandoned."

"It doesn't matter," decided Lynn. "Our job is to find the mausoleum. We'll have to use the flashlights when we get outside, Alvarez."

Taking the toolhouse as a base, the two started a new search outside. This time, they made cautious use of the flashlights. They discovered an old path and followed it. The ground leveled; a mass of ghostly whiteness loomed suddenly ahead.

Lynn doused his flashlight; Alvarez did the same. They crept toward the whitened object, placed their hands against a stony wall.

"The mausoleum!" whispered Lynn. "Whew! It's spooky here! Let's find the door to it and finish up this job."

GROPING along, they passed a corner. Their hands found a crevice. Prying together, they swung a heavy door that groaned on rusty hinges. The sound was sepulchral; almost like a voice that protested against this entry. Lynn could hear Alvarez mutter low words in Spanish. He knew that his friend also felt the chill of this ghostly spot.

Nevertheless, both had the same idea the moment that they had entered. Together, the pair groped for the door that they had opened and drew it shut behind them. Again, hinges grated; this time, the sound brought hollow echoes from the interior of the mausoleum. The new groan was even less assuring than the former one.

Lynn used his flashlight. Its glare was ample. All about were white walls. The floor, like the walls, was of stone; it gave a solid *click* as Alvarez walked toward the rear wall. There, he stooped, beckoned for Lynn to approach with the flashlight.

It was obvious that this mausoleum had never been used for a burial. Any ordinary visitor would have regarded it simply as a structure of solid stone and would not have troubled to search the interior. That fact showed the wisdom of old José Rentone. Alvarez's grandfather had made an excellent choice in using this abandoned building as the blind for a treasure vault.

In fact, as Lynn watched Alvarez probe the floor, he felt that the quest would prove useless. Stones were fitted so closely together; they seemed so solid, that it was difficult to believe that an opening could exist. However, Alvarez must have received exact instructions from his cousin Estaban.

Pressing one hand against the lowest stone of the wall, the other against a section of the floor, Alvarez manipulated them like the panels of a tricky Japanese box. The wall stone clicked; receded slightly. Pushing his fingers into the space, Alvarez found hidden springs and pressed them. Other wall stones slid aside.

Alvarez pushed the floor stones inward. Entering the wall, they left an opening that measured two feet by three. Lynn eagerly turned the rays of the flashlight down into the space below. The light showed a drop of five feet. Alvarez slid his feet over the edge and dropped into the space beneath.

There, he beckoned to Lynn. Watching Alvarez, Lynn saw his friend stoop and crawl through an opening that led beneath the rear wall of the mausoleum.

Lynn came through, down into the space that Alvarez had left. He saw his companion's flashlight blinking from a flight of rough-hewn stone steps that led down into a lower passage. Lynn joined Alvarez; the two stood erect in a narrow corridor that ended in a heavy metal door.

They were more than six feet underground. The top of the passage had been reinforced with metal crossbeams and cemented stones. Though crumbly, the roof was strong enough to support the weight of the ground above.

THE pair approached the door. Above a rough-ened knob, they saw a mass of heavy wax. Implanted in that wax was a mark of a seal that Lynn immediately recognized. It was the seal of José Rentone, identical with the one that Alvarez carried in his watch fob.

Alvarez gripped the doorknob, tugged at it. The door did not open; Lynn found the reason when he ran his flashlight along the crevice. There was a hidden catch that held the door tight. Lynn could barely detect its glimmer, for the catch was behind the heavy seal.

Producing a penknife, Lynn jabbed at the seal. It cracked; he thrust the knife blade into the crevice. He forced the catch back; motioned for Alvarez to pull the knob. The door swung this time. Drawing it wide, the young men played their flashlights into the vault beyond.

They saw a close-walled room, fashioned of rough stone. The chamber measured about eight feet in each dimension. It was reached by a descent of three stone steps. At the far wall rested the object that they sought: a metal coffer the size of a large trunk.

Alvarez sprang forward with eagerness. Lynn, more cautious, remained upon the steps to satisfy himself that the door could not swing shut. Finding it tight upon its hinges, he joined Alvarez. He aided him with the heavy bands that girded the coffer. The bands were of metal; clamped, not locked.

"In a few minutes more," promised Alvarez, breathlessly, "you will see my grandfather's heirlooms! I know what some of them will be; for he told me about them, often.

"The silver sword belt, that was worn by Balboa; the candelabra that belonged to a former Spanish viceroy; medallions, once the property of Simon Bolivar. They are of rare value, Lynn; but most important are those promissory notes, that will bring a million dollars to the cause of liberty in Santander!

"Come! Help me with this last band. There! It is loose! Hold the flashlight close, while I raise the lid —"

As Lynn glimmered the light, Alvarez suited his words with actions. He jolted the lid of the coffer upward and backward. It nearly snapped its hinges from the force of the jerk that Alvarez gave it.

Instantly, Lynn Jefford uttered an inarticulate cry.

The contents of the coffer were not those that Alvarez had promised. Instead, the metal box contained a gruesome object—that made Lynn Jefford sag away in instinctive horror.

Packed within the coffer, twisted into a shape that seemed no longer human, was the corpse of a man who had died in fearful agony.

THE face that stared from above contorted shoulders had once been handsome; but in death, it was terrible. White eyeballs showed from shrunken sockets; dark pupils had narrowed to the size of tiny beads. Black hair looked like withered grass. Sallow features were drawn like tightened parchment.

Lynn could see that the dead man's face must have shown a demoniacal expression soon after death. Its leer, however, had shrunken into a mummified grin, from which teeth stood out against brownish, withered gums.

Shaky as he held the flashlight, Lynn managed to turn his eyes from the terrible sight within the coffer. He looked toward Alvarez, expecting to see his companion crouched back in awe. Instead, Alvarez was rigid.

The young man from Santander was leaning above the coffer, looking straight down upon the face that mocked him with its hideous upward glare. No horror was registered by Alvarez; nor was his expression one that denoted inability to turn his eyes away.

Alvarez's face was toned with a profound sorrow. Though strained, his eyes were watery. His lips, alone, were quivering; as though ready to utter piteous words. Lynn gained sudden realization as he noted Alvarez's emotion.

In strained tone, Lynn queried: "You know him?"

Alvarez nodded; his movement was slow and mechanical. Lynn waited for Alvarez to speak. When words came from Alvarez's saddened lips, they were solemn despite their chokiness. More than that, they carried an astonishing statement that left Lynn Jefford dazed.

"I knew this man," pronounced Alvarez, his eyes fixed on the face below. "I knew him, trusted him, depended upon him more than any other man alive!"

Then, in a tone that might have been a knell, Alvarez Rentone added: "This man was my cousin Estaban!"

CHAPTER IX
STRANGERS FROM THE DARK

FLOODING thoughts surged through Lynn Jefford's brain, when he heard the dead man's identity. Disjointedly, Lynn began to piece together the circumstances that had led up to the discovery of the corpse.

Estaban Rentone had been safe in Santander, in a town called San Luis. From there, he had sent a letter to Alvarez, telling him of this treasure vault. There could be no question regarding the authenticity of the letter.

Alvarez would have recognized a forgery. Moreover, Estaban alone knew that Alvarez had come to America in search of buried wealth.

Fate, nonetheless, had provided a grim surprise for the finish of Alvarez's quest.

Behind such fate, Lynn began to see the plotting of a human brain. A mind that well might belong to a demon. Some master hand of evil had delivered a series of amazing strokes.

Estaban Rentone was dead. His grandfather's treasure was gone. In its place was Estaban's body, its shrunken face grinning in irony at Alvarez. The master criminal who had prepared this climax must know everything.

That final thought made Lynn turn to Alvarez. In one instant, Lynn could see that he and his companion stood in a spot of danger. Lynn gulped words; Alvarez did not notice them. He still stood staring at the cramped body of his dead cousin.

"Alvarez!" Lynn added emphasis to his cry by shaking his companion's shoulder. "Alvarez! Snap out of it! We can't stay here!"

The shouted words echoed within the vault. They came back with ringing shudder that seemed loath to cease. Lynn, startled by the reverberations of his own cries, stood in startled silence. The echoes seemed ugly, inhuman in this vault.

"Alvarez—"

Lynn repeated the name in lower tone. Again, there were echoes. They were uglier than before; from them came new words that Lynn had not uttered. Snarled words, that made Lynn spin about.

... The metal box contained a gruesome object ... twisted into a shape that seemed no longer human ...

Alvarez came with him, as they heard a voice pronounce the words:

"Alvarez Rentone! I have expected you here!"

STANDING upon the stone steps that marked the entrance to the vault was the man who had uttered the sneering announcement. Lynn saw a face that showed evil against the framed light of a lantern that was held by someone in the outer passage.

The face was vulture-like. Its nose was high-bridged, beakish. The face itself was full, with high forehead; adding to its heavy effect was a spade-shaped beard through which fierce, ruddy lips formed a merciless smile.

The identity of the arrival was plain to Lynn Jefford, even before Alvarez blurted the name:

"Emilio Zenjora!"

Zenjora chuckled at the recognition. His tone was satanic. His teeth showed in tigerish ferocity as he spread his lips to laugh. Then Zenjora's manner changed to harshness; though his words were purred, the vault gave them a deep rumble.

"You expected to find treasure," announced Zenjora. "Something that your grandfather valued. You should not be disappointed, Alvarez. Your grandfather thought much of your cousin, Estaban."

A pause. Alvarez glared his defiance. He countered with the accusation:

"You murdered Estaban! You tortured him to make him speak!"

"No!" Zenjora shook his head as he spat the word. "I did not murder Estaban; nor did I torture him. He was killed by these."

Zenjora beckoned. From beneath the muzzles of guns that bristled from the corridor came two hunched figures—apish men who scampered down into the vault and stood with grinning faces. Each gripped a pointed shaft of feathered bamboo. Alvarez recognized the men and their weapons.

"Jibaros!" he exclaimed. "They killed Estaban with their poisoned weapons!"

Zenjora nodded.

"They slew Estaban," he declared. "They brought me the letter that he had written to you. So I came to this country by plane, bringing Estaban's body with me. Once I had learned of this treasure vault, I felt that I should substitute something for the wealth that I intended to acquire.

"My Jibaros came with me, along with other followers. They killed Manuel Fendoza; for he had learned of Estaban's death and was coming to inform you. Tonight, they killed another man: Nick Broggoletta, evidently a friend of Fendoza's. It was unwise for you to learn that Estaban had died."

There was significance in Zenjora's tone. The answer dawned on Lynn and Alvarez, even before Zenjora gave the explanation.

"Your death," stated Zenjora, "might have caused too much comment. It might have alarmed James Oakbrook, whose promissory notes I now hold. So I decided to let you come here, Alvarez, hoping that you would bring your friend Jefford with you.

"The trap was simple. I merely mailed your cousin's letter, before I left Bogota. The envelope was opened, then sealed again, but too well for you to notice it. By coming here, you have aided my plans. Your disappearance will not cause the comment that your death might.

"Especially since you were staying undercover. That was something that you probably told Oakbrook, when you saw him today. Oakbrook, I understand, has left New York. That will not matter. I shall await his return."

THE completeness of Zenjora's measures left Alvarez astounded; and Lynn shared his friend's amazement.

Zenjora spoke in a strange tongue, giving a command to the Jibaro headhunters. Alvarez and Lynn expected thrusts from the deadly bamboo shafts. Instead, the headhunters lowered the weapons; they bounded forward and began to search the helpless men. While the Jibaros pulled articles from the pockets of Lynn and Alvarez, Zenjora added a final touch.

"We might have trapped you outside this vault," he sneered, "but that was not necessary. Fortunately, I had this"—he held up a circular object of gold—"a replica of your grandfather's seal, which we found upon your cousin's body. I used it to seal the vault after I had taken the treasure.

"When I depart, the seal will again be applied. Sometime, years from now, someone may find this vault again. The seal will be the same as ever. Only there will be three skeletons—not one—within this death pit!"

Walls echoed back the evil prophecy. The Jibaros had finished their search of the trapped men's pockets. They brought the collection to Zenjora, who pocketed all papers and letters. When he examined watches and money that the two men had carried, Zenjora gave a contemptuous shrug of his shoulders. He ordered his servitors to return them to the doomed prisoners.

Mechanically, Lynn and Alvarez accepted the trifles that the Jibaros thrust into their hands. Zenjora explained his action with an ugly chuckle.

"I am Emilio Zenjora," he declared, proudly. "I never rob the living. I prefer the dead."

With that, he clucked an order to the headhunters. The Jibaros retired; Zenjora stepped back. Leveled gun barrels parted to make way for him. Zenjora placed a brawny hand upon the metal door. His bearded face showed a final surge of devilish malice. His arm slung; the heavy door clanged into place. The automatic catch clicked from above the steps.

Lynn and Alvarez were standing in the feeble glow of the flashlights that they still held. The brilliant lantern was gone with Zenjora and his followers. The trapped men saw what their intended fate would be. Zenjora had spared them the thrusts of Jibaro spears, evidently considering such strokes as useless.

Buried alive, Lynn Jefford and Alvarez Rentone could count the few minutes that remained to them. Zenjora had left them flashlights and watches so that they could clock the time until their doom arrived.

That interval would not be long.

Already, the air of the vault was stifling. The oxygen in a room as cramped as this one could not last two men more than a few hours, at best. The vault, however, lacked the qualities of an ordinary room. Its air supply was already bad.

LYNN JEFFORD groaned, as he foresaw the death that was to be. Then, gaining determination, he sprang to the door. Beyond it, he heard scraping sounds: Zenjora was restoring the seal. Lynn looked for the catch that held the door tight. It could not be reached from this side.

Since the door closed from the corridor, a metal frame had been designed to stop it. That frame covered the crevice. In addition, the door hinges were on the outside. Despairingly, Lynn turned about to ask Alvarez for suggestions.

Alvarez had none. He seemed resigned. Lynn saw him gaze at Estaban's body. Perhaps the sight of his cousin's upturned face gave Alvarez the courage to meet death. For Alvarez stood rigid, concerned only with the sight before him.

Lynn sat on the stone steps and mopped his forehead with a handkerchief that Zenjora had allowed him to keep. He held his flashlight loosely, let the glow play toward Alvarez. Sniffing the air, Lynn noted its rankness.

"We're through, Alvarez," he said, slowly. "Half an hour will do us in. Well, the only thing to do is face it. My only regret is that Zenjora is free to go ahead with further dirty work."

No comment from Alvarez. Lynn put a question:

"What about James Oakbrook? Is he the man you saw today? The one who has the money?"

Alvarez heard Lynn's query; he nodded. He no longer had reason to keep Oakbrook's identity a secret.

"I hope Oakbrook keeps clear of Zenjora," remarked Lynn. "Naturally, Oakbrook will be allowed to live until he forks over the cash. I suppose he will have to recognize Zenjora's claim on the cash."

"He will," spoke Alvarez, turning away from the coffer that held Estaban's body. "Oakbrook will have no other course, once Zenjora finds him. When I am dead, the new régime in Santander can claim possession of all that belongs to me.

"And when Oakbrook has paid—"

"Zenjora will murder him. Let us hope, therefore, that Zenjora does not find him. But there are others, Lynn, who will suffer, regardless of what happens to Oakbrook."

"You mean your grandfather's friends?"

"Yes. A list of their names was with the heirlooms. Zenjora will kill them because of his hatred for my grandfather. He may have another reason, also. If he does not find Oakbrook, he will hunt those men down, one by one, to learn if they know where Oakbrook is."

LYNN came to his feet. The stifling air made him gasp from his effort. Approaching the coffer, he wrenched away one of the iron bars that had clamped it. Driving upward, he began to chop vainly at the ceiling. He chipped one stone; then ceased his effort. He stood panting beside the wall.

"We cannot aid those other men," announced Alvarez, in a stoical tone. "I do not know their names. I was dependent upon the list. All were old friends of my grandfather's, whom he knew before I was born. He never mentioned their names to me."

"We can help ourselves," retorted Lynn. "We've got to get out of here, Alvarez!"

With that, Lynn began new efforts. He wielded the bar with fury. Two minutes of effort tired him. He waited for a few minutes; then began again. This time he cracked a stone; a few more lunges caused a chunk to clatter to the floor beside him. Gasping, Lynn turned his flashlight upward. He saw another layer of stone above the insignificant hole that he had made.

Lynn sat wearily upon the steps, and Alvarez joined him. Glancing at his watch, Alvarez calmly remarked:

"Zenjora has been gone for fully fifteen minutes. Even he would not be present to hear your hopeless efforts. We have but a few minutes to live, Lynn. Let us spend them in quiet contemplation."

Lynn nodded with effort. His flashlight was dying; its fading rays barely showed the coffer that contained Estaban's body. Thought of Estaban made the next few minutes easier. After all, suffocation would be a better death than the poisoned doom that Zenjora had meted out to Estaban.

"Death will be comfortable," promised Alvarez. "Each breath will come harder." He paused, gasped a moment for air, and added: "At last, breath will not come. That will be all—"

Lynn's hand groped to grip Alvarez's arm. Gasping, Lynn panted:

"Listen!"

From somewhere above came a slow crunching sound—the bash of metal against resisting rock. It jarred its muffled grind through the very stones that formed the roof above this vault of doom.

"Someone has heard us!" panted Lynn. "He is working to rescue us!"

"It is too late!" gasped Alvarez, his voice calm despite its effort. "No need to hope, Lynn!"

Lynn did not accept Alvarez's opinion. He wobbled to his feet; used the iron bar to pound at the ceiling. Though his strokes were few and feeble, they gave another signal to prove that life still existed within the vault.

LYNN sagged to the floor and lay there, his breath coming in long sighs. Above, the grind came louder. Alvarez flicked his flashlight to the ceiling.

A cry of jubilation came from his parched lips. Until now, he had not believed rescue possible; but what Alvarez saw told him that it was reality.

Mortared stones cracked. Fragments clattered to the floor. The end of a metal pipe poled into view. It shoved two feet downward; stopped. Whoever had driven it knew that the pipe had reached the hollow space of the vault.

Again, Alvarez uttered an elated cry. The echoes of his shout must have carried through the pipe, for there was a response from above. A weird, commanding tone issued from the mouth of the pipe, like a voice through a speaking tube. Alvarez was awed by the compelling power of that strange whisper.

Rescue had come to the doomed men in the vault. The being who had brought that rescue was The Shadow.

CHAPTER X
TRAILS IN THE NIGHT

WAVERING through lack of air, Alvarez dropped his flashlight and gripped the welcome pipe. Too excited to remember his usually perfect English, he gasped words in Spanish to the rescuer above. There was no response; Alvarez suddenly understood why.

He had babbled that he needed air. He had it. Inhaling from the opening of the pipe, Alvarez obtained the oxygen he needed. The mouth of the pipe was two inches in diameter; as a result, the pipe formed an excellent air shaft.

Alvarez remembered Lynn. He stooped, found his companion groping on the floor beside him. He hoisted Lynn to the pipe, helped his friend to puff fresh air. Taking turns, each man revived. They could feel a draught of fresh air that crept downward.

The Shadow had seen the need for an airline, the moment that he had heard raps from below. From the toolhouse, he had brought short pipes and long ones. With the short pipes, he had pounded a wedge through stone and mortar; he had finally driven the long pipe through.

Calmly, Alvarez began to talk through the pipe. In brief words, he told the location of the vault; how it could be reached through the mausoleum. The response was an encouraging whisper from The Shadow. After that, there was a period of silence, while Alvarez and Lynn continued to obtain fresh air.

Soon, they heard sounds at the door of the vault. The barrier swung outward; a flood of fresh air entered. Alvarez and Lynn blinked into the glare of a flashlight. They heard The Shadow order them to follow him above. Gladly, they came from the vault and took the stairs up to the mausoleum.

There, they caught a hazy glimpse of their rescuer; for The Shadow purposely turned the flashlight toward himself. The rescued men gaped as they saw the weird shape in black. Lynn could tell from Alvarez's awed whisper that his friend half believed The Shadow to be some supernatural being who inhabited the mausoleum.

Certainly, there seemed no other explanation for The Shadow's presence. Neither Lynn nor Alvarez guessed that The Shadow had trailed them from Lynn's garage; that his car had actually been behind the coupé outside the gates of the Kincaid estate.

Because of Lynn's tactics on the driveway, The Shadow had been unable to trail them farther by car. Coming on foot, The Shadow had been belated. He had not reached the mausoleum until after Zenjora had entered and departed.

The Shadow knew who had trapped the prisoners. Zenjora's evil hand was apparent throughout this plot. The words that The Shadow put formed a question; but it sounded more like a command to Lynn and Alvarez. The Shadow's tone was sibilant:

"State Zenjora's purpose!"

"ZENJORA rifled the treasure vault," explained Alvarez, wondering how The Shadow had learned the name of the master crook. "He learned of it when he murdered my cousin, Estaban, whose body we found in the coffer. Zenjora holds promissory notes that call for a million dollars. Those funds belong to Santander. They are held by—"

Alvarez paused, loath to reveal Oakbrook's name, even to this rescuer. It was Lynn who supplied it. He had heard it from Zenjora. To Lynn, it seemed obvious that The Shadow, so amazing a rescuer, must be the only person who could prevent Zenjora from committing further evil.

"James Oakbrook has the money," stated Lynn. "He is a wealthy New Yorker. Alvarez warned him today that there might be danger. Oakbrook has left New York, carrying the funds with him."

There was a pause. The flashlight fell squarely upon the rescued men, as they sat against the inner wall of the mausoleum, near the yawning opening which The Shadow had not yet closed. Lynn saw an object leaning against the wall. It was the sledgehammer from the toolhouse. The head of the hammer was wrapped in a cement sack.

Lynn understood how The Shadow had pounded the pipeline through to the vault. He realized also that the sack had served as muffler, so that no outside listeners could have heard the blows.

"State who placed the seal upon the vault."

The Shadow's words were addressed to Alvarez. In reply, Alvarez drew his watch from his pocket, opened the fob and gave the seal to The Shadow. Alvarez explained that it was his grandfather's seal; that Zenjora had found a duplicate on Estaban's body. After a moment's thought, Alvarez added:

"Zenjora could not have guessed that I also carried one of these seals. If he had, he would have searched me until he found it."

A whispered laugh chilled the mausoleum. Despite the fact that they knew The Shadow for a friend, Alvarez and Lynn felt a creepy chill. Then came commanding words. They nodded as they heard them.

"Remain here," ordered The Shadow. "Be on guard. Soon I shall return."

He pressed automatics into the hands of the rescued men. His cloaked form showed momentarily, as he edged downward through the opening in the floor. Lynn and Alvarez saw the flashlight blink below. Its rays vanished. Lynn whispered to Alvarez.

"He has gone back to the vault!" expressed Lynn. "To close it and affix the seal!"

"As Zenjora did," responded Alvarez. "The wax can be softened with a single match. Once the seal is applied, it will harden."

"And be as Zenjora left it. If Zenjora returns, he will not guess that we were rescued from the vault."

SOON, The Shadow's flashlight reappeared. The task was done. When he came from the floor, The Shadow turned about and used his flashlight while he clicked the stones back into position. That accomplished, he whispered to Alvarez and Lynn, telling them to follow. The flashlight went out. In darkness, The Shadow opened the outer door of the mausoleum.

A drizzle had begun. Night seemed to be impenetrable. Nevertheless, The Shadow picked his path without a single blink of the flashlight. His low-toned whispers guided the men behind him. They reached a spot where the slight rain slackened.

Lynn recognized that they were at the spot where he had left his coupé; but the car was gone. Zenjora and his men had taken it. Lynn remembered that a Jibaro had given the car keys and licenses to Zenjora.

The Shadow's whisper commanded further progress. The group reached the drive; took another course across a soggy lawn. At intervals, the lessening of the drizzle told that they were passing beneath clustered trees. At last, there came a guarded

blink of the flashlight. The Shadow had brought the rescued men to a side road, off the edge of the estate. Sheltered behind a cluster of bushes was a high-speed roadster.

The Shadow took the wheel; Lynn sat beside him, with Alvarez on the outside. In darkness, he started the motor; its rhythm was scarcely audible. Lynn began to understand how his coupé had been trailed; for this car was remarkably silent. Further understanding came to Lynn when The Shadow eased the car out to the road.

Without the slightest difficulty, The Shadow nosed the roadster through pitch darkness, feeling the rough road by the touch of the front wheels. He eased the car down the slope and reached the highway. There, he turned on the lights and headed in the direction of the gates that marked the entrance to the Kincaid estate.

As the car rolled slowly ahead, The Shadow spoke to Lynn. With gloved hand, he passed a key to the man beside him.

"Go to the Atlas Apartments in New York," ordered The Shadow. "This key is for Apartment 5-G. Remain there until a visitor arrives, tomorrow. His name will be Harry Vincent. You may trust him fully."

The roadster had covered a quarter mile. It was slowly nearing the gates. Peering straight ahead, The Shadow must have noted the glimmer of a light, even though Lynn did not spy it. Slowing the roadster, The Shadow opened the door on the left; he drew Lynn over to the wheel.

"Speed past the gates," ordered The Shadow. "Drive straight into New York. No one will overtake you."

An instant later, The Shadow was gone. The *click* of the door told that he had dropped off to the road.

THE gates were just ahead. Lynn stepped on the accelerator. He was amazed by the sudden response that the big roadster gave.

Like an unleashed hound, the car launched forward in a joltless burst of speed. As it passed the gates, a cluster of men sprang from the side of the road. Revolvers flashed in the glimmer of the roadster's lights. Lurkers had come from ambush.

Two factors offset the trap that Zenjora had laid.

The first was the whippet speed of The Shadow's super-powered roadster. The car had idled up to the gates; when Lynn gave it gas, it had covered the intervening space at a pace that the lurkers had not deemed possible.

The other factor was The Shadow himself.

The Shadow was ready with a brace of reserve automatics. He saw the enemy, by the glare of the roadster's lights, the moment that Zenjora's henchmen leaped forth from cover. Before a single foeman could loose a shot, The Shadow opened fire.

Bullets burned through the drizzle, big slugs that found immediate marks. Two of the foemen staggered. The others forgot the roadster and whipped about to return The Shadow's fire. The taillight of the speeding car dwindled into nothingness. Thanks to The Shadow's timely barrage, Lynn Jefford had run the gantlet.

A car roared forth from farther up the road. It was a sedan that was manned by others of Zenjora's men. It was taking up the roadster's trail—a useless task. Underslung, with widened body, equipped with a gigantic motor, The Shadow's car could do a hundred miles an hour, when handled by an ordinary driver.

The Shadow knew that Lynn would outdistance the sedan. Within five miles, the chase would be a farce. Lynn knew the road, for he had driven here.

Gunfire ceased temporarily after the cars had sped away. The slight patter of the drizzle was audible, as crouched men waited tensely. Then came a strident laugh that made this lonely spot seem a haunted place. That mirth arose in long and sinister mockery. The laugh was The Shadow's; a challenge to the lurkers who sought to locate his position.

In addition to its challenge, The Shadow's laugh carried other import. It told men of crime that they had been thwarted by The Shadow's design. The roadster's easy escape stood as reason for The Shadow's mirth.

In addition, it conveyed the news that The Shadow himself was here. It gave the impression that the men in the roadster must be agents whom The Shadow had brought with him. Zenjora already knew that The Shadow was in the game. As a result, the master crook would believe that his own men had been trailed by The Shadow. Zenjora would not suspect that Alvarez Rentone and Lynn Jefford were the ones who had actually blazed The Shadow's path to this lonely terrain.

THE SHADOW'S laugh brought spasmodic shots from foemen. Their fire was wide. No one could have guessed The Shadow's exact location from the deceptive shudder of his eerie laugh. The shots that Zenjora's men delivered were as bad for them as boomerangs. Even while their guns echoed, The Shadow returned the barrage. He had targets: the flashes of the revolvers.

Cries sounded as The Shadow clipped foemen in the darkness. There were shouts; scurrying sounds along the road. Shifting his position, The Shadow blazed new bullets; then shifted again. No one returned the fire. Evil henchmen were seeking darkness, anxious to elude the superfighter whom they could not see.

As The Shadow made a circuitous advance, another car suddenly started from a spot beyond the gates. The Shadow snapped quick shots as he saw the lights come on. The driver zigzagged; his car wallowed through the ditch at the left side of the road.

The maneuver was a lucky one. It carried the escaping car on a line beyond the gates; prevented The Shadow from taking new aim until the fleeing machine was out of range.

Alone, The Shadow laughed. He was not disappointed by the car's escape. The Shadow knew that Zenjora must have gone ahead; that these were mere underlings left in reserve. The sooner the news of The Shadow's fight reached the supercrook, the better it would be. The Shadow could foresee what Zenjora's next step would be. It was one that suited The Shadow's plans.

Passing through the gates, The Shadow headed for the old mansion. He reached the house, kept onward and arrived at the mausoleum. There, he made a brief inspection; he carried away the sledgehammer that he had left. Going to the rear of the white-walled building, he found the spot where he had drilled the air hole into the vault. The Shadow covered all traces of the work after he had drawn the six-foot pipe from the ground. Carrying odd lengths of pipe, he returned to the toolhouse and stacked the articles there.

Waiting under the shelter of the toolhouse roof, The Shadow listened for tokens of an approach. Time passed slowly amid the drizzle; yet The Shadow scarcely moved from his position. After an hour, he heard a stealthy, creeping sound from a spot close by. Silently, The Shadow moved through the rain.

Ghoulish visitants had arrived; enemies against whom The Shadow did not care to risk a battle under these circumstances. He knew who the stealthy men must be. They were Jibaro headhunters, sent here by Zenjora. Though The Shadow had sensed their presence, he knew that these jungle lurkers could use darkness almost to equal advantage with himself.

Unquestionably, they would be equipped with poisoned shafts. Moreover, they had subtle ways of

body sagged; it toppled sidewise to the floor and sprawled motionless. Doom had struck Dundee despite the fact that he stood within a room equipped with barred shutters and bolted door.

The murderous power of Emilio Zenjora had seemingly stretched from nowhere to prevent the law from learning the name of James Oakbrook. Howard Dundee had died before dawn; before The Shadow had arrived to save him.

CHAPTER XIII
THE SHADOW'S STROKE

TO Joe Cardona, the sudden death of Howard Dundee was an unaccountable phenomenon. As he stooped beside the dead man, Cardona was ready to believe in the impossible.

Dundee's face still held its grotesque stare. Blinking, Cardona looked about the room. For a moment, he thought that some ghostly manifestation could have occurred within this room; that Dundee might have died in horror, at some sight he had viewed.

The room, however, was empty, except for Cardona and the corpse. The meager furniture of the study offered no hiding place for even a midget. Barred shutters were tight in place. The bolts of the door were closed.

Dundee's body rolled rigidly as Cardona shifted it. The fixed face turned downward; one shoulder sagged. Staring squarely at the dead man's back, Cardona saw something that made him utter a low grunt.

Projecting from a spot near Dundee's spine, plain against the dark smoking jacket that the dead man was wearing, Cardona spied a yellowish sliver that looked like a large thorn. Gripping it, Cardona plucked the needlelike object from Dundee's flesh.

It was a thorn, and a long one. It had buried itself an inch deep in Dundee's back. Cardona knew that the thorn must have come from some peculiar tropical tree, for it was as unpliable as a metal nail. The point was long and sharp.

As Cardona held it to the light, he noted that the sharp tip was stained with some brownish substance. Cardona guessed instantly that the thorn was poisoned. That guess gave credence to Dundee's story. It told that Fendoza and Broggoletta had died from similar thrusts. It proved the possibility of Jibaro headhunters, rampant in New York. For the moment, however, it did not explain how Dundee had become a victim.

Cardona arose; he placed the thorn carefully upon the desk. He looked toward the window and shook his head. He stared at the door, but remained as puzzled as before. Eying the position of Dundee's body, Cardona pictured the exact spot where the victim had last stood. Joe visualized Dundee between himself and the door; he remembered that Dundee had been facing him when the stroke had come.

His revolver gripped in his right hand, Cardona slowly lifted his eyes on a direct line. His gaze again rested on the door; this time, Cardona's eyes halted. He was looking straight for a spot that he had forgotten. That was the keyhole of the bolted door.

PERHAPS Joe would not have realized that the keyhole offered a solution to the riddle of Dundee's death, if he had not seen it at this precise moment. It chanced that as Cardona gazed, an action occurred at the keyhole. A tiny object thrust inward; Cardona saw the rounded opening of a hollow reed, no larger than a peashooter.

With that, Cardona had the answer; but it came too late for his own comfort.

A Jibaro killer had slain Dundee by blowing the poisoned thorn through a long stalk. The murderer had easily inserted the improvised blowgun through the keyhole. The Jibaro had been in the house when Cardona arrived, but he had reserved death for a later moment. Evidently, the Jibaro had been instructed to deal with Dundee before any other victim.

Dundee was dead. The Jibaro had bided his time outside the door. Peering through the keyhole, the killer had watched Cardona. The Jibaro had deemed it time to take another victim. Cardona was in the exact spot where the headhunter wanted him.

Doom's finger pointed straight at Joe Cardona, in the shape of the same jungle blowpipe that had finished Howard Dundee. The fact struck Joe instantly; dazed him to the point where his own actions seemed slow motion.

Springing forward, Cardona came up with his revolver, to aim for the keyhole. His thoughts were speedier than his moves. Instinctively, Cardona knew that his attempt was futile. The Jibaro had the bead; already the killer's lips were starting the puff that would speed the poisoned thorn to its new victim. Cardona's action was no more than a frantic, hopeless effort to save his own life.

Two amazing things happened while Cardona's gun was coming up. First, there came a muffled report from somewhere outside the room—a gunshot that seemed like a previous echo of the one that Cardona intended to deliver. Simultaneously, the hollow reed quivered in the keyhole. The projecting end twisted at an upward side angle. A yellowish sliver sped from the tiny muzzle; but its path was wide.

The thorn skimmed past Cardona's shoulder, hit the wall and dropped somewhere on the floor. Cardona's finger tugged the revolver trigger after all that happened.

While his own gunshot echoed in the steel-shuttered study, Cardona saw the useless damage that his bullet had done. The shot had plowed the woodwork of the heavy door above the keyhole and inches to one side of it. In fact, the shot was so close to the door frame that it could not have reached a person on the other side of the door.

Nevertheless, the blowgun had not delivered death. More than that, it was sliding away from view, vanishing through the keyhole in a downward direction. As Cardona reached the door, he realized that someone had spotted the Jibaro from the hall and had dropped the killer ahead of Joe's own shot.

CARDONA ripped back the bolts, yanked the door inward. The light from the study showed a sprawled shape on the threshold. Cardona saw an apish face, staring upward in an agonized expression that meant death. The huddled creature answered Dundee's description of the Jibaro who had been outside the house.

Vaulting the Jibaro's body, Cardona reached the hall. He swung toward the front door, expecting to see it open. As he gazed, Cardona heard a warning hiss. From the blackened wall, a cloaked figure whirled to view, delivered a sidearm swing that sent Cardona rolling toward the passage from which he had come.

Cardona's head banged back against the wall. Dimly, he sensed what followed; for he knew the identity of the person who had thrust him back. Joe's rescuer was The Shadow.

Arrived at Dundee's, The Shadow had picked the house as the one which Zenjora probably intended to visit. He had passed Markham's car without being spotted by the detective sergeant. Inside, The Shadow had discovered Lakiki, the English-speaking Jibaro, crouched outside the door of Dundee's study.

Knowing that Lakiki's purpose was to deliver death, The Shadow had dropped the Jibaro before the staring killer knew that he was watched. Dundee's death was avenged; Cardona's life was saved. But The Shadow had not waited to examine that situation.

He knew that another Jibaro might be present— the one called Miquon. Hence The Shadow had wheeled back into the hallway. Cardona's opening of the study door had brought light to the rear end of the darkened hall; though not enough to show The Shadow, the glow had outlined Cardona when the latter reached the hall.

Therefore, The Shadow had thrust Cardona downward and backward. The Shadow, in turn, made a dive in the opposite direction. His quick moves were necessary. A snarl sounded from the curtains at the side of the front hall; a bamboo javelin whizzed through the air, straight for the spot where The Shadow had intercepted Cardona.

It was Miquon's thrust; though speedy, it failed. Halfway between Cardona and The Shadow; above the heads of both, the poisoned shaft struck the hall, to bounce back harmlessly and strike the floor.

The Shadow's automatic blasted an answer. Cardona heard two shots, quick ones that came while The Shadow aimed in darkness, both directed uncannily toward the curtains from which Miquon had hurled his weapon. But the Jibaro had sprung away, the moment that he had loosed the missile. The clatter of a window told that he was making an escape outside.

The front door swung inward. A flashlight blinked in the hand of Detective Sergeant Markham. Just inside the doorway, Markham saw The Shadow. Before Cardona could shout for Markham to stay his gun, The Shadow sprang upon the newcomer.

With one hand, The Shadow plucked the flashlight from the detective sergeant's grasp; sent the lighted torch bouncing off through the room where Miquon had fled. With his gun arm, The Shadow gave a swing like the one he had handed Cardona. The blow swept Markham from The Shadow's path. It bowled the amazed detective sergeant away from the door.

AGAIN, The Shadow had acted just in time. As he sprang outside and leaped to the side shelter of the stone steps, shots ripped from the lawn. Zenjora and Cardell had arrived, a horde of imported outlaws at their heels. The Shadow's shots had brought them to a quick attack.

Markham would have been their first target, had The Shadow failed to shove him from the doorway. The flashlight was the very sort of indicator that Zenjora's fighters wanted; but The Shadow had disposed of it. Again, he was opening battle in darkness with men who had given him their positions by the spurts of their own guns.

This time, however, the gunmen shifted. They were trained to guerrilla warfare, these outlaws from Santander. They had learned a lesson in their first encounter with The Shadow. They tried his own tactics: quick shifts in the darkness after every shot.

Meanwhile, The Shadow kept up a wary fire from in front of the house. No shots came from inside. He guessed the reason. Cardona had dashed back into the study to put in a call for police reserves. That done, Joe would wait with Markham, to resist an onslaught. Cardona was a cool head when battle started. He would deem it better to maintain a stronghold to which The Shadow could retreat, than to break out from the house with a useless attempt at aid.

Counting upon Cardona's tactics, The Shadow continued a spasmodic fire. Gradually, he shifted away from the wall; ceased his shots altogether. Reaching the lawn, The Shadow knew that he was almost in the midst of Zenjora's outspread men. They had also ceased their fire, waiting for The Shadow to disclose his own position.

Moving across the lawn, The Shadow stopped short. One of the enemy was close at hand; The Shadow could hear the man moving in the drizzle. A shoulder jostled The Shadow's; he heard a snarled oath in a foreign tongue. Instantly, The Shadow shifted; he fired a quick shot toward the wall where he had previously been.

The ruse was perfect. An encounter with this ruffian would have told the others that The Shadow was among them. The shot toward the house made them think that the person who fired it belonged to their own clan.

The outlaw who had jostled The Shadow gave a growled laugh; muttered approving words to the fighter whom he thought was a companion. For good measure, the ruffian aimed and fired a shot of his own.

Timed with the recoil of the fellow's gun, The Shadow slugged downward with a .45. His sledged blow clipped the gunman's skull. The enemy plopped without noise upon the softened turf. No others were close enough to hear this aftermath. Zenjora's band numbered one less.

CROUCHED beside his vanquished foeman, The Shadow sensed the sound of creeping enemies. They were closing toward the house, prompted by some order from Zenjora, whose location was hidden. Another revolver spat from darkness; dispatched a futile shot toward the house.

The Shadow saw the game.

Zenjora believed that his cordon had closed sufficiently to trap The Shadow. Soon there would come a massed onslaught—a vicious drive in which a dozen fierce fighters would attempt to overwhelm a single foe. None had guessed that The Shadow was safely away from the house.

The Shadow waited, letting his enemies creep on ahead. They would be due for a double surprise when the right moment came.

The time arrived.

Flashlights burned suddenly from the drizzle. Guns began to roar, all along the line. Zenjora's squad surged forward, blasting the house steps with a withering fire. Though the space ahead looked vacant, they believed that The Shadow was there; that they had dropped him with their barrage.

All the while, they had watched the white door of the house; they knew that it had not moved, hence The Shadow could not have gone inside. Nevertheless, as Zenjora's men revealed themselves, that door ripped open. From inner darkness, two marksmen fired for the approaching flashlights.

Cardona and Markham had entered the fray. Their shots were timely. One of Zenjora's henchmen sprawled as the others dived away, flinging their flashlights from them. Thinking that The Shadow had been eliminated, the vicious attackers aimed for the house door.

An instant later, shots ripped from behind them. The Shadow was commencing a rear attack, using two mammoth automatics against the men who thought him dead. Outlaws wheeled; they fired too late. The Shadow was speeding across the lawn at an angle. He gained the shelter of Markham's car.

Two fires burned the ranks of Zenjora's men. They were boxed between the house and the car. Like The Shadow, Cardona and Markham riddled a flank of the attacking line. Crooks broke and ran; their attack had become a rout.

They were heading for cars out near the entrance, running pell-mell across the lawn. Huddled figures lay behind them, unseen in the darkness. The Shadow had accounted for three; Cardona and Markham had dropped a pair. Others were wounded, but still able to run.

Cutting across the lawn, The Shadow came suddenly upon the starting cars. The first were away; but as they sped from the road outside the gates, they were met by new arrivals. Police, called by Cardona, had come to halt the flight. A machine gun blasted from a police car as it swung beside the road.

Crooks would have fared badly as they ran the gantlet, except for the intervention that came from a standing car. Shots crackled from that machine; rifle bullets raked the police car. The driver of the police car ditched it, to avoid the bombardment. The machine gun went out of play.

It was The Shadow's countercharge that ended the rifle barrage. Seconds more, and the police car would have been riddled and its occupants killed. As the car that held the riflemen started forward, The Shadow reached its running board. He sprang upon the step, into the midst of bristling gun barrels.

A gloved fist sledged its heavy .45 straight for the heads of sharpshooters. Rifles dropped as their owners sagged. They could not swing the long barrels to cover their unexpected adversary. The car jolted forward; its driver, crouched low, gave it the gas. The car sped ahead in high-speed second gear, The Shadow still clinging to its side.

The Shadow swung for the driver's skull. An arm shot forth above the man who gripped the wheel. The Shadow's gun clashed metal. Half into the car, his eyes came close to a bearded face that showed above the dashlight.

The Shadow had found Emilio Zenjora.

BY a quick parry with a revolver, Zenjora had luckily stopped the blow that The Shadow had aimed for the driver's head. Coming up above the top of the front seat, Zenjora snarled as he aimed for his cloaked opponent.

Simultaneously, The Shadow swung far out from the side of the car. Clutching an open rear window with his left hand, he let his body fall from view. His right hand planked its gun muzzle on the window ledge; the mouth of the weapon tilted toward Zenjora.

A death duel was at hand. A split-second could decide it. The Shadow, however, had outmaneuvered Zenjora. The Shadow had dropped away while his enemy had come upward. The quick shift completely changed the odds. Both guns were due to roar; but the most that Zenjora could do would be to wound The Shadow. Zenjora, however, had become a sure target. At that instant, his death seemed certain.

It was the driver who changed matters, without knowing the importance of his deed. Huddled over the wheel, riding the car at thirty miles an hour, the driver saw cars ahead as they took a sharp turn into a lane on the right. Instinctively, he picked the same course. He gave the steering wheel a hard twist just as The Shadow and Zenjora were about to tug their triggers.

The car careened as it skidded and swung its nose to the right. The Shadow's left hand nearly lost its precarious grip upon the door. As he sought to maintain his hold, the door itself swung open. The Shadow pulled the trigger; but he was already hurtling to the road. His bullet whined wide of Zenjora's bearded face.

At the same instant, Zenjora fired; his shot, too, was useless. It was high; it proved that Zenjora would not have clipped The Shadow, even if the car had not made the sudden swing. Accident had saved Emilio Zenjora from The Shadow.

The speeding car did not halt. As its taillight vanished in the drizzle, shots boomed from the road behind. They were proof that The Shadow had been uninjured by his fall; that he had come to his feet, to begin a last barrage. The pursuing shots smashed into the rear of the car, but the range was too great for The Shadow to find the gas tank or the tires.

Zenjora was gone, carrying his groggy crew of riflemen. His other minions had gone ahead, some of their number wounded. Back on Dundee's lawn lay others, who were either dead or prisoners of the law. The Shadow's stroke had been a heavy blow to Emilio Zenjora.

The Shadow hoped to follow up his victory. Hurrying along Brisbane Avenue, he came to an open spot, where he blinked a signal with his flashlight. Lights answered; they were from Moe's cab. The Shadow boarded the vehicle, ordered Moe to speed him into Manhattan.

ONCE in the city, The Shadow paused to contact Burbank. He learned the location of Zenjora's apartment, from Burbank's search of telephone numbers. The Shadow sped to that new destination. He knew that he must be ahead of Zenjora; for the crook had taken a roundabout route through muddy lanes.

From darkness across the street, The Shadow studied darkened windows that he knew must be Zenjora's. He waited half an hour; there were no signs of returning men. Dawn was appearing, despite the drizzle. The Shadow decided to make final investigation.

Entering the apartment house, he ascended by an automatic elevator. He found the door of Zenjora's apartment unlocked. Entering, The Shadow discovered nothing but the furniture. Zenjora had taken no chances with a trail for either The Shadow or the law.

The supercrook had abandoned this headquarters when he had started for Long Island. Once again, The Shadow must begin a hunt for the bearded man of crime. Yet, as he stood in the gloom of Zenjora's abandoned lair, The Shadow delivered a whispering laugh.

Tonight, The Shadow had gained the key to Emilio Zenjora's schemes. From now on, he could play an equal game. Though Zenjora had managed the murder of Howard Dundee, the supercrook would be too wary to attempt similar crimes that he might have intended.

Zenjora would have but one objective: a meeting with James Oakbrook. It would be The Shadow's task to anticipate that meeting. That new goal offered opportunity to deal finally with men of crime.

The Shadow knew.

CHAPTER XIV
ZENJORA'S EMISSARY

EARLY afternoon found Alvarez Rentone and Lynn Jefford seated in their new apartment. With them was a man who had just arrived; a visitor whom the pair had expected. He was Harry Vincent, agent of The Shadow. Harry's appearance, his firm handshake, had impressed both rescued men.

Laying a stack of newspapers to one side, Harry smilingly remarked that he was ready to answer questions. Lynn grinned and put the first one:

"Who rescued us last night?"

"The Shadow."

Harry's calm reply brought an exclamation from Lynn Jefford. That young man had heard of The Shadow's ability at hunting down criminals and bagging them like big game. Lynn questioned quickly:

"Do you know who The Shadow is?"

"I serve The Shadow," replied Harry, "but I have never learned his actual identity. He saved my life; in return, I accept all duties that he assigns to me."

"We are willing to do the same," put in Alvarez. "We know that only The Shadow can combat Emilio Zenjora."

"Very well," declared Harry, briskly. "Here is the first test. Read these evening newspapers— editions that have just appeared on the street. A man named Howard Dundee was slain last night by a Jibaro headhunter. The death has been linked with those of Fendoza and Broggoletta—"

"And I am mentioned as the man behind the crimes!" cried Alvarez, scanning a newspaper. "New men support the police theory! Here are their names; they are men who expected gifts from my grandfather. They think that I have tried to rob them. This is an outrage! Zenjora is the perpetrator of those crimes! The Shadow knows it. He should have cleared my name!"

"Zenjora found the list of your grandfather's friends when he looted the treasure vault," explained Harry, calmly. "He had three reasons to want to murder them. Profit, for one; vengeance, for another. But the third and vital reason was information. Zenjora believed that one of those men might give him a lead to James Oakbrook."

Nods told that Alvarez and Lynn agreed.

"Zenjora chose Dundee first," continued Harry, "because he had heard from Fendoza. Though The Shadow did not save Dundee, he rescued Inspector Cardona. That cracked the case. Dundee had talked to Cardona. The police knew that the stiletto stabbings were faked. The Shadow left them a dead Jibaro to clinch the case.

"The law knows only the first name of James Oakbrook. They have not learned his full name from your grandfather's friends. Zenjora will therefore learn that those men are useless as informants. Since they have revealed themselves to the law and are protected, it is better that they should regard you as their enemy. Zenjora will feel secure. The Shadow can hunt him more effectively and the law will not bungle the search."

HARRY'S words carried weight. Alvarez saw other points. He recognized that Zenjora would desist from crimes that meant but small profit and minor vengeance, particularly since Zenjora believed Alvarez dead. Zenjora would prefer to let old crimes be blamed on Alvarez, without risking new deeds that might lead a cross trail to himself. Harry Vincent added another point.

"James Oakbrook will read the newspapers," he declared. "He will stay under cover; he will understand that this is Zenjora's work. You must tell me, though, what plans you have made to hear from Oakbrook."

Alvarez hesitated; then decided to answer. Briefly, he explained how Oakbrook was to place an advertisement in the evening *Sphere,* offering property for sale under the name of Thomas Rustwick. He added that the location given in the ad would tell Oakbrook's residence; while a repetition would call for a visit from Alvarez.

As Harry was about to leave, he added a question which he put to Alvarez:

"What about Nick Broggoletta? Can you account for him being a friend of Manuel Fendoza?"

"I thought, perhaps, that Broggoletta had a message," replied Alvarez. "One that Fendoza failed to bring; perhaps about Estaban's death. That seems weak, though. Fendoza might have chosen an adventurer for a friend, but scarcely a paid assassin like Broggoletta."

The question of Broggoletta puzzled Harry, after he had put in a call to Burbank. Harry knew that Zenjora had introduced the fake Italian angle; but he had done it through his Jibaros. Zenjora would not have sent Broggoletta purely to bluff the law. His policy had been hands off regarding Alvarez, for Zenjora had already arranged the treasure vault as Alvarez's place of doom.

The only answer that Harry could see was the one that Alvarez had rejected: namely, that Broggoletta had been a friend of Fendoza. His duty done, Harry wondered how much he had accomplished for The Shadow. He would have been pleased, had he known.

Though the facts that Harry relayed through Burbank did not pave the route to Emilio Zenjora, they would soon enable The Shadow to choose the proper battleground for a final conflict with the bearded master of crime.

FOR the present, Zenjora was secure. He was gone from Manhattan, vanished with his tribe of followers. In some new stronghold, the bearded outlaw leader was free to plot new mischief. The Shadow knew only that Zenjora must have been crafty in his choice of a new headquarters. The Shadow's opinion was correct.

Forty miles northwest of Manhattan, the setting sun shone upon a crew of desperadoes who outrivaled any that had ever visited American soil. These cutthroats were assembled in a rocky glen that bordered a rugged ravine. They were congregated away from the gorge, under the shelter of larger trees; for only saplings lined the brink of the ravine.

The stronghold was perched in a remote section of the New Jersey hills. The outlaws numbered a dozen; men of mixed nationalities who had served Zenjora in Santander. Some looked like Americans who had become soldiers of fortune. Others might have been French convicts, escaped from Devil's Island. A few were *mestizos*—half Spanish, half Indian.

Their babbled jargon, which mixed one language with another, ran the gamut of many dialects. They were like pirates, these *banditti;* but they had chosen land in preference to ocean. The ugly appearance of the renegades had been increased by last night's skirmish with The Shadow. Three had bandaged heads; two carried arms in slings; another was propped against a tree, too crippled to move about.

Their growled epithets included a name. Those who spoke French referred to *L'Ombre* and added the expression *"Le Diable."* Those who used Spanish uttered the titles: *"El Ombre"* and *"El Diablo."* Translated, the expression meant that The Shadow, in their opinion, was one with the devil.

One huge ruffian glowered as he watched two others build a fire in the circle. The glowering man was Bandrillo, Zenjora's chief lieutenant. Bulky of form, with ugly eyes that glowered from a square, pock-marked face, Bandrillo was impatient as he listened to talk of The Shadow.

Curbing his anger, Bandrillo arose to examine the wounds of his men. He had crude skill at surgery; that was one reason why Zenjora had first raised him to the rank of lieutenant. After attending the man who lay against the tree, Bandrillo showed new malice.

Facing his men, he delivered a savage tirade that included every language known to the group. From his belt, Bandrillo drew a machete. He flourished the knife as if he intended to carve the next man who mentioned The Shadow in any tongue.

The group silenced. Bandrillo paused in his outburst. Before he could resume, he heard a purred voice behind him. Turning, Bandrillo faced Zenjora. The master of crime had stalked up silently to join the group.

AS he stood close by the firelight, Zenjora appeared more demoniacal than any mortal whom that cutthroat crew had ever seen. His face carried a ferocity that surpassed the death-frozen countenances of victims who had cried at the hands of his Jibaros.

Ruffians shifted uneasily; even Bandrillo quailed. They watched Zenjora as he eyed them. Beyond their chief, they saw the three headhunters: Quinqual, Incos and Miquon.

Lakiki was missing. The absence of that Jibaro told of The Shadow's power. But the circled crew was not thinking of The Shadow. To a man, they were awed by their sight of Zenjora.

"Ah, Bandrillo!" The smoothness of Zenjora's tone seemed all the more insidious, when it issued from his twisted, ruddy lips. "So you think it unwise that the men should talk of The Shadow? Perhaps you are right, Bandrillo. Perhaps you are not. Listen, while I question the men themselves."

Turning to the group, Zenjora spat a medley of words that all could understand. Each man who heard words in his own language grinned and nodded his agreement. Zenjora was telling them that they would meet The Shadow again; that the time would come very soon. He was urging them to look forward to that meeting.

Elated snarls were their replies. Men rose to foment, as they shook their fists in the firelight; whipped revolvers into view, to signify their readiness for new battle. Even the wounded man against the tree made effort to join in the enthusiasm.

"You see?" Zenjora's face had calmed when he turned to Bandrillo. "You should not misunderstand them. They are more than eager, Bandrillo. Let them talk about The Shadow. It will sharpen them for the next encounter."

Henchmen resumed their growled palaver. Zenjora stepped close to Bandrillo. He lowered his voice below the babel of sound and said:

"Come! Let us go to the main cabin. Cardell is there. We have much to discuss."

With the Jibaros following as escort, Zenjora and Bandrillo took a path that led to a group of tumbledown cabins. These building explained the nature of the place that they had chosen for their headquarters. This was an abandoned summer colony, long since forgotten. Zenjora had located it soon after he had uncovered the buried treasure vault. This deserted settlement was within fifteen miles of the old Kincaid estate.

These shacks explained how Zenjora had kept his polyglot crew undercover; yet had them available for any call. He had kept a few in Manhattan; but the rest had remained here. Instead of returning to his apartment, Zenjora had simply come to join his men.

No place could have been better suited to an outlaw band like Zenjora's. Used to the hardships of the Santander mountains, these bandits considered themselves in luck, with roofs above their heads. The battered bungalows were their idea of luxurious living quarters.

Zenjora and Bandrillo arrived at the central cabin. They entered its square main room, stepping into the glow of hanging lanterns. A man awaited them. It was Cardell. He nodded to Bandrillo, then joined Zenjora and the lieutenant at an old table that was scarred with carved initials.

Zenjora planked his hand upon a stack of newspapers that Cardell had brought. Scanning them, he uttered an ugly chuckle that was for Bandrillo's benefit.

"The police!" sneered Zenjora. "Bah! They are as stupid in New York as in Santander! Luck has enabled them to find out how men have died; it has spoiled my plans of vengeance upon others like Dundee. Beyond that, however, it has served me."

From his coat pocket, Zenjora produced a folded paper, spread it to show a list of names.

"I have marked death for these men," he declared. "I delayed their doom once, until I had settled with Alvarez Rentone. I shall postpone death again, until after I have disposed of James Oakbrook. Look—one name is off the list; that of Howard Dundee. Someday, you shall see lines drawn through the other names as well."

PAUSING, Zenjora put away the list; he lowered his voice to a harsh growl.

"For the present," he declared, "Oakbrook is most important. The police are stupid fools; they think that Alvarez Rentone is responsible for Dundee's murder. They do not know that Alvarez is dead. I do not want them to learn the fact. That is why we must use the utmost strategy."

Zenjora looked to Bandrillo and Cardell as if inviting questions. Cardell put one.

"What about The Shadow?" asked the light-haired rogue. "Does he know that Alvarez Rentone is dead?"

"The Shadow's part is plain," assured Zenjora. "He is a fool who hounds crude criminals. He was watching Nick Broggoletta; saw the Italian meet Manuel Fendoza. The Shadow followed Fendoza to the Hotel Goliath; heard him ask for Alvarez Rentone.

"Believing that Fendoza was the man we murdered that night, The Shadow came to the hotel himself. Like a parrot, he asked for a message from Alvarez. He was wise enough not to open it. Instead, he gained an encounter with Marinez and Quinqual.

"There, his trail ended. He went back to watching Broggoletta. That brought him to the Clearview Hotel, where he battled Quinqual and Incos. He managed to follow them; that is how he came to be at the Kincaid estate, too late to rescue Alvarez and Jefford."

Zenjora had delivered a series of erroneous statements; but in his egotism, he thought that he had struck the truth. He was allowing a connection that Alvarez doubted; namely, a friendship between Fendoza and Broggoletta. Sure that he was right, Zenjora continued with more mistaken declarations.

"The Shadow was not at the mausoleum when Quinqual and Incos returned there," he announced. "He could not have followed them had he been there, for I gave them strict instructions to avoid all followers. Where was The Shadow? I shall tell you. He was back in New York.

"There, he learned that Inspector Cardona had gone to see Howard Dundee. So The Shadow went there himself. He had the luck to surprise Lakiki, to kill him and save Cardona's life. All this is the result"—Zenjora tapped the newspapers—"because Cardona lived to tell what Dundee had said."

CARDELL and Bandrillo were fully satisfied with Zenjora's incorrect analysis. They gazed in awe at their bearded chief, impressed by his ability to piece unknown facts.

"We must find Oakbrook," growled Zenjora, suddenly. "There is only one man whom I can risk sending to New York. That is you, Cardell. The Shadow will be looking for Oakbrook. You must learn facts before The Shadow."

"Suppose"—Cardell hesitated, to mop his forehead with a handkerchief—"suppose I run into The Shadow?"

Bandrillo snarled, taking Cardell's question as a sign of weakness. Zenjora raised a silencing hand. He faced Cardell.

"If you encounter The Shadow," purred Zenjora, "you will meet with no harm. He will know that you are a link to me. He seeks me, as well as Oakbrook. Should you find The Shadow, or believe that he has discovered you, simply rejoin me here. That will bring The Shadow on your trail."

"The Shadow went past our men before!" put in Bandrillo. "They cannot stop him in darkness. If he sees their lights, he will—"

Again, Zenjora's hand was raised. This time, it pointed to the doorway. Bandrillo and Cardell saw Quinqual and the other headhunters seated outside the door. The ape-faced trio were engaged in a curious task. They were weaving long strips of canelike wood into an odd-shaped matting.

"A jungle trap," chuckled Zenjora. "Tonight, the workmanship will be superior. There will be no need to dig a pit. There are gullies all about, where streams have cut their way to the gorge."

Rising, Zenjora gestured for Cardell to start his journey to New York. The spy saluted; turned and strode past the Jibaros. Soon Zenjora and Bandrillo heard the muffled sound of a departing automobile.

"All will be well, Bandrillo," purred Zenjora in Spanish. "The Shadow came alone before; he will venture alone again. This time, his own stealth will lead him to sure disaster."

With that promise, the evil chief beckoned his lieutenant to follow him. Together, they went out to join their mongrel followers at the campfire. Though Zenjora's theories were wrong, his prediction was one that seemed certain to come true.

In sending Cardell upon his mission, Zenjora had chosen a perfect bait to snare The Shadow.

CHAPTER XV
CHANGED TRAILS

IT was late afternoon the next day when Cardell entered a secluded restaurant just off Broadway to partake of an early dinner. Picking an isolated corner of the cafe, Zenjora's spy made sure that no one was watching him. Thereupon, he produced a memo pad from his pocket.

Cardell had listed his progress in the search for James Oakbrook. Last night, immediately upon reaching Manhattan, he had gone to Oakbrook's apartment house; he had made inquiry, with no result.

Later, he had called Oakbrook's club, with the same bad luck. Afterward, Cardell had registered at a hotel; this morning, he had stopped at Oakbrook's Wall Street office, to represent himself as a customer who wanted advice on bonds. Cardell had insisted that he must talk with Oakbrook in person. He had been told that the broker had gone away and had left no word regarding his destination.

Though Cardell had not guessed it, he had been under almost constant surveillance from the first step onward. Outside of Oakbrook's apartment house, a small crafty-faced man had spotted him. That was "Hawkeye," who served The Shadow.

A cab had stopped to pick up Cardell. The taxi was Moe Shrevnitz's. It had carried him to the store where he made a telephone call; the same cab, slightly altered in appearance, had Cardell as a fare to his hotel.

At the breakfast, Cardell had been watched by Harry Vincent, who sat at another table. When he visited Oakbrook's office, an elderly man had noted him, hobbled to the elevator just behind him, making good progress with a cane. That watcher had been The Shadow, in disguise.

While Cardell lunched, Moe's cab had been outside. Cardell had been trailed all afternoon; it was known that he was in this restaurant at present. In fact, Cardell had scarcely ordered his meal before a tall, calm-faced individual entered, took a seat at a nearby table and unfolded a copy of the evening *Sphere*.

This chance diner was The Shadow. He sat almost unnoticed by Cardell. As soon as he had given his own order, The Shadow sat back and turned to the real estate ads. His attention centered upon the newspaper.

Halfway down a column, The Shadow noted an advertisement that he had hoped to find. It stated that a fine lodge was for sale, in the foothills of the Catskill Mountains. The ad described the lodge as being three miles northwest of the town of Mercer; it specified that the property included forty acres, ten of which had been cleared as an emergency landing field for airplanes; that one portion of the grounds bordered a fair-sized lake.

The owner's name was given. It was Thomas Rustwick.

FROM that moment, a singular policy was adopted by The Shadow. He folded the newspaper, laid it aside and stared suspiciously at Cardell.

Zenjora's spy was quick to observe The Shadow's action; but he caught no glimpse of The Shadow's face. The Shadow turned away too soon.

When the waiter arrived with the first course, The Shadow began a complaint, always avoiding Cardell's direct observation. Tossing money on the table, The Shadow arose and stalked from the restaurant, still keeping his face turned from Cardell's view.

Cardell became uneasy as soon as The Shadow had gone. He pocketed his memo pad; began to think about his own departure. He finally decided to finish his meal. When he was halfway through it, he saw another man enter the restaurant.

This fellow looked like a reporter—which, in fact, he was. The arrival was Clyde Burke; he had come in response to a call from Burbank. Clyde's first action was to give a quick glance toward Cardell. The spy turned his head. Clyde sat down, ordered a dinner and began to drum the table. He looked toward a corner telephone booth and gave a grin.

Soon, Clyde arose and sauntered to the booth. He entered it and closed the door, just as Cardell was paying his check. The spy arose, came toward the door of the restaurant. He was within six feet of the telephone booths. The temptation was too great.

Cardell used a trick that he had worked before. He stepped to the booth next to Clyde's, entered it and shifted low. Listening, he could hear the reporter's words.

"He's the man all right!" Clyde's tone was emphatic... "No. There's no use to trail him. We know where he's stopping... What's that? You'll leave the report for me? About Oakbrook?... I won't be able to pick it up for an hour...

"All right, leave it anyway... Yes. Room 608 at the Marmont. I left the door unlocked, in case you came there... What's that? You're at the Marmont now?... Good! Then you can leave the report right away... I'll get it in about an hour..."

Clyde hung up, stepped from the booth and glanced toward Cardell's table. The spy saw his action; smiled as he watched Clyde go from the restaurant. Coming from his own booth, Cardell could scarcely cover his elation.

Cardell was sure that he had spotted two agents of The Shadow, who were doing double duty: covering him and searching for James Oakbrook. Apparently, they had learned important facts concerning the missing broker. Anytime after the next ten minutes, those facts might be available in a report that could be found in Room 608 at the Marmont Hotel. That report would be available, in an unlocked room, for nearly an hour to come.

CARDELL hurried from the restaurant and boarded Moe's cab, which came along in timely fashion. Cardell took the precaution of looking at the hack-driver's license; saw that the name and photograph were different from those in cabs that he had previously taken.

That was because Moe also took precautions. He put in new cards every time he dropped Cardell.

The spy ordered Moe to take him to the Marmont Hotel. Fifteen minutes later, they arrived there. Cardell entered the hotel.

Moe rounded the block, changed the license inside his cab and came back. He nosed into the hack stand just in back of a waiting cab. Moe figured that the other taxi might be gone by the time Cardell came out. If it still happened to be there and picked up Cardell, Moe could simply trail it.

When Cardell entered an elevator in the hotel, he experienced a sudden attack of jitters. The car did not start at once; the operator held it to take aboard a belated passenger; then waited for a few others. Each time that that door joggled and halted, Cardell became impatient. His lips twitched; his hard face paled. Cardell shifted as other passengers glanced curiously toward him.

The delay had sapped the spy's nerve.

Cardell recalled how effectively he had been covered at the restaurant. He knew that The Shadow was on his trail. He had two duties: one, to learn facts concerning Oakbrook; the other, to lure The Shadow to Zenjora's new lair. Cardell began to wish that he had forgotten the first job and concentrated only on the second.

The door of the elevator clanged shut. The operator called for floors. Cardell spoke nervously when he uttered "Six." He fancied that several passengers noted him. Any of these might be other watchers, posted by The Shadow. Cardell felt a sudden doubt of Zenjora's assurance that The Shadow would adopt a hands-off policy.

Cardell remembered Marinez and Lakiki. Zenjora had expressed no great regret for the deaths of his lieutenant and the Jibaro. To Zenjora, one henchman more or less was a matter of but little consequence. In fact, Zenjora was so proud of his own prowess that he had often made it evident that he could replace anyone who served him. In Santander, Cardell had seen Zenjora shoot down some of his most valuable men when they disobeyed minor orders.

When the door opened at the sixth floor, Cardell stepped off in halting fashion. He quivered like a victim going to a sacrifice. It was not until he felt sure that he stood unwatched that Cardell rallied. Looking along the corridor, he saw a turn that led to Room 608.

Cardell sneaked to the short passage. He noticed that it was unlighted. Dusk had settled; the entire corridor was gloomy. That gave Cardell mingled sensations of doubt and assurance. At last, Cardell steeled himself, moved to the door of 608 and opened it.

A floor lamp was illuminated; by its glow, Cardell saw an envelope that lay upon a writing desk. The envelope was unsealed.

Leaving the door open, Cardell drew a gun and edged across the room. His nerves were at high pitch; he did not dare to let his finger touch the hair trigger of his revolver, for fear the gun would go off. He reached the desk, rested one shaky hand beside the envelope.

One moment more, Cardell would have taken the bait. But before he could steady his hand, he heard a sound from somewhere in the outside corridor. It was the closing of a door.

HAD Cardell waited and reasoned, he would have picked the true source of that sound. Some hotel guest had simply stepped from his room and closed the door behind him.

Cardell, however, no longer possessed a sense of reason. He sprang away from the writing desk as if it had been electrified. He darted out into the short passage.

There he halted, crouching with his gun. He heard the *clang* of an elevator door; it was simply taking the guest on board. Again, Cardell's strained senses deceived him. He fancied that the elevator had let off men who had come here to trap him. Completely victimized by his own imagination, Cardell shrank back. His revolver nearly wobbled from his hand.

Two minutes passed. Cardell regained some of his spent nerve. He looked back to 608; made an effort to return to the room, then changed his mind. Instead, he crept toward the main corridor; gasped his relief when he saw that it was deserted.

Cardell spied the dial above an elevator, noted that a car was descending from the tenth floor. Seized with a sudden phobia, he shoved his gun into his pocket and made a bolt for the elevators. Wildly, he pressed the button in time to halt the descending car.

The elevator stopped. Cardell entered it. The door clanged shut. That sound carried through the sixth floor. It caused an action across the hall from Room 608. Another door opened; a cloaked figure stepped into the gloom of the passage. The Shadow, listening in another room, had sensed Cardell's flight.

The Shadow's first move was to enter 608. There, he picked up the unsealed envelope. He carefully drew a paper from it; there was a slight resistance to The Shadow's pull. He had affixed the paper in the envelope with a tiny dab of gum.

The paper was simply a small sheet that had Oakbrook's want ad pasted to it. A ring was drawn in blue pencil around the name of Thomas Rustwick; below was the written notation:

This is James Oakbrook. Wait for a repeat ad tomorrow.

For some strange reason of his own, The Shadow had desired that this information should reach Emilio Zenjora. That was why The Shadow had played hide-and-seek with Cardell. The Shadow, through some deductive process had foreseen that Oakbrook would soon advertise his whereabouts. As soon as he had seen the ad in the *Sphere*, The Shadow had changed tactics with Cardell.

The Shadow had made the spy's task an easy one. He had planned that Cardell should gain the message and rejoin Zenjora. The Shadow would then have had no need to follow Cardell, for he could have avoided a trip to Zenjora's headquarters. The simple course would have been to go to Oakbrook's new abode, to await Zenjora's eventual arrival.

Cardell's sudden fright had changed all that. The bait might not work again. The Shadow's only alternative was to find Zenjora as soon as possible; that meant that he must take up Cardell's trail.

THE SHADOW picked up the telephone and called Burbank. He received an immediate report—one that proved the efficiency of his agents. Moe had picked up Cardell as a fare outside the hotel. Cardell had told the taxi driver to take him to a West Side garage. It was obvious that Cardell was going to obtain a car of his own.

Moe had scrawled this information on a slip of paper, unnoticed by Cardell. He had flicked the paper, wadded, from the cab window. Hawkeye, who was slouched near by, had snagged the paper and phoned the news to Burbank.

The Shadow knew that Moe would dawdle on the trip to the garage, choosing streets where traffic was heavy and delay unavoidable. Calmly, The Shadow replaced the baited envelope that Cardell had failed to take. Doffing his cloak and hat, he placed them over his arm, so that they appeared as ordinary garments.

With that, The Shadow strolled from the room. He was on his way to gain his own car, that same speedy roadster that he had used before. He had time to reach the garage before Cardell arrived there. Darkness had almost settled; The Shadow would find it easy to pick up Cardell's trail when the man started out in his own car.

Tonight's trail was to prove easier than The Shadow supposed. Cardell's actual fright had lulled him; prevented The Shadow from divining the real truth behind the spy's hasty action. Cardell's quick flight foreboded trouble that The Shadow did not foresee.

The Shadow was faring to a spot where the odds would be hopelessly against him. He was heading straight for an invisible trap that Zenjora's head-hunters had prepared. Tonight, The Shadow was to find new evidence of Jibaro cunning.

Changed trails had swung the game in Zenjora's favor.

CHAPTER XVI
THE DOUBLE TRAP

DARKNESS lay thick amid the Jersey hills when a coupé stopped near the end of an old abandoned road. The driver turned off the ignition switch; he lighted a match with shaky hand and applied it to a cigarette. The glowing flame showed the strained face of Cardell.

Zenjora's spy had reached the spot where he must begin a trail on foot; but he was not satisfied that his work was done. This time, it was doubt that made Cardell nervous. All along the route, Cardell had watched the mirror for signs of a following car. At times, he had believed that he had spotted one; but he was not sure.

The Shadow had again used the trick of following by the headlights of the car ahead. At this precise moment, he was stowing his smooth-motored roadster in a place well off the road. The Shadow had picked a winding path that led to lower ground beside a wide stream. He was bringing his car almost on a line with Cardell's, without the fellow's knowledge.

Cardell finished his cigarette. Extinguishing it, he stepped from the coupé. He started along a path that led upward, then turned and led back toward the creek, but on a higher level. After a hundred yards, Cardell stopped.

The spy grunted a troubled laugh. He realized that he stood a good chance of putting himself in Zenjora's bad graces. Cardell did not intend to mention the episode at the Marmont Hotel. He knew that Zenjora would show no mercy to an underling who had turned yellow in a pinch. Nevertheless, the knowledge of his failure rested heavily upon him. To cover it, Cardell had hoped to bring The Shadow here. He began to feel that he had not succeeded.

Inspired by a failing hope that The Shadow might possibly have followed, Cardell stopped to light another cigarette. He let the tiny coal glow in the darkness; then strolled slowly ahead, flourishing the cigarette as he went. A bit farther on, Cardell used a flashlight, blinking it at intervals.

These beacons served better than Cardell had supposed. Eyes had spotted them from the path. The Shadow had seen opportunity to close the trail. Coming speedily, but silently, the cloaked follower moved within a dozen paces of Cardell. The Shadow expected trouble. The closer he came to it, the better, under circumstances such as these.

Cardell had nearly reached the cabins when his

feet crunched underbrush that lay upon the path. Cardell remembered this spot. Previously, it had marked a hollow cut by heavy rains; wide boards had been laid across the space. Those boards were gone.

Though the path seemed solid, Cardell guessed what lay beneath. He was treading upon the weaved matting spun by the Jibaros. Thin poles lay beneath the weave; underbrush had been gathered and spread above.

Just as Cardell reached the far side of this stretch, he detected motion beside him. The Jibaros were crouched in darkness. The instant that Cardell passed, they reached down to cut thongs that held the poles in place. They were preparing the trap for Cardell's follower. Their purpose was to have the matting loose, so that an arrival would tumble the moment that he struck it.

There was one flaw to the plan. Neither Zenjora nor his cunning headhunters had supposed that The Shadow would be so close upon Cardell's trail.

The Shadow's foot struck the underbrush before Cardell was fully past it. One step more told The Shadow that he was upon treacherous footing. His keen ears caught sounds ahead; as he took a long stride, he felt a quiver beneath him. Lunging, The Shadow gave a long spring forward. He was too late.

UNDERBRUSH crackled; the matting dropped as poles were loosened. The Shadow's plunge went short; his hands failed to reach the farther bank. There was a crash as debris plunged into an eight-foot gully; twisting downward. The Shadow was swallowed into the pit.

One factor alone had favored The Shadow. His leap had carried him almost to the far side of the gully. As he sprawled, he was still spinning forward. His shoulder struck the far side of the pit. His fall was broken as he slipped down to the bottom.

Something scraped The Shadow's back. Lying prone, he probed in darkness. He learned instantly that he had escaped death by hairsbreadth. The object against his back was a stout pole, driven deep into the bottom of the pit. The Shadow's gloved hand found the upper end of the pole. It had been whittled to a sharp point.

Reaching farther, The Shadow found another wooden spike. He realized that the pit was full of them. Any ordinary plunge would have impaled its victim upon one or more of these spearlike prongs. Chances were that all of them were dyed with Jibaro poison.

Though The Shadow's spring had not carried him beyond the trap, it had at least saved him from death. It gave him a chance for battle; and The Shadow expected such strife soon. Already, he could hear elated shouts from back along the path by which he had come.

Zenjora's outlaws had heard the crash. They were coming in from the woods to view the pit. Flashlights began to glimmer. The Shadow could see them through the remnants of the underbrush.

The pit would be a death trap of a new sort when those enemies arrived. Though The Shadow might thin them with bullets, they would gain the final victory if he remained in the cramped space where he had fallen. The Shadow's only course was to climb from the pit, on the side toward the cabins.

With an upward lunge, The Shadow gripped the claylike bank, clawed his way to the top. Each slip of his hands offered disaster, for a backward fall would impale him on a spike. Lights were coming closer every second; any delay would mean death from outlaw guns. The Shadow had eight feet to go. He made it by superhuman effort.

Each time one hand slipped, the other was quick to grip a higher spot. Before his body slid slowly back to its former level, The Shadow gained a temporary grip that pulled him closer to the solid ground above. One hand came over the brink, caught a twisted tree root. The other hand joined it; The Shadow hoisted his body into the clear by virtue of one tremendous pull.

AS The Shadow rolled upon solid turf, lights burned downward from the other side of the trap. Outlaws gave fierce snarls when they saw vacancy. One spied the muddy stretch of bank where The Shadow had clawed his way to freedom. The rogue turned his flashlight to the far edge of the pit.

The glare was just in time to show The Shadow coming to his feet. The outlaw shouted; the others swung their guns, but did not fire. The Shadow had scrambled away to farther darkness. Wildly, Zenjora's henchmen began to circle the pit, hopeful that this time they could surround The Shadow and down him with their guns.

Ordinarily, The Shadow would have stopped to meet them; but he knew that another menace existed in the darkness. The Jibaros were on his side of the pit. If any one of the three should gain a chance to fling a poisoned dart, The Shadow's doom would be assured. What The Shadow needed was a temporary stronghold. He came upon one in the darkness.

The Shadow had found a cabin, with door and windows closed. He was beside the door; as he listened, he could hear the creep of Jibaro headsmen, plain despite the more distant shouts of outlaws. Gun in one hand, The Shadow gripped the knob of the cabin door with the other. The door loosened; The Shadow flung it inward and dived with it.

Instantly, he was in the glare of lanterns. The tight door, the shuttered windows had hidden the glow. Yet the light did not deter The Shadow. He whipped the door shut behind him. He wheeled to face any foemen who might be within. As he swung, The Shadow saw a man seated at a table. He covered the fellow instantly; then eyed his foeman.

The man at the table was Zenjora. Eyes glaring, a distorted smile upon the lips that showed from his heavy beard, the supercrook was gloating at The Shadow's arrival. Zenjora's arms were folded. His ugly gaze expressed no fear.

An instant later, The Shadow learned the reason for Zenjora's composure.

Windows swung wide on either side; the door whipped inward. The Shadow saw apish faces to left and right; he knew that another stood behind him. Each was ready with a poisoned bamboo javelin. Death threatened The Shadow from three directions. Zenjora had not trusted to the Jibaro pit alone. He had prepared this second trap.

IN order to give the headhunters full opportunity to gain their posts, Zenjora had stationed himself within the cabin. His ruse had worked well. The Shadow, entering, had looked for an occupant; hence had concentrated on Zenjora. Timed to perfection, the headhunters had arrived to back their master.

Another move was due, according to Zenjora's calculations. Ever crafty, he had remained unarmed. His guess was that The Shadow would swing in futile attempt to shoot down the Jibaros. Zenjora did not expect him to clip a single one of them; for the headhunters were set to dodge from the windows as they launched their javelins.

This time, Zenjora was wrong.

The Shadow's first actions had been logical; for every one had offered him some advantage. Sighting the Jibaros, The Shadow saw a hopeless situation. Had he swung about, or made a single mistaken shift, death would have struck upon the instant.

Instead, The Shadow took advantage of the only flaw in Zenjora's snare. Finger upon the trigger of his .45, he held steady aim toward Zenjora. To give it emphasis, he moved forward to the table; faced the bearded crook almost eye to eye.

The Shadow had not allowed a fraction of time for Zenjora to spring away while headhunters made their thrusts. The moment that a bamboo javelin winged the air, he could pull his trigger. If death should be The Shadow's, Zenjora would share it.

The Shadow had produced a stalemate. Zenjora knew it; he babbled frantically in high-pitched dialect. The Shadow recognized that he was calling to his headhunters, telling them to restrain their weapons.

To The Shadow, however, Zenjora snarled in English:

"Kill me, you will die!"

The Shadow's answer was a sinister laugh that crept through the pine walls of the cabin. The game worked either way. The Shadow's mockery told that he had no fear of death; that Zenjora's dilemma was the same as his own.

Nevertheless, The Shadow foresaw that he might lose his equal status. Though the Jibaros stood motionless, there were others: those outlaws whom The Shadow had escaped. They were creeping toward the cabin. At any time, they might poke gun muzzles through knotholes in the pine boards. If rifles crackled from the hands of sharpshooters, their bullets could kill with speed.

There was one way to end this changing situation that could become worse for The Shadow. That was to give Zenjora a reason to call off his hounds of death. Calmly, The Shadow spoke unexpected words.

"My death," pronounced The Shadow to Zenjora, "will mean yours. My death would end your schemes. I hold facts that you can never learn. I, alone, can tell you where James Oakbrook may be found."

A sudden glint came to Zenjora's eyes; his optics glittered below the beads of perspiration that had formed upon his bulky forehead. Zenjora snapped up The Shadow's proposition.

"Your life for mine," he bargained. "Your freedom, later, when you have told me where Oakbrook is!"

"Agreed," announced The Shadow. "Order your men to lower their weapons."

ZENJORA hesitated; then leered in confident fashion. His men were too numerous for The Shadow, with this cabin a trap instead of a stronghold. Zenjora delivered two orders; the first to the Jibaros, the second to the outside outlaws.

The Shadow stepped back from the table, placed his automatic beneath his cloak. Instantly, Zenjora whipped out a revolver to cover him. While Jibaros stood at the windows, outlaws surged through the door; they surrounded The Shadow and disarmed him.

Zenjora ordered them to tie the prisoner hand and foot. The brigands obeyed, using lengths of ropes and leather thongs. They sprawled The Shadow in a corner, thrusting him there with kicks and jeers.

Zenjora ordered his motley crew outside. Standing above The Shadow, he was joined by two men: Bandrillo and Cardell. With these witnesses present, Zenjora snarled his ultimatum.

"I have allowed you to live," he sneered to The Shadow. "You shall have freedom after my plans are complete. Tell me where Oakbrook is. That will complete our bargain."

"Our bargain is complete," responded The Shadow, calmly. "We are both alive. As for freedom, I no longer request it. Find Oakbrook for yourself."

Zenjora scowled. He realized what The Shadow had gained. Death was no longer a weapon for Zenjora, until he had learned the facts he needed. Torture was the one instrument that the crook could use.

"You think that you will not speak?" purred Zenjora. "Ah, we shall learn that for ourselves. You have not yet tasted the medicine that Emilio Zenjora can give. It may take hours, days perhaps; but you will speak before I have finished!"

Cardell saw a sudden chance to hold his chief's favor. In concise fashion, the spy began to tell of the episode at the Marmont Hotel. He softened the story, to make it appear that danger had been too great to enter the hotel room. At first, Zenjora showed an outburst of anger.

"You failed!" he snarled. "You fool! You know the fate of those who fail me!"

"Let me return," pleaded Cardell. "I brought The Shadow here, as you wanted. He is your prisoner; the way is safe. The message may still be where I saw it."

Zenjora stroked his beard; his eyes glistened approval as he nodded.

"Go, Cardell," he ordered. "After you have searched for the message, call by telephone to the little store two miles from here. Bandrillo will be waiting there to receive your message."

Cardell strode from the cabin. Zenjora's eyes gleamed triumph. Beckoning to Bandrillo, Zenjora drew the lieutenant to the table; there, the two sat down to discuss future deeds.

Men of crime had reached their zenith. With The Shadow a prisoner, success seemed certain to Emilio Zenjora.

CHAPTER XVII
JIBARO TORTURE

IN the minute that followed Cardell's departure, The Shadow summed the present circumstances and found that they offered little. The Shadow had gained respite from death; but he knew that the interval would not be long.

When he bluffed Zenjora, The Shadow had hoped that a period of imprisonment would give him opportunity to work out an escape. He had been willing to take doses of Zenjora's tortures, if they came as part of a campaign for freedom.

Cardell, however, had crossed The Shadow's plans. The spy had taken a chance that The Shadow had expected him to avoid. Zenjora, in turn, had curbed his wrath, and had agreed to let Cardell return to his former mission.

In about one hour, Cardell would be back in Manhattan. He would find the room at the Marmont exactly as The Shadow had left it. Soon after that, Bandrillo would receive the telephoned message, stating the news concerning James Oakbrook. Once that word was brought to Zenjora, the crook could pronounce doom for The Shadow.

Looking ahead, The Shadow considered the vital hour that still remained to him. No minutes could be wasted. The only course was to force a change in present circumstances.

Half rising in his corner, The Shadow began to struggle against his bonds. His hands were securely tied behind him. It would take a long time to loosen them. Nevertheless, The Shadow used great effort, twisting about until his back was half toward Zenjora and Bandrillo. The two halted their conference to watch the motions of The Shadow's wrists.

While he fought against the rigid bonds that held his hands, The Shadow used his ankles also; but the watchers scarcely noticed that fact. The Shadow had deliberately attracted their attention to his wrists. He had a reason; he knew that he could free his feet sooner than he could his hands. Therefore, he wanted to divert attention from his ankles.

When the outlaws had bound him, The Shadow had managed to cross his feet. By shifting his ankles, bringing them side by side, he could gain slack at will. Ropes and thongs were still too tight to be slipped; but steady pressure might eventually loosen them.

Zenjora and Bandrillo returned to their conference, satisfied that The Shadow's struggle were hopeless. They had nothing to fear; for headhunters were close at hand, ready for immediate call. Nevertheless, the crooks could still hear The Shadow's struggle on the floor; and that fact caused Zenjora to deliver occasional glares toward the corner.

At last, Zenjora stopped the conference with a snarl. He gesticulated impatiently to Bandrillo.

"Bah!" exclaimed Zenjora. "We waste time talking! What good are plans until we know where we must go? When we hear from Cardell, then we can make plans."

There was a pause, while Zenjora eyed The Shadow, who had temporarily ceased his struggles. Sight of The Shadow made Zenjora express new thoughts.

"What if Cardell finds nothing?" he demanded, savagely, with a gesture to Bandrillo. "What shall we do then?"

Bandrillo made no answer. Zenjora replied for himself.

"We must torture him," the supercrook declared, pointing to The Shadow. "We must make him speak as soon as possible. Perhaps"—Zenjora smiled with relish as The Shadow began a new struggle against the bonds—"ah, perhaps it would be good to start the torture now."

RISING, Zenjora walked to The Shadow's corner,

glared down at the huddled prisoner. The Shadow's eyes met Zenjora's; they showed a blazing challenge that brought a snarl from the crook.

"You ask for torture, eh?" queried Zenjora, angrily. "Very good. You shall have it!"

Wheeling to Bandrillo, Zenjora gave an order. He told the lieutenant to go outside and summon four outlaws. As Bandrillo started, Zenjora added:

"Send the men here. Then go to the little store and wait to hear from Cardell."

Two minutes after Bandrillo had gone, four ruffians entered the cabin. Zenjora ordered them to carry The Shadow, while he led the way. As the banditti hoisted their living burden, Zenjora called an order from the doorway. His three headhunters scrambled from their posts, joined their evil chief and followed him.

Zenjora led the way to the glade, where other outlaws sat about their campfire. The throng arose with ugly murmurs as they saw four of their fellows bringing The Shadow on their shoulders. Zenjora beckoned; all followed.

Zenjora strode to the brink of the ravine. There, he turned about; his face glowed with demonish malice; the light from the campfire gave that bearded visage a satanic ruddiness.

The four men dropped The Shadow at Zenjora's feet. Prone and motionless, on the very edge of the gorge, The Shadow could hear a roar from far beneath, where the wide stream surged through the gap between the slopes.

The Shadow had ceased his struggles with the bonds. Given a dozen minutes more, he could have loosened those about his ankles. Zenjora had unwittingly blocked that move. At present, new struggles would be more than futile. They would lead the outlaws to tighten the bonds more fully.

Calmly, The Shadow watched Zenjora. He knew that the supercrook must have picked this spot for some definite reason; one that undoubtedly included torture. Zenjora's eyes saw The Shadow's gaze; the crook's ruddy lips formed a devilish leer.

Like a showman upon a platform, Zenjora summoned his Jibaros. He pointed to a stout sapling that was rooted on the very edge of the gorge. With chattered response, the headhunters started up the tree like monkeys.

As the first Jibaro neared the top, the slender tree wavered. As it swung toward Zenjora, another Jibaro scrambled beside the first. The sapling bent down toward the high ground; the third Jibaro added his weight to the top branches. In one mass, the headhunters carried the slender treetop to the ground; they held the doubled sapling in its new position.

Another gesture from Zenjora; a pair of husky outlaws stepped up and held the bent tree where it was. Zenjora pointed to a second sapling, only a dozen feet from the first. The Jibaros repeated their process; brought the second treetop downward. Again, a pair of outlaws took over the task of holding it.

ZENJORA had evidently tested this device beforehand; for other preparations had been completed earlier. Stooping to a spot beside The Shadow, Zenjora pushed away a small pile of brush. The action showed heavy timbers sunk deep in the ground, and weighted by huge stones. From the logs projected the ends of a massive leather strap.

The Jibaros knew what was due; for this was one of their own jungle tortures. Without a word from Zenjora, they dragged The Shadow to the sunken timbers. They pushed a strap end between The Shadow's ankles, over the bonds that held them. Zenjora, himself, buckled the strap; saw that it was firm.

Shoving The Shadow to a seated position, the Jibaros cut the bonds that held his wrists. Instantly, Quinqual seized one of The Shadow's arms, while Incos grabbed the other. They raised The Shadow's hands above his head. Miquon tightened a leather thong around one of The Shadow's wrists; then bound the other wrist with the same cord, leaving a stretch of stout leather between.

One such bond was not enough. Miquon added more, with Quinqual and Incos helping him; for they no longer needed to hold The Shadow's arms. They nodded to Zenjora; babbled harsh words of glee.

Outlaws maneuvered the tops of the bent saplings between The Shadow's upheld arms. Gradually, they released the pressure. The trees, stiffening upward, drew The Shadow upright. He was stretched like a rod that restrains the action of a powerful spring. The outlaws still held the bent trees to relieve the strain.

Zenjora faced The Shadow, whose back was toward the edge of the ravine. With his headhunters clustered beside him, Zenjora described the torture that was to come.

"I have seen this in the jungle," he told The Shadow. "Once my men have taken away their weight, your body will bear the strain of four. Perhaps for a while, you will have the strength to resist it. Once that is ended, you will learn how horrible death can be.

"Perhaps an easier death will suit you better. I can promise you less pain. Speak, while the time still offers. Tell me where I shall find James Oakbrook. I shall give you until Bandrillo returns; no longer."

Outlaws were weakening; The Shadow could already feel the tug of the pulling saplings. The strain reached his feet; he felt a quiver of the cords that bound his ankles. The Shadow's reply to

Rising from the desk, Oakbrook looked about with satisfaction. His three servants were stationed out of sight. Lynn and Alvarez were behind the tapestries. A desk drawer was pulled half open; within it lay a .38 for Oakbrook's own use.

"Be ready," he spoke for Lynn and Alvarez to hear. "Come from the tapestries when I raise my left hand thus. Cover Zenjora when you appear. My servants already have their instructions."

With that, Oakbrook went to the front door and listened. He heard the purr of a motor coming along the drive. The gray-clad man smiled his confidence. Lynn and Alvarez watched him from the edges of the tapestries.

So intent were all those in the room that they failed to notice something else that happened. There was a slight rustle at one of the curtained passages at the rear of the room. Soon afterward, there was semblance of motion at the second passage.

Those occurrences were ominous, coming at the exact time of Emilio Zenjora's arrival. They signified that trouble could have come to Oakbrook's body-guards; first, to the man at the back door; afterward, to each isolated servant who was stationed in a passage.

The rustle of curtains was ended. Like tokens of death, they had appeared; then vanished. The draperies were stilled when footsteps crunched outside the front door of the lodge. Unwitting of the happenings within the lodge itself, Oakbrook placed his hand upon the doorknob.

Calmly, the gray-clad man opened the portal and stepped back from the threshold to extend a hand of greeting to Emilio Zenjora.

CHAPTER XIX
THE CLAIM OF WEALTH

EMILIO ZENJORA had arrived alone. He was suave and friendly as he bowed from the doorway of the lodge. On this occasion, the bearded bandit had masked his evil pose. He was the Emilio Zenjora who had formerly been well received in the capitals of South America.

Glare was gone from eyes of evil. Ruddy lips were pleasant in their smile. Zenjora's hand faked sincerity in its grip when he received Oakbrook's shake. Still bowing, the bearded visitor followed Oakbrook as the broker conducted him to the desk.

When Oakbrook's back was turned, however, Zenjora's eyes showed an avaricious flash. The bearded man had spied the safe behind the broker's desk. Zenjora guessed that the safe was the reposi-tory for the million dollars that he had come here to acquire.

"I presume that you are from Santander," remarked Oakbrook, as he sat down and passed a box of cigars across the desk. "In fact, Senor Zenjora, I have heard of you in the past."

"Ah!" Zenjora shrugged his shoulders. "Anyone may be heard of in Santander. I hope that you did not believe all that was told you."

"I understood," said Oakbrook, "that you belonged to a faction opposed to my former friend, José Rentone."

"Ah, no!" Zenjora shook his head. "Much was misunderstood. I was a friend to the late dictator; but it was difficult for either of us to state that fact. Politics are serious business in Santander. It is not wise always for friends to appear too friendly."

"I understand," nodded Oakbrook. "Perhaps, then, senor, you can tell me what has become of Alvarez Rentone. I have expected word from him; but it has not come—"

"You have read the newspapers?"

Oakbrook hesitated; then answered: "Yes. But I was not ready to believe their reports."

"You should not believe them," declared Zenjora. "They tell of another man who has been misunderstood. Alvarez Rentone is not a criminal. The crimes of others have been placed upon him. But he has been forced to leave this country. That is why I have come here in his place."

Oakbrook feigned surprise. Zenjora smiled; reached into his pocket and produced the sheaf of promissory notes. He spread them on the desk in front of Oakbrook.

"I have brought these," he declared. "Once you have given me the money, I shall carry it to Alvarez Rentone. I, alone, know where to reach him and his cousin Estaban."

ZENJORA veiled the insidious significance of his words. Oakbrook gave no sign that he suspected the true meaning. Instead, he simply examined the promissory notes; turned about and pulled the door of the safe.

The door was unlocked; it swung wide. From the safe, Oakbrook produced the same box that he had shown Alvarez in the Wall Street office. He tendered the wealth to Zenjora.

"These notes," declared Oakbrook, "are canceled." He tore them; tossed the pieces into a wastebasket. "The entire amount is there, senor; all negotiable. I trust you to deliver it to its proper owners."

Zenjora completed a quick counting of the funds. He arose; Oakbrook did the same. The broker waited until Zenjora tucked the box under his arm and turned toward the door; then, with a quick move, Oakbrook raised his left hand.

Tapestries swept aside. Lynn and Alvarez leaped from their hiding places, with ready revolvers. At the same instant, Oakbrook whipped his .38 from the desk drawer. He gave a sharp call to Zenjora.

They saw Zenjora seize the dying broker and swing him as a shield ... The Shadow pumping bullets from both automatics ... found Zenjora as ... target ...

The bearded crook wheeled. His eyes glared as he saw himself within a triangle of guns. He gazed at the men who held the weapons. A dumbfounded look registered itself upon Zenjora's bearded visage.

For seconds, no one spoke. It was Zenjora himself who broke the silence. He let the money box fall to a chair; slowly, he raised his hands above his head. His tone was an ugly purr that came from curling lips.

"So The Shadow rescued you," he said to Lynn and Alvarez. "That is how he learned so much concerning Oakbrook. Bah! The Shadow did not profit by his interference. Perhaps, my friends, you will soon join him!"

Stolidly, Alvarez reached for the money box. As he picked it up, Oakbrook spoke, telling him to place the million dollars on the desk. Alvarez did so. Oakbrook gestured for him to again cover Zenjora with his gun. Alvarez obeyed.

"So it is you," sneered Zenjora, facing Oakbrook, "who arranged this trap! You are a fool, Oakbrook! You have lost one million dollars. Perhaps you and I could have made a bargain for that wealth."

A hard smile showed on Oakbrook's lips. The gray-haired man kept his revolver leveled straight toward Zenjora.

"No bargain is necessary," declared Oakbrook, his tone a rasped one. "Stand where you are, Zenjora! I have you covered! As for you, Alvarez, and your friend Jefford, I order you to make no move! The two of you are covered by the servants whom I placed behind the curtains!"

LYNN and Alvarez stared in surprise. One look at Oakbrook's face told them that he meant his words. Oakbrook's glare was as fierce, as evil as Zenjora's.

"Why did I need to give up a million dollars?" demanded Oakbrook. "Two men alone knew the secret of its hiding place. You were one, Alvarez; your cousin Estaban the other. The day I left New York, I prepared to deal with both of you.

"To eliminate Estaban, I sent an anonymous cablegram to Santander, telling the authorities that they would find him at San Luis. I learned tonight that the step was unnecessary. Zenjora had already seen to your cousin's death.

"For you, Alvarez, I prepared a death that fitted with Fendoza's; one that would further mystify the law, by continuing the Italian angle that Zenjora had started. I hired an assassin to kill you with a stiletto thrust."

The truth struck Alvarez before Oakbrook finished.

"Nick Broggoletta!" Alvarez exclaimed. "You sent him to murder me at my hotel!"

Slowly, Oakbrook nodded. An appreciative chuckle came from the bearded lips of Zenjora. He admired the craft that Oakbrook had shown. Oakbrook smiled at Zenjora's approval.

"No one guessed my part," sneered Oakbrook. "Not even the man you call The Shadow. But Broggoletta failed to kill. That was why I brought you here, Alvarez. The newspapers told that you were wanted by the law. Very well. The law will find you. You will lie dead, here in this lodge. I and my servants will be congratulated for having disposed of a public enemy."

Lynn Jefford saw Alvarez stare, half dazed. To Lynn's brain came a sudden understanding; he realized why he and Alvarez had been told to remain in New York.

The Shadow had divined the part played by Nick Broggoletta. The Shadow had seen that a paid assassin must have come from some definite source. Only Oakbrook could have sent him; for— outside of Zenjora—only Oakbrook knew that Alvarez was at the Clearview Hotel.

Alvarez, by confiding in Oakbrook, had given the broker a chance to turn to crime. Oakbrook had grasped it; and The Shadow had seen the answer. That was why The Shadow had wanted Alvarez to take the burden of Zenjora's crimes, so that Oakbrook would feel confident enough to reveal his evil hand.

Lynn saw more; he saw that Zenjora must also have come here through information that The Shadow had enabled him to gain. The Shadow had planned a showdown, crook against crook. Zenjora, with the promissory notes; Oakbrook, with the money that they represented. The Shadow wanted the two to meet and battle while he arrived to pluck the spoils and restore them to Alvarez Rentone.

Dully, Lynn realized how he and Alvarez had blundered. He stared toward Oakbrook; then looked at Zenjora. A shiver suddenly seized Lynn as he saw a demoniacal smile appear upon Zenjora's lips. Oakbrook was speaking; he was sealing Zenjora's doom; but the bearded crook was unconcerned.

"You, Alvarez," spoke Oakbrook, "and you, Jefford, can have one satisfaction. Your guns are trained upon Zenjora. When I give the word, you can proceed to riddle him with bullets. My own men will slaughter you, immediately afterward; but the joy of dealing with Zenjora will lessen your own burden of doom. I am ready with the order—"

A TERRIFIC clatter interrupted Oakbrook's statement. Three windows shattered simultaneously. In from the dark sprang a trio of apish men; one from the front, two from the sides. They were Zenjora's Jibaro tribesmen.

They had passed Keller, at the gate. Outside the windows, they had caught a signal from Zenjora. As they smashed the glass and hurtled inward, their arms were raised to throwing positions. Each had a feathered bamboo shaft; each had a potential victim.

Quinqual and Incos were prepared to strike down Alvarez and Lynn. Miquon, at the front window, was driving his limber arm toward Oakbrook. An instant later, three javelins would have winged the air; but only one of those shafts was destined to take flight.

Timed with the crashing entry of the head-hunters, the curtain of a passage doorway was swept aside. A gloved hand jabbed toward Quinqual; a .45 boomed as a finger pressed the trigger. Swinging to the opposite angle was another hand, that held a second automatic. It waited only as blazing eyes turned to sight along it. The second automatic flashed.

Quinqual sprawled to the floor, his javelin in his fist. Incos tumbled as his arm began its heave; his fingers loosened, the shaft fell from them. Rolling, the Jibaro lay across his poisoned weapon.

Miquon alone dispatched his dart. The shaft found its victim: Oakbrook. The broker took the point deep in his shoulder; he staggered behind his desk. Miquon leaped for the window; Alvarez and Lynn saw The Shadow spring from the curtained passage. An automatic boomed its lethal message. Miquon tumbled, headforemost, through the window, dropped in his final dive for safety.

The Shadow had arrived to witness the meeting between Oakbrook and Zenjora. He had escaped from the gorge; freed his chafed wrists and had reached his hidden car. He had called Burbank, to dispatch Crofton with an autogiro from Newark Airport. In that ship, The Shadow had reached the landing field in back of the lodge, ahead of Zenjora's arrival.

Coming to the lodge, he had overpowered Oakbrook's servants in silent fashion, one by one. He had taken his place behind the curtain, ready to deliver his own thrusts when the moment arrived.

ZENJORA saw The Shadow. The bearded crook went berserk. Springing from between Lynn and Alvarez, he leaped for the desk, vaulted it and fell upon Oakbrook's swaying form. Lynn and Alvarez fired late and wild. They saw Zenjora grab Oakbrook's gun; seize the dying broker and swing him as a shield.

The move had been amazing in its swiftness. Already, Zenjora had begun to stab wild shots toward The Shadow. His aim was shaken by the sway of Oakbrook's body; and that gray-clad form failed utterly to serve him as a shield.

The Shadow was pumping bullets from both automatics. They came in a blazing stream, riddling Oakbrook, to reach the man beyond. That deadly hail was overwhelming in its power. Pummeling bullets literally chopped away the human shield. Unstopped slugs found Zenjora as their target.

Oakbrook was dead at the beginning of The Shadow's fire. The Jibaro shaft had doomed him with its poisoned dye. As the bullet-riddled corpse sank to the floor, Zenjora floundered upon the desk. He made a last effort to rise; Lynn and Alvarez added their bullets to The Shadow's.

Zenjora's hands clawed a last tattoo upon the desk. His bearded face plopped from sight.

Emilio Zenjora lay dead across the body of his rival in crime, Oakbrook.

The Shadow was reloading his automatics. The move was timely. Shots were sounding outside. Bandrillo and the outlaws had driven past the gate; Keller was firing as they went by. Ordering Lynn and Alvarez to remain in the lodge, The Shadow opened the door and headed out into the night.

There, his sinister laugh sounded its challenge to approaching foemen. As revolvers barked, The Shadow's guns responded. Once again, he was tonguing death from darkness. Banditti scattered before the double-barreled volley.

Members of the band were sprawling as they fled. Bandrillo was among the ones who dropped. Leaping into a lone car, a leaderless crew took flight. They passed the gate unscathed, for they had settled Keller with the loss of two men.

As the outlaw machine swept past the gate, a car roared up to block it. New guns opened fire. The Shadow's agents had arrived to stop the flight. The driver of the bandit car was felled; uncontrolled, the machine hurtled from the road, rolled down a long slope and wrecked itself completely when it struck a high stone wall.

WITHIN the lodge, Lynn and Alvarez heard the end of gunfire. They heard the distant rumble of a car, that faded off along the road below. Soon afterward, they caught the sound of a roaring motor; it throbbed upward, faded and was lost in the night air.

The Shadow had sent his agents from the field of battle; they had traveled away in their car. He, in turn, had left by autogiro. Crooks had met their doom. The Shadow's task was done.

Alvarez Rentone and Lynn Jefford stood by the desk where the million dollars rested. That wealth; the torn notes in the wastebasket; the dead forms of Zenjora and the Jibaros were all they needed to prove their case when the law arrived.

Oakbrook's body, too, was evidence. The broker's servants, bound and gagged, would testify to the crime that their master had planned; for they knew the power of The Shadow, and would not care to risk his future enmity.

But although The Shadow had accomplished this task for the law against great odds; although he was leaving behind him a living sermon that crime does not pay, he was bound to meet even greater obstacles before the aftermath of this crime had passed.

Not one man, not one family, but a whole city would be his next objective—a *City of Crime* in which the roots of gangdom had grown so strong that they held almost every citizen in their clutch. From the least important citizen to the most prominent civic leader, the guilty finger pointed its way. Only some tremendous outside force could clear this evil; only someone with the power of The Shadow could hope to battle such outstanding odds. The *City of Crime* was soon to have this scourge of the underworld, this amazing being of the darkness, as a much-needed guest!

THE END

POSTSCRIPT *by Will Murray*

One of the most intriguing aspects of The Shadow was his long-running impersonation of Lamont Cranston. When first introduced in the second Shadow novel, the New Jersey millionaire was a typical member of the wealthy set. He summered in Europe and wintered in the tropics. This was one reason why The Shadow found usurping his face, identity and New Jersey mansion so convenient. The real Cranston was hardly ever home.

Over time, Walter Gibson expanded his depiction of the absent globetrotter. Cranston was invariably off exploring the far corners of the earth. Whether on Safari in Africa, braving the wilds of Borneo, or navigating the Amazon River, he rarely got in The Shadow's way.

Through his infrequent descriptions of the real Cranston's whereabouts, Gibson painted a portrait of an individual who might be compared to Frank "Bring 'Em Back Alive" Buck, the famous big-game hunter of that era. Buck hunted wild animals all over Asia and South America and elsewhere, fetching them back for display in the world's zoos. His 1930 bestseller, *Bring 'Em Back Alive,* was filmed in 1932—the same year Lamont Cranston emerged as a great white hunter.

In his impenetrable disguise as Lamont Cranston, The Shadow often spoke of his experiences among savage tribes and native peoples. It was hard to know where the actual Cranston ended and the true Shadow—Kent Allard—began. For Allard too was a man familiar with distant dangers and ferocious cultures, as Gibson ultimately revealed in *The Shadow Unmasks.* For Gibson, the line between the two primary identities of his phantasmal protagonist clearly became blurred over time. But when The Shadow (as Cranston) spoke of being a legend known to faraway peoples as "White Chief," "Child of the Moon" or "Smoke Man," it was really the unrevealed Kent Allard talking.

The novels selected for this volume find The Shadow dealing with archeological mysteries and primitive foes worthy of the long-lost explorer Colonel P. H. Fawcett (on whom Kent Allard was modeled) and Doc Savage. Or for that matter, Indiana Jones!

The Blue Sphinx show-

The Shadow looms over Lamont Cranston and Henry Arnaud.

cases Clyde Burke, whom Gibson named after a reporter from his Philadelphia newspaperman days. Although Burke loses his job at the New York *Classic* in this exploit, he will be back at the old stand in future stories. Which is more than can be said for interim Police Commissioner Wainwright Barth. Introduced by Gibson because he felt Ralph Weston was getting too close to Lamont Cranston (and therefore The Shadow) at the Cobalt Club, Barth was finally phased out and Weston reinstated, as he clearly is by the time of *Jibaro Death.*

If the name Santander rings a bell, the tiny fictional South American republic figured in 1933's *Shadowed Millions* as an emerging nation. Here, it lies in the background of this otherwise unrelated adventure. It turns up again as the name of a steamer in 1946's *Malmordo.*

Early in the Dark Avenger's career, he created another alternate identity. Henry Arnaud was a wealthy businessman, and thus had entrée into the world of commerce where Cranston, as a merely rich idler, might not be able to penetrate.

The Shadow first assumed the Arnaud role in the eighth Shadow novel, *The Black Master.* As he had with Cranston, the Master of Darkness took over another man's true identity. This was a fact that Walter Gibson seems to have forgotten over the years. In any event, no more was ever said in the pages of *The Shadow Magazine* about the true Arnaud. He became simply another convenient cover creation of The Shadow.

In later years, Gibson revealed the inspiration behind Henry Arnaud: legendary New Orleans restaurateur "Count" Arnaud Cazenave. A Frenchman who emigrated to America, Cazenave founded Arnaud's Restaurant in 1918, influencing and defining French-Creole cuisine to this very day. Arnaud's is still in business, although for a period it was padlocked while the self-described "count" languished in jail for serving alcohol during Prohibition.

By a curious coincidence, The Shadow resorted to being Henry Arnaud exactly 28 times in the course of his recorded career—which is the precise number of times he appeared as Kent Allard. •